Praise for

Body Work

"*Body Work* is the kind of book that sucks you into the pages and won't let you go until the end. It's edgy and different, with a strong hero and heroine who don't fit the usual mold."
—*New York Times* bestselling author Linda Howard

"Brand tells a disturbing, engrossing tale of murder and madness, adding her own unique touches of eroticism and humor. An excellent read."
—*Romantic Times BOOKreviews*

Praise for

Touching MIDNIGHT

"Brand's extraordinary gifts as a storyteller are very evident here. This story is a rare and potent mixture of adventure, mystery and passion that shouldn't be missed."
—*Romantic Times BOOKreviews*

Also by

FIONA BRAND

DOUBLE VISION
BODY WORK
TOUCHING MIDNIGHT

*Watch for Fiona Brand's
upcoming novel*

BLIND INSTINCT

Available February 2008

KILLER
FIONA BRAND
FOCUS

MIRA®

MIRA®

ISBN-13: 978-0-7783-2563-5
ISBN-10:   0-7783-2563-6

KILLER FOCUS

www.MIRABooks.com

Printed in U.S.A.

Acknowledgments

Once again, thank you to Jenny Haddon, a former bank regulator, for her advice and the fascinating insight into the world of international banking, Claire Russell of the Kerikeri Medical center, New Zealand, for supplying the medical details and for helping me find the right drug to fit the crime, and to Pauline Autet for kindly answering my questions about the French language and providing the perfect phrases. Heartfelt thanks also to my editor, Miranda Stecyk, and the team at MIRA Books.

For Dad.

Prologue

Portland, Maine
October 12, 1984

The powerful beam of a flashlight probed the darkness, skimming over breaking waves as they sluiced between dark fingers of rock. Hunching against an icy southerly wind and counting steps as she picked her way through a treacherous labyrinth of tidal pools, a lean, angular woman swung the beam inland. Light pinpointed the most prominent feature on the exposed piece of coastline, a gnarled, embattled birch that marked the beginning of a steep path.

Breath pluming on the chill air, she followed the track to the rotted remains of a mansion that had once commanded the promontory, and which had burned down almost thirty years ago to the day.

Memories crowded with each step, flickering one after the other, isolated and stilted like the wartime newsreels she'd watched as a child. The wind gusted, razor edged with sleet, but the steady rhythm of the climb and the purpose that had pulled her away from a warm chandelier-lit room and an ambassadorial reception to this—a mausoleum of the dead—kept the autumn cold at bay.

Thirty years ago, the man who had hunted her, Stefan le Clerc, had almost succeeded. The Jewish banker turned Nazi hunter had tracked her and her father and the *Schutzstaffel,* the SS officer who had been tasked with caring for them, through a series of international business transactions. Somehow le Clerc, a former banker, had broken through the layers of paper companies that should have protected them and found their physical address.

Dengler had shot him, but not fatally. In the ensuing struggle, le Clerc had turned the tables on Dengler, wounding him. Then he had shot her father at point-blank range. She had had no doubt le Clerc would have killed her if she hadn't barricaded both Dengler and le Clerc in the ancient storeroom, where they grappled together, and set it ablaze.

The fire had been terrifying, but it had served its purpose. The two men and her father's body had been consumed within minutes. In the smoking aftermath, any evidence of gunshot wounds the skeletal remains might have yielded had been wiped out by a series of substantial bribes. The weeks following her father's death had been difficult but, once again, money had smoothed the way and, at eighteen years of age, she had been old enough to conclude all of the legal requirements and make arrangements to secure herself.

Ice stung her cheeks as she paused by a small, sturdy shed and dug out a set of keys from the pocket of her coat. A gust flattened the stiff oilskin against her body and whipped blond strands, now streaked with gray, across her cheeks, reminding her of a moment even further in the past.

Nineteen forty-four. She had been boarding the *Nordika*.

She shoved the key in the lock, her fingers stiff with cold. She had been…seven years old? Eight?

She didn't know why that moment had stuck with her. After years of heady victory, then horror, it hadn't been significant. The wind had been howling off the Baltic, right up the cold alley that Lubeck was in the dead of winter, and it had been freezing. Aside from the lights illuminating the deck of the *Nordika* and the dock—in direct contravention of the blackout regulations—it had been pitch-black. After hours spent crouching in the back of a truck, sandwiched cheek by jowl with the other children, the lights and the frantic activity had been a welcome distraction but hardly riveting.

And yet, she remembered that moment vividly. A crate had been suspended above the ship's hold as she'd walked up the gangplank, the swastika stenciled on its side garishly spotlighted, the crane almost buckling under the weight as the crate swayed in the wind. The captain had turned to watch her, his eyes blank, and for a moment she had felt the power her father wielded. The power of life and death.

Slipping the shed key back into her pocket, she stepped inside out of the wind, pulled the door closed behind her and engaged the interior locks. She played the beam of the flashlight over the dusty interior of the shed, then reached down and pulled up the hatch door that had once been the entrance to the mansion's storm cellar. Her flashlight trained below, she descended to the bottom of the ladder, crossed a cavernous, empty area, ducked beneath a beam and unlocked a second door.

Here the walls were irregular, chiseled from the limestone that formed a natural series of caves, some that led down almost to the sea. The beam of the flashlight swept the room. It was a dank and cold museum, filled with echoes of a past that would never be resurrected and a plethora of unexpected antiquities.

A dowry to smooth their way in the new world and ensure their survival.

Moldering uniforms hung against one wall. For a moment, in the flickering shadows, they took on movement and animation, as if the SS officers they had once belonged to had sprung to life. Her father, Oberst Reichmann. Hauptmann Ernst, Oberleutnant Dengler, *leutnants* Webber, Lindeberg, Konrad, Dietrich and Hammel.

It was a terrible treasure house but, despite the fact that by right of her heritage she had become the custodian, she wasn't locked in the past; the future was much too interesting.

Provided they were never discovered.

She'd studied the news reports over the years as one after the other of their kind had been cornered and killed, or imprisoned in various countries, but she was too disciplined to let emotion or bitterness take hold. She was nothing if not her father's daughter.

Crouching down, she unlocked a safe. Her fingers, still stiff with cold, slid over the mottled leather binding of a book. Relocking the safe, she set the book down on a dusty table and turned fragile pages until she found the entries she needed. *Names, birth dates, genetic lineage, blood types. And the numbers the institute had tattooed onto their backs.*

The older entries, written in an elegant copperplate hand, had faded with time. The more recent additions, the false names, IRS numbers and addresses, were starkly legible.

The documentation of the link they all shared was an unconscionable risk and a protective mechanism. They were all ex-Nazis and illegal aliens; the surviving *Schutzstaffel* were gazetted war criminals. Collectively, they were all thieves. They had stolen the spoils of war from a dozen nations to cushion a new life, and murdered to secure it.

Every one of them was vulnerable to discovery. The agreed penalty for exposing a member of the group or compromising the group as a whole was death.

She turned to the last section of the book, and the half-dozen names noted there, and added a seventh: Johannes Webber, now known as George Hartley. It was an execution list.

Slipping a plastic bag from the pocket of her coat, she wrapped and sealed the book, which was no longer safe in this location. She would make arrangements in the morning to relocate the rest of the items, and destroy those that couldn't be moved.

Cold anger flowed through her as she locked the door of the shed and started down the steep path, hampered by the powerful wind and driving sleet. She hadn't used the book for almost a decade. But then, as now, the need to use it had been triggered by a betrayal. Webber, the old fool, had talked.

After all these years, the *Nordika* had been located.

Cancun
October 14, 1984

She stepped into the foyer of a popular resort hotel, took a seat and waited. Seconds later, she was joined by a narrow-faced Colombian. Her Spanish was halting and a little rusty, but her lack of fluency scarcely mattered. Mendoza spoke English and he already knew what she wanted.

The conversation concluded, she got to her feet and left, leaving an envelope on the seat. She didn't turn to check that the man had picked up the envelope. He was there for the money—a very large sum of money. Twenty-five percent now, seventy-five percent when the job was done. She had found that if she paid fifty percent up front, the hitter invariably took the money and ran. With the majority of the money on hold, greed guaranteed completion.

A street urchin trailed the blond *gringa* through the streets. She was easy to spot but not so easy to follow. Unlike most of the tourists who crowded the resort town, she checked her back every few seconds.

She entered a crowded market. Sidling close, he snatched at the large tote bag she was carrying. She spun, her fingers hooked around the strap, preventing a clean getaway. Surprised, he yanked. The strap broke and he stumbled back. She reacted with unexpected ferocity, lunging after him. Bony fingers closed on one arm, hard enough to bruise. A fist caught him in the cheek, the impact snapped his head back and made his ears ring, but he'd been hit worse, and for a lot less money. With a vicious jerk, he yanked the bag from her fingers, twisted free and darted down a side alley.

Automatically scanning the narrow streets for *policia,* he sprinted across the road, through a darkened, almost deserted cantina and out onto another dusty street. He could hear the *gringa* behind him, her heels tapping sharply on the cobbles. That was another thing that was different about her. Most women screamed and made a fuss, they didn't chase after him.

Ten minutes later, as arranged, he met the man who had paid him to steal the *gringa*'s bag on the beach. Tito Mendoza was narrow faced and feral, with a reputation as a killer.

Heart pounding, avoiding Mendoza's stare, he handed over the bag. Mendoza examined the contents, drew out a musty old book wrapped in plastic, then slipped his hand in his pocket and handed over a wad of bills.

The following evening, Mendoza stepped out of a dim, smoky bar and made his way through streets filled with strolling tourists. The beach was dark and empty, the absence of the moon making the night even darker.

He reached the rendezvous point, the shadowy lee of a rock formation, and settled in to wait, gaze drawn to the faint luminosity of the breaking waves, the empty stretch of sand. He was early, but with the money at stake, he didn't want to leave anything to chance, and the Frenchman had a reputation for being exacting.

A faint vibration drew him up sharply. He could hear two men, not one, as agreed, and a primitive jolt of warning had him reaching for his gun.

The first slug caught him in the stomach; the second went higher. Mendoza clawed at his chest, his legs buckling. His gun discharged as he hit the ground, the round plowing uselessly into the sand.

Pain sliced through him as he was rolled over in the sand and the rucksack, which contained the book, was stripped off his shoulders. More pain as he was kicked onto his back. A spreading numbness in his legs, the fire eating into his chest and stomach.

Cold, dark eyes met his. *Muerte.* Death.

He must have lost consciousness; when he came to, the Frenchman was leaning over him, his palm jammed over the wound in his chest. He could hear sirens, the babble of voices.

Xavier le Clerc's gaze was fierce. "The book. Where is it?"

Mendoza coughed, pain spasmed. "Gone." He couldn't breathe; his mouth kept filling with blood.

"Who took it?"

Mendoza spat a name.

Faces appeared. The pressure on his chest eased, and le Clerc melted into the shadows. Someone, a doctor, set a bag down beside him. A uniform sent an automatic chill of fear through him. He recognized Franco Aznar, a senior detective. The questions started.

The doctor muttered something sharp.

Mendoza caught the phrases, *collapsed lung, lacerated intestine.* The numbness was spreading. He was a dead man; he had nothing more to fear.

Choking on his own blood, he began to talk.

Ten miles off the coast of Costa Rica
October 21, 1984

The anchor dropped through murky blue-green water and lodged on the reef bed sixty feet below. The rope went taut, stopping the drift of the chartered launch as it swung south, pushed by the current and a stiff offshore breeze. In the distance a fishing boat moved slowly against the chop, reeling in a long line. Closer in, another charter boat trolled for marlin and tuna.

Lieutenant Todd Fischer eased a single scuba tank onto his back, buckled up, slipped the snorkel into his mouth and flipped backward off the railing. Seconds later, the other seven members of the naval dive team were in the water, leaving Rodrigo, the charter skipper, to man the launch. After pairing off, they replaced the snorkels with regulators and began the descent, following the anchor rope down.

Minutes of patient grid-searching later, the encrusted hull of the *Nordika* loomed where it perched on the edge of a deep trench.

The ship had broken into three pieces. The hull had snapped in two and everything above deck had sheared off and fallen into the trench. Todd's interest sharpened when he noted the way the steel hull had ruptured. The blast pattern was unmistakable, indicating that the ship hadn't foundered; it had been scuttled. There was no sign of the ship's name, but near the stern three numbers were still visible. They matched the Lloyd's Register number for the *Nordika.*

Removing the lens cover from his underwater camera, he began to take photos. The visibility was poor, but all he needed was proof that the *Nordika* was there. Archival records compiled from an eyewitness report and the shipping records at the Baltic seaport of Lubeck stated that the *Nordika* had disappeared on the sixteenth of January, 1944, allegedly hijacked by SS officers just weeks before the fall of the Third Reich. The unsubstantiated report had claimed that the

Nordika had been bound for South America, loaded with passengers and an unspecified cargo. Intriguing as those facts were, it wasn't enough to spark the interest of either the coastguard or the U.S. Navy. But a report from a civilian source that Nazi war criminals had been involved with drugs and gunrunning, liaising with U.S. military personnel and using the scuttled carcass of the *Nordika* as a drop-off point, had been enough to make someone in the admiralty curious.

Todd's brief was to investigate gunrunning with a possible military link, and, crazily enough, the weird slant that there *was* a Nazi connection even after all this time. South America was a known haven, but Todd was no Nazi hunter. Despite the fact that their information had supplied him with documents dating back to 1943, his money was on drugs, and possibly weapons, attached to a buoy or a wreck that might or might not be the *Nordika*.

He moved through the ship, snapping pictures. After finding no evidence of any cargo, forty years old or more recent, he swam through the blasted area and into the detached stern. The four diesels were still bolted down in the engine room, the name *Wiesen Bremerhaven* still legible. He took more photos, checked the luminous dial of his watch, then swam back the way he'd come. From what he'd seen, the ship *was* quite possibly the

Nordika. The tonnage was right, and the four Wiesen diesels matched the *Nordika*'s specs.

He passed through the hold and swam out onto the deck area. Thirty minutes had passed. At this level he could spend longer, but with nothing more to investigate there wasn't much point. It was possible they would do a second dive down into the trench, just in case the stash point was farther down, but that wasn't likely. According to the charts, the trench was more than two hundred feet deep. As a stash site, it was neither safe nor convenient.

He swam around the side of the *Nordika,* searching for his dive buddy, Verney, and the rest of the team. Verney had followed him into the cargo hold, but he'd disappeared shortly after. None of the other divers were in sight. Mathews, Hendrickson, McNeal and Salter were supposed to be grid-searching the reef. Brooks and Downey should have been checking along the edge of the trench. He glanced at his watch again. Thirty-five minutes had now passed. At this depth they were easily good for forty. Unless he'd given the order, the rest of the team should still be working.

A diver appeared over the lip of the trench and swam directly toward him. For a split second Todd was certain it was Downey, then something wrong registered; the neoprene suit and the gear were regulation, but the mask and the tank weren't. Adrenaline pumped. It was possible the stranger was a diver from the charter launch that had been trolling in the area earlier. He couldn't hear the sound of the launch's engine, which meant they could have dropped anchor nearby, but recreational diving wasn't compatible with game fishing, especially not this far out and with the visibility so poor.

The second possibility was that the diver was one of the bad guys, protecting their drop site. Instinctively, he depressed the shutter on the camera, then reached for the knife sheathed at his ankle. The diver veered off to one side. Todd spun in the water as a second diver swam up out of the trench. A hand ripped at his face mask. Salt water stung his eyes and filled his mouth: his oxygen line had been cut. An arm clamped around his neck. He slashed with the knife. Blood clouded the water and the arm released. With a grunt, he kicked free, heading for the surface. With a lungful of air he could make twice the distance with ease.

A hand latched around his ankle, dragging him back down. Jackknifing, he dove at the man, slicing with the knife. Blood and air erupted. He glimpsed the camera as it drifted down to the seabed, the strap cut in the struggle, and he registered that the other diver had also used a knife.

Vision blurring, he grabbed the limp diver's regulator and sucked in a lungful of air. He had a split second to register a third diver, then a spear punched into his shoulder, driving him back against the hull of the ship. Shock reverberated through him; salt water filled his lungs. Arm and shoulder numbed, chest burning with a cold fire and his throat clamped against the convulsive urge to cough, he kicked upward.

Sixty feet above, the ocean surface rippled like molten silver. Sunlight. Oxygen.

A sudden image of his wife, Eleanor, and small son, Steve, sunbathing in their backyard in Shreveport sent a powerful surge of adrenaline through his veins. He cleared the edge of the hull.

A split second before his vision faded, he spotted Mathews and Hendrickson, floating. Distantly, he felt hard fingers close around one ankle, the cold pressure of the water as he was towed down into the trench.

Shreveport, Louisiana
October 21

Eight-year-old Steven Fischer dropped the ball.

"Aw, Steve. Didja have to—"

His cousin Sara's voice was high-pitched and sharp as Steve stumbled to a halt. It was the middle of the day in his cousin's backyard. Despite the fact that it was autumn, the sun was hot enough to fry eggs and so bright it hurt his eyes, but that wasn't the reason his vision had gone funny. He could see a picture of his dad, staring at him, which wasn't right. His dad was away, down south somewhere. Having another holiday on the navy, Granddad Fischer had joked.

This time he'd promised to bring Steve back a sombrero.

Fear gripped him. As abruptly as it had formed, the picture faded, like a television set being turned off, and the tight feeling in his chest was gone.

"I'm not playing anymore." He stared blankly at Sara, who was looking ticked. He was going home. Something had happened. Something bad.

Shreveport, Louisiana
November 20, 1984

Eleanor Fischer watched the coffin as it was lowered into the grave and fought the wrenching urge to cry out.

The gleaming oak box was filled with Todd's clothing and a few mementos that had meant something to him. Silly bits and pieces she had hardly been able to part with: a snapshot of Todd, darkly handsome in full dress uniform; a wedding photo; a disreputable old T-shirt she'd tried to throw away half a dozen times and which he'd stubbornly retrieved from the trash can; his favorite baseball cap.

Knowing that the box didn't contain his body, and that his remains would most likely never be recovered, didn't make the grieving any easier. She still couldn't accept Todd's death; she didn't know if she ever would. A part of her expected him to come home with some wild explanation as to why he and the rest of the guys had gone AWOL, wrap her in his arms and blot out the horror of the past month.

Jaw clenched, she dropped a white rose onto the coffin lid, and gently squeezed Steve's hand to let him know it was his turn. Steve's rose dropped, the stem broken, the petals crumpled, as if he'd gripped it too tightly.

Swallowing the sharp ache in her throat, she hugged him close in an attempt to absorb his pain. His shoulders felt unnaturally stiff, his spine ramrod straight.

Since the day he'd come home insisting that she find out where Todd was and check that he was all right, he'd been…different. He hadn't wanted to play with any of his friends, or swim; instead he'd stuck close to home, staying within earshot of the telephone. When they had finally heard that Todd was missing, presumed dead, Steve had simply gone to his room and had sat staring at the wall, his focus inward.

The doctor had said that children coped with grief differently from adults, but he didn't understand that Steve had known Todd was in trouble *before* they'd been informed he was missing.

Commodore John Saunders handed Eleanor Fischer the folded flag that had draped Todd's coffin, his expression grim.

This was the second ceremony he'd officiated at this week, and there were six more to go. Eight men lost at sea, nine men lost in all, if you counted the launch skipper, and none of the bodies had been recovered. When that many men disappeared on a peacetime mission, it was difficult to stop the speculation, and so far the media had had a field day, calling the incident a bungled mission.

To compound the embarrassment, the civilian who had instigated the hunt, an old crony of Admiral Monteith's, had also died, a victim of a heart attack after drinking too much at an official function. When the news had broken, Monteith had run like a rat, hiding behind his medals and his Boston connections and taking early retirement. He had refused to be questioned over the affair. Monteith's secretary and his personal aide had also resigned, leaving the office in disarray. The file on the mission had been conveniently "lost" and had somehow never made it onto the Admiralty's new computer system.

As far as Saunders was concerned, the whole affair had been a wild-goose chase from start to finish, and a waste of taxpayers' money. And he had lost eight good men.

He would carry out an investigation. Regulations demanded that a proper reporting process had to be adhered to, but with Monteith's defection, the likelihood that they would come up with any satisfactory conclusions was close to nil.

The launch had broken up on the rocks, and to date only a small part of the wreckage had been located. The life raft had been found farther along the coast, fully inflated and equipped, which had added to the speculation. Something had gone seriously wrong, and Saunders wasn't buying into the accidental-drowning scenario.

Fischer had been a seasoned veteran, and so had every member of his team. They should have survived what had amounted to a recreational dive on a sunken wreck in calm waters. With no witnesses other than a fishing boat that had seen two launches in the vicinity, and no bodies or evidence beyond the wrecked launch and the life raft, there was little chance that answers would ever come to light.

But he did know one crucial piece of the puzzle that the press hadn't stumbled on yet. Todd Fischer's team hadn't only been searching for a cache of drugs and guns; they had been hunting Nazis.

Saunders's ulcer burned every time he thought about the briefing for the mission. Monteith must have been senile.

He would make it his personal mission to ensure

that that particular piece of information never saw the light of day. The media had already done enough damage. It was better that Fischer and his team were perceived as deserters than that the U.S. Navy was made into a laughingstock.

One

Lieutenant Commander Steve Fischer stepped
into the records room of the Jackson Naval Air
Station, Florida, and handed the clerk a list of the
files he wanted to view. There were nine in all.
Eight didn't require a security clearance; one did.
On request, he produced his ID and security clearance and waited for his details to be verified
against the computerized register.

Several minutes later, the files were deposited
on the counter, checked and signed off by a second
records officer and Fischer was cleared to carry
them through to the cramped work cubicles that
ran the length of one wall.

Taking a seat, he placed the eight files he had

chosen at random, and in which he had no interest, to one side, and selected the file labeled *Akidron*. In a recent overhaul of the filing system, Akidron had suddenly appeared. The reference number tied it in with a group of files containing material on operations in the Middle East, but the coincidence that *Akidron* spelled backward was *Nordika* had been enough to pique his interest.

He examined the security classification and a seal that had been put in place in 1984 and had never been broken, indicating that he was the first person to view the file since it had been taken out of circulation. The fact that the file had been off-limits for over twenty years and had a high security rating was notable but not unusual. Jacksonville was the center for the Southeast Command, which included twenty-one naval installations, among them Guantanamo Bay and Puerto Rico. With Cuba on their doorstep, a number of files contained sensitive material that could affect the security of the United States.

He broke the seal and opened the file. On the first page *Akidron* was reversed to spell *Nordika*.

He skimmed the pages that detailed the information supplied by George Hartley, a wealthy manufacturer based in Houston, and which had been passed on to Monteith. Hartley claimed that ex-Nazi SS officers, in league with Marco Chavez, head of a major Colombian drug cartel, were involved in smuggling arms and drugs. The arms were bound for terrorist and military factions in South America and Cuba, the cocaine was moving stateside. Military personnel were reportedly involved, although Hartley hadn't been able to supply a list of names. When the divers had gone missing, an attempt to follow up on the details Hartley had supplied had been stalled by Hartley's unexpected death. According to the coroner's report, the fatality had been caused by a lethal cocktail of prescription medications and an excess of alcohol, and had been deemed an unfortunate accident.

Suddenly the lack of information available on the wreck of the *Nordika* and the disappearance of eight navy personnel made sense. Monteith had not only run from the scandal of the loss of an entire SEAL team and the ridicule that would result from a failed Nazi hunt, he had been afraid for his own life. Hartley had been executed, and Monteith had recognized that he would be next.

In a botched attempt to kill the affair, he had concealed all the evidence he'd obtained by renaming the file and closing it. He had banked on the fact that twenty years after the *Nordika* tragedy, there was likely to be little interest in a follow-up investigation. Monteith had died just eighteen months later, reportedly of natural causes.

The back of his neck crawling, Steve flipped through the last set of pages, which contained the mission brief and the orders issued to Todd Fischer and his men. The documents had been signed off by Monteith. As he turned the last page, an envelope attached to the rear file cover with tape that was cracked and perished by age detached. Glossy prints and a set of negatives spilled across the desktop.

The first photo—a splash of bright turquoise and the primary yellow of a mask and snorkel—was of himself at age eight, underwater, in the family swimming pool. The second was a shot of his best friend, Marc Bayard, the third of his cousin, Sara.

The fourth print was of Todd Fischer, sitting on the bottom of the pool, holding his breath and waiting patiently while Steve had fooled with the camera, trying to get a cool shot of his dad.

Chest tight, he picked up the print, careful to handle only the edges, and stared into a piece of the past he had never expected to find. He remembered the afternoon the photos had been taken as clearly as if it had been yesterday. It had been approximately two weeks before his father had disappeared. The weather had been hot and sultry and his dad had been home on leave, giving them snorkeling lessons and, when they'd pestered him, a lesson on underwater photography. Normally, they weren't allowed to touch the camera, because it was an expensive piece of equipment and the shutter release was ultrasensitive.

In the next photo the luminous turquoise of pool water changed to cool blues and lilacs. Seawater. The absence of red and yellow tones in the coral indicated the depth as being from between forty to sixty feet, maybe a little more.

Through the murk he registered the focal point of the shot, the stern of a vessel and three numbers. The reason Monteith had kept the film, which should have been passed on to Eleanor Fischer, was now obvious. The numbers, remnants of Lloyd's Register numbers, were familiar. Two years previously Steve had spent a few days in Costa Rica, chartered a launch and had found the wreck of the *Nordika*. Because of its remoteness, the site was not a popular dive location, but it was noted on the sea charts. He had dived on the wreck and had taken almost the exact same photo.

A set of prints depicting the cargo hold and the ancient diesels in the engine room followed. The sensation, as he flipped through the prints, was eerie as he viewed the same scenes he had photographed, only this time seen through his father's eyes.

The next photo made the tension in the pit of his stomach escalate: a diver and, off to the side, the shadowy, encrusted shape of the *Nordika*'s hull. The final two snapshots were markedly different. The first was an off-center flash of a face distorted by a diving mask and a cloud of dark fluid—*blood*. The second, aimed upward, as if the camera had dropped to the sea bottom and the shutter mechanism had triggered, capturing the divers suspended above, one arching back as a spear punched into his shoulder.

Steve stared at the print. The snapshot was skewed, but the picture it had produced was sharp enough. He could make out the U.S. Navy marking on the wounded diver's scuba tank, as well as the tattoo on Todd Fischer's bare shoulder—the same tattoo that was visible in the holiday snap of his father sitting in the bottom of the Fischer family swimming pool.

For a split second the image of his father that he had "seen" more than twenty years before was superimposed over the print. He had never told his mother, or anyone, the full truth, that somehow in the last few seconds of his life Todd Fischer had reached out and connected with him. That he had experienced the moment of his father's death.

The phenomenon had been singular and frightening. As the days following his father's disappearance had passed and the search had continued, Steve had waited for news, aware that even if they did find his father it was too late. Todd Fischer had died on October 21, 1984, at approximately three o'clock in the afternoon.

The weeks of waiting for confirmation of what he had already known had burned deep. But just days after the funeral, when the press had published a leaked naval report citing Fischer and his men as deserters, Steve had been stunned. He had grown up with a number of calm certainties in his life. One of those had been that his father was a bona fide hero and a patriot. There was no way Todd Fischer would have deserted his family, his command *or* his country.

Shortly after the funeral, he had overheard his uncle discussing the fact that Todd had been working on something sensitive enough to hit a nerve with naval command, and the possibility of a cover-up. At eight years old, Steve hadn't grasped the concepts of collateral damage and expendability fully, but he had understood enough. Something had gone wrong and his father had been sacrificed. He could understand his father giving his life for his country—Todd Fischer had talked about that risk often enough—but he couldn't accept that sacrifice going hand in glove with the disgrace of being labeled a traitor.

He hadn't known all of the men who had died, but he had met some of them. They were mostly married with families. They hadn't been any more *expendable* than his own father had been, and he was certain that in no way had justice been served.

Now, finally, he had proof. Instead of investigating the crime, Monteith, along with his personal staff, had covered the deaths up and walked out.

Extracting a notebook from his briefcase, Steve

made a note of the personnel who had been involved, not only with the mission but with the reporting process, including the filing clerk who had authorized the closing of the Akidron file.

Maybe it was overkill, but Monteith, a decorated admiral, had been frightened enough by Hartley's death to not only resign, but to commit an act of treason by concealing a threat to national security, and an indictable offense by concealing evidence of a mass murder. Steve could only put that fear down to two things. Monteith had obtained further information that wasn't contained in the file, and he had been afraid for his own life.

Replacing the photographs and the negatives in the envelope, he slipped them into his briefcase along with the file, locked it and returned the remaining files to the front desk. After all these years the possibility that he could find his father's remains was remote, but at least he had clarity on one point: Todd Fischer and the seven men under his command had been murdered while serving their country.

Frowning, the clerk counted the files, checked them against the register then recounted them. "Sir, there's a file missing."

He stared at the space Lieutenant Commander Fischer had occupied on the other side of the counter just seconds before. He was talking to air.

Fischer had already left.

* * *

Two days later Fischer walked into an interview room at the office of the Director of National Intelligence in Washington, D.C., and handed a copy of the Akidron file to Rear Admiral Saunders. The only other occasion he had met Saunders had been at his father's funeral, although he was well aware of Saunders's career path. Since 1984, Saunders's rise through the ranks had been swift, moving from commodore to rear admiral with a raft of commendations and honors for active service in the Gulf. Following a stint in naval intelligence reporting to the Joint Chiefs, his career had shifted to another level entirely when he had been headhunted by the Director of National Intelligence.

Saunders invited Fischer to take a seat and opened the file. Minutes later he placed the photos that had accompanied the file in a neat pile beside the open folder. The photos were dated, numbered and indisputably had come from Todd Fischer's underwater camera. The first four photos were family snaps, the next ten, working shots of the *Nordika.* The final three clearly depicted a murder in progress.

Saunders's jaw tightened at the frozen violence of the last two photos. He had known Todd Fischer personally, and liked him. He had never found it easy to stomach the actions that had been necessary to keep Monteith's Nazi-hunting junket under wraps. The fact that Monteith had gotten his men to the scene, recovered Todd Fischer's camera and sealed away evidence that would not only have cleared Fischer and his men of all charges but sparked a murder inquiry, was an unpleasant shock.

The even more unpalatable fact that he now faced public exposure for his actions in the *Nordika* cover-up was a very personal and immediate threat. He reported to the Director of National Intelligence, who advised the president and oversaw the entire intelligence community. When it came to matters of national and international security, the slightest miscalculation on his part could cost him his job. "I presume you have the originals."

Fischer's gaze was remote. "And the negatives."

Saunders steepled his fingers and studied Steve Fischer's tough, clean-cut features, the immaculate uniform. Todd Fischer had been competent, likable and damned good at his job. His son was in another category entirely. In anyone's terms, Steve Fischer was a high achiever. He had cruised through basic training, completed BUDS without a hitch and graduated from the College of Command and Staff with honors. With a string of awards and medals for active service with the SEAL teams in the Gulf and Afghanistan, he had fast-tracked his way through the ranks. A lieutenant commander already, according to the assessments of his superior officers, Fischer would make commander by the time he was thirty-five. If a new theater of operations opened up, the promotion would be effective immediately. "What do you want?"

Fischer slid a letter outlining his resignation from the navy across the polished walnut of Saunders's desk. "A job."

Two

Washington, D.C.
Eight months later

The barnlike chamber of the library was chilly, the central heating cranky and inconsistent, so that some areas were warm and others existed in a flow of icy air. FBI Agent Taylor Jones was unlucky enough to be sitting in a room with a windchill factor somewhere in the arctic range.

Huddling into the warmth of her lined woolen coat, she scrolled the microfilm until she reached the date she was searching for and began to skim newspapers that had been published more than fifty years ago. Outside, the night was black, the wind fitful, driving sporadic bursts of rain against tall, mullioned windows. Somewhere a radiator ticked as if someone had just turned up the heat. The sound was comforting and oddly in sync with the yellowish glow of the lights, and walls lined with books that had moldered quietly for decades.

She made a note on the pad at her side then continued to scroll. A clock on the wall registered the passage of time. One hour, then two. The ache in her shoulder and wrist that had developed from hours spent making the same small movement over and over became more insistent. Taylor dismissed it in favor of sinking into the familiar cadences of sifting through information, and the well-worn comfort of being in utter control of her world. If the pain became sharp enough to interfere with her concentration, she would take a break and do a few exercises to free up the muscles.

Somewhere behind her a chair scraped on the tiled floor. The measured step of the only other occupant of the room, a thin man wearing bifocals, registered. The double click of a briefcase unlocking was distinct in the muffled quiet of the room.

A terrible alertness gripped her.

Eyes glued to the screen, she concentrated on controlling her breathing. *Stay calm. Stay focused.* The tightness in her chest and stomach, the sour taste flooding her mouth, were a mirage, leftover symptoms from a nightmare that had ended months ago. A nightmare she had worked hard to forget.

She had read the psychiatric reports on the

effects of the four days she had spent as a hostage; she'd had the therapy. She had even gone back for further sessions so she could understand and control the anxiety attacks which, according to her therapist, were her mind and body's remembered response to the experience. The way out was simple: instruct the mind that there was nothing to fear and so invalidate the body's responses.

Inhaling again, she forced her focus outward, away from the coiled tension, away from the memories. Her gaze skated over shelves of books, a wooden stepladder, and snagged on her own reflection, white faced and strained, in a window.

Not a dim, claustrophobic shed with bars at the window. Endless shadows, the snick of a briefcase, the sting of a needle. The smothering paralysis as the drug anesthetized her body, leaving her formless, floating, eyes wide, staring into a darkness that shifted, reformed—

Stop.

Don't let the mind go back.

It was late. Instead of working she should have gone home and eaten dinner. She was tired; her therapist had warned her that tiredness and stress were, in themselves, triggers.

As dangerous as briefcases and needles.

She drew in another controlled breath and checked her watch, anchoring herself in the normality of that small gesture. The hostage crisis was over, finished. Earl Slater was behind bars, Diane Eady and Senator Radcliff, the man whose property she had been held on, were both dead. She had escaped; she was safe. But Alex Lopez, head of a Colombian drug cartel, and the man who had drugged her with a powerful hallucinogen called ketamine hydrochloride, had gotten away.

Rain swept against the windows, and the sense of cold increased.

Don't go back.

But in order to catch Lopez, she had to.

He was dangerous, a psychotic killer, and she needed him caught. When he had injected the first dose of ketamine he had stated that he would kill her, regardless of whether Rina Morell—Lopez's former wife and a federal witness—handed herself over in exchange for Taylor or not. The only question was when.

Normally, that kind of rhetoric wouldn't have shaken Taylor. Lopez was powerful and influential; if he had wanted her dead, she would be dead. But caught in the grip of a hallucinatory drug, her normal reasoning process hadn't worked. She would never forget the experience, and she was going to make sure it didn't happen to anyone else.

Apart from her own determination to capture him, her appetite for the hunt was further whetted by the fact that Rina Morell was a personal friend. The damage Lopez had done the Morell family was a matter of record now, but that didn't alter the horror of the ordeal Rina and her parents had endured.

She registered a second click as the briefcase was closed. Jaw tight, she swiveled around in the chair and studied the owner of the briefcase who was strolling toward the front desk, the box of microfilm he had been studying tucked under one arm. He was midforties, about one hundred and forty pounds, six feet tall, give or take an inch. Height was always the most difficult detail to estimate.

She wondered what he had been doing here this late on a Sunday night, but the flare of curiosity was brief. It was automatic for her to notice people. The clinical assessment was part of the job, but for as long as she could remember she had been aware of the people around her, how they looked and what made them tick. Her mother's standard complaint had been that she hadn't produced an eight-pound baby girl, she had given birth to a cop. It had been a mild form of rebellion for Taylor to become an agent instead.

Still on edge, she returned to the screen. A heading caught her attention, drawing her once more into the past. None of the key search words she had noted down were included, but the name was familiar.

She flipped through the files in her bag until she found the relevant one. It contained research she'd done while she was recovering from the hostage situation and the depressive effects of the ketamine. Locked out of the office for a month on mandatory sick leave, she'd had nothing better to do than attend therapy sessions and try to break open the Lopez/Morell case, which had unaccountably stalled.

She'd combed FBI files, the Internet and microfilms of old newspapers for anything to do with Lopez who, aside from drugs charges, was wanted for illegal entry into the United States, collusion in the theft and sale of decommissioned missile components, fraud, grievous bodily harm and murder.

Lopez's real name was Alejandro Chavez, and he had been living in the States under a false identity from the age of twelve, courtesy of a brutal series of mass murders in Colombia that had made it impossible for him to live in his own country. Marco Chavez, Lopez's father, had orchestrated the murders to force his son's release from prison. Marco had succeeded in obtaining a pardon for Alex, but with the public outcry surrounding the massacres and a number of death threats, Alex had been forced into hiding.

She was also searching for anything to do with Marco Chavez, now deceased, and—just to pull this one into the region of the seriously weird—international banking and Nazis. The Nazis, according to the testimony of Slater—one of the few arrests they had made in the case—formed the backbone of a secretive cabal that had bankrolled Lopez and his cartel.

She opened the file, found the reference and returned her attention to the microfilm, a Reuters report dated 1954. Noted Jewish banker and self-professed Nazi hunter Stefan le Clerc had disappeared and fears were held for his safety. His last known location, New York, had been established from a letter he had posted to his wife, Jacqueline le Clerc, who was appealing for any information about her husband's whereabouts. Apart from the years he had spent in international banking, le Clerc had founded an organization that worked to reunite families separated during the war and help survivors recover family money and assets. He was also noted for his campaign to track Nazi war criminals, and had been searching for a group of SS officers who had escaped Berlin in 1944 just weeks before Hitler had committed suicide in his bunker.

According to le Clerc, the officers had hijacked a cargo ship, *Nordika,* from Lubeck and escaped, taking with them an enormous quantity of looted goods and a group of children with IQs that ranked them as geniuses, part of a research project designed to establish a superior genetic seed pool for the Reich.

Taylor didn't know how common the name le Clerc was, but the fact that Stefan had been Jewish and in banking made the likelihood that he was related to the le Clerc who had surfaced in the Lopez case stronger.

Xavier le Clerc was a Jewish banker turned international thief. He was infamous for collapsing a Swiss bank that had had a large base of Nazi investment, then having the audacity to make a clean getaway. Interpol had an old sheet on him, but despite that he was still at large. It was suspected, although not proved, that Esther Morell, the wife of one of Lopez's business partners and a former international banker herself, had used her connection with le Clerc to pull off a multibillion-dollar theft, emptying Alex Lopez's main operating account. The money had since been recovered by the feds but after more than twenty years, any trail that might have led to le Clerc was gone.

She leafed through the information she had collected on Xavier le Clerc, and found the connection she was looking for. Xavier was Stefan le Clerc's son.

She made a note, then read through the Reuters report on the screen again, double-checking the name of the ship, a second reference that made the article even more interesting.

Two weeks ago, she had found an article that had been printed in 1984, about the wreck of a ship purported to be the *Nordika,* which had been discovered off the coast of Costa Rica. A naval team that had dived on the wreck had disappeared and had been presumed drowned. There was no mention of any cargo, but the fact that Costa Rica wasn't far from the coast of Colombia and was well within Marco Chavez's sphere of influence had been enough to pique her interest.

The tie-in was tenuous. She wasn't certain any of it would add up to anything productive, but she couldn't ignore the picture that was building. The disappearance of the *Nordika* from Lubeck had been a wartime mystery that had stumped a lot of people, including Stefan le Clerc. Marco Chavez was known to have harbored German nationals after the war. Crazily enough, the pieces of that old wartime puzzle seemed to be fitting into the Lopez case.

She hit the Print button. While the article fed out, she repacked her bag, then walked through to the front desk and paid to have the document scanned and saved to disk.

An hour later, Taylor settled down at the computer monitor in her apartment with a carton of hot noodles and a double-chocolate brownie from the all-night bakery at the end of the block.

Outside, the wind had increased to a steady howl. Hail rapped against the windows, a sharp counterpart to the clicking and humming of her computer as she slipped the disk into the drive and opened up the file that contained the articles she'd had scanned.

Long minutes passed while she ate noodles and read through the articles again. The hail changed to sleet, the cold palpable as it reached through thick, lined drapes into the comfort of her sitting room, sending the temperature plummeting as she made a written prècis of the information. It wasn't as fast as typing, but she'd found over the years that sometimes her brain worked better when she had a pen in her hand.

Fingers stiff with cold, she left her desk to turn up the heat and strolled through to her bedroom to pull on a sweater. Taking a fleecy blanket from the end of her bed, she returned to the computer.

With the blanket wrapped around her middle, she sat back down and noticed that at some point she had eaten all of the noodles *and* the brownie. Somehow, the fact that she couldn't remember tasting a brownie that was justifiably famous for at least a ten-block radius seemed symptomatic of her life. She had had her cake, she just couldn't remember eating it.

Until those hours spent locked in the dark, Lopez turning her blood to ice every time he had injected what could have been a fatal dose into her veins, she hadn't realized how empty her life had been, or how desperately she wanted to live, despite that emptiness. Coming that close to death had been like slamming into a brick wall. It had stopped her in her tracks, forced her to assess, to need more than a career that had somehow expanded to fill every waking hour.

The change, radical as it was, hadn't happened overnight. For a self-confessed workaholic from a dysfunctional family, trying to picture herself fitting into a scenario that involved a husband, kids, maybe even a house and garden, was difficult. For most of her adult life she had sidestepped the issue, denying that she wanted the family values that most people clung to. It was disorienting to discover that she needed them.

Tossing the empty noodle carton and the paper bag that had contained the brownie into the trash can beside her desk, she accessed the Bureau Web site. She entered her code and password then dialed up a Bureau search engine, typed in a list of search words and stared at the list of hits.

Great. Boring *and* weird.

Huddling into the blanket, she began to read.

At one in the morning, on the point of giving up, she found an article about a Colombian drug dealer and hit man, Tito Mendoza, who had been murdered for a book. Mendoza had been shot at point-blank range but hadn't died immediately. The Costa Rican *policia* had questioned him at the scene, but he had slipped into a coma and died before they had gotten more than a few basic details. The newsworthy part was that he had claimed that aside from names and addresses, the book had contained other details: blood types, numbers that had been tattooed onto the backs of a group of German ex-nationals—Nazis—and an execution list.

The report, though bizarre, meant nothing on its own. But coupled with the fact that Mendoza had been involved with Marco Chavez and that he had been murdered the same week the naval team who had dived on the *Nordika* had disappeared, suddenly, the implications began to pile up.

In her research, Taylor had found out a lot of information she never, ever wanted to know, including the fact that SS soldiers had routinely had their blood types tattooed onto their chests. A practical solution for the battlefield, it had proved to be a liability after the Allies had invaded, because the tattoos had made them easy to identify.

The tattoos Mendoza had mentioned didn't sound like blood types—he had said *numbers,* not letters—but the connection was there.

Maybe it was a leap to imagine the book had anything to do with the SS soldiers who had hijacked the *Nordika,* and even more of a leap to connect it to the missing naval divers, Lopez or the Nazi cabal Slater had mentioned, but it was a possibility.

She saved a copy of the article and, out of habit, saved a copy to disk, which she labeled, dated and slipped into a storage box that contained copies of all of the archival information she had researched on Lopez. After the internal security leaks concerning the case, two of which had resulted in failed busts, and the more mundane fact that occasionally information had a habit of disappearing off the scope in the Bureau's system, she liked to keep her own separate set of records.

Stifling a yawn, she hit the send button and e-mailed a copy to her work computer.

Just before she went to bed, she reread the article and made a brief note. The wintry chill seemed to intensify as she studied what she had written.

Mendoza had had a book. The book had been important enough that he had died because of it.

Three

A week later, Taylor leaned back in her office chair and skimmed a page of Alex Lopez's file. She'd studied the information found on Lopez's computer after the unsuccessful raid on his estate at Winton on the West Coast until her eyes ached. Legitimate company accounts, tax legislation and a bunch of legalese about property-development trusts.

The information, most of which had been supplied by an unnamed South American source eighteen months previously and which had formed the basis for the FBI's investigation into Lopez, should have put her to sleep, but Taylor refused to be lulled by the familiarity of the material.

She needed to find something—anything—that would provide a lead on a man who had killed almost everyone who had ever gotten close to him.

The list had included Lopez's own father; his business partner and father-in-law, Cesar Morell; and, at the age of twelve, his own bodyguard.

Exhaustion, the product of another late night spent surfing government databases and the Internet, sucked at her as she read. Her mind began to drift, slide sideways.… She blinked, staring at the page, not seeing the words, suddenly on the verge of—

A sharp thud jerked her head up.

Mike Colenso, the agent occupying the adjacent desk, was rummaging through the box of files he had just dropped onto the floor.

Stifling a yawn, she tried to recapture the moment. When the relaxed mood wouldn't come back, courtesy of Colenso opening and discarding files, she went over what she'd just read. After skimming the page a second time, then a third, she stopped trying to force the knowledge. Whatever it was that had gotten her antennae twitching was obscure enough that she wasn't going to find it by focusing harder. It was entirely possible that what she was looking for wasn't on the page, but the result of information triggering her mind to make a connection.

She checked her watch and set the file down. She would get that moment back, and now she was going to have to do it on her own time, not the Bureau's. Marc Bayard, her boss and a newly appointed division head, had been saying for weeks now that she was too close to the case, that she had lost her perspective and needed to back off. In fact, this morning he had *ordered* her to back off.

According to Bayard, the Lopez case had redefined her commitment to her job in "an unhealthy way." The only reason she had been assigned to the Lopez task force in the first place was her connection to Rina Morell. He had assigned another agent in her place. He had been polite but he hadn't pulled his punches. Her psychiatric report detailed post-traumatic stress disorder, insomnia, chronic fatigue, paranoia and evidence of obsessive behavior. Bayard had enough material to suspend her on medical grounds if she didn't fall into line.

She had argued the point on the "obsessive behavior." Driven, maybe. Bayard hadn't seen the distinction.

She pulled out Lopez's psychological profile and studied it. He was clinically organized and successful, but he had made significant errors in judgment, notably in underestimating the Morell family. Years ago, Esther Morell had outsmarted him, Cesar Morell had worked with him, but only under duress, and their daughter, Rina, had come close to bringing him down.

Lopez was also eccentric. Amongst a list of known traits, it was noted that while he used computers in his business, he didn't trust them. In a way, that was understandable, since Esther Morell, in partnership with Xavier le Clerc, had relieved him of billions of dollars through a series of electronic transactions.

A pen rolled off Colenso's desk and dropped onto the floor, but this time the elusive feeling that she was about to get something didn't vaporize.

Taylor stared at the sentence she'd just read. That was it.

So far they had gleaned zilch from Lopez's computer files. In a nutshell, he didn't store his information on any electronic system they'd found. They had assumed that he had the information stored on a computer somewhere. It was possible he had an encoded system and they simply hadn't found it, but what if he stored information in another way?

Feverishly, she turned pages. Mendoza had had a book, and there had been a mention of a book in Earl Slater's testimony.

She found the page and ran her finger down the margin until she located the piece she was looking for. According to Slater, Lopez had recently retrieved a book from a bank vault in Bogotá. Slater didn't know what the book contained, just that it had been important enough for Lopez to make a trip to collect it. It was possible it had been a rare antique, an easy asset to liquidate when he'd needed—

Colenso's chair creaked as he rocked back and propped his expensively shod feet on the desktop.

He jerked his head toward the file she was reading. "Thought Bayard pulled you off the case."

"He did." She indicated a pile of paperwork occupying one corner of her desk. "In theory I'm working on operation Update the Filing System."

His gaze sharpened. "You've found something."

Several heads turned. Taylor closed the file. "Maybe. Nothing that isn't already on file."

And nothing that she was prepared to talk about yet.

The fact that there had been a serious leak connected with the Lopez case—in effect, a mole in the Bureau—made her wary. According to her own private snooping, the information leaks were exclusively related to the Lopez case. That meant Lopez had either corrupted someone in the FBI, or else he had managed to hack into the Bureau's information systems. She trusted everyone in the office…to a degree.

Colenso looked disgruntled. "You're giving me that schoolmarm look again."

"Get used to it. I've applied for Bayard's old job. You could be looking at your new boss."

"After what happened on the West Coast?"

Colenso's amused expression set her teeth on edge. Taylor picked up a file detailing Slater's successful prosecution and tossed it onto his desk. After "what happened" in both Eureka and Winton, she had zero tolerance for assholes. Someone had hemorrhaged information, compromising the operation on more than one occasion, with the result that Lopez had slipped the net. She had been caught off guard and taken hostage on the heels of the last spoiled operation. "Correct me if I'm wrong, but my *mistake* was the only investigative break we had."

His hands shot up in surrender. "I hear you, Yoda."

A reluctant smile twitched at her mouth. Lately, she'd gotten a lot of wisecracking about "the force," courtesy of her crusade against the "evil empire"—Lopez.

Gail, one of the clerks from administration, sorted through the bundle of mail she was carrying and dropped a letter onto Taylor's desk.

Frowning, Taylor retrieved a paper knife from her drawer and slit the envelope. A business card slid out, and for a moment her mind went utterly blank. There were no words, just a crude symbol in the shape of a jaguar's head stamped onto the card. The stamp lacked detail, it was the kind kids bought from bargain outlets and toy stores, but the fact that it was a jaguar's head made her skin crawl.

Lopez had had a jaguar tattooed on the back of one of his hands. The tattoo was no longer visible. He'd had it lasered off years ago, but Taylor had seen a grainy photo of it.

"What is it? What's wrong?"

"Someone just sent me a calling card. A jaguar's head."

Feeling light-headed and a little strange, she turned the card so Colenso could see it, then slipped it back into the envelope so as not to further compromise any prints.

Colenso frowned. "It's got to be a prank."

"I'm not laughing." The thought that it could have been Lopez made her freeze inside. If it was a bona fide calling card, the precursor to a hit—

He shrugged. "Sorry, wrong word. I'm not trying to trivialize it, but I've never heard of Lopez or the Chavez cartel using mafia tricks."

Taylor dropped the envelope into a plastic bag, her mind automatically going over the list of people, aside from Lopez, who could hold some kind of grudge against her. Slater's ex-wife and his hooker girlfriend. A number of Lopez's security staff who had been arrested in Eureka following the bust on Senator Radcliff's place, and who were presently standing trial. It had to be someone who knew about Lopez's tattoo and who knew that she would recognize the significance of the jaguar's head.

It could have been sent by Lopez.

The probability sent a shaft of raw panic through her. Until that moment she hadn't realized how much she never wanted to see Lopez again. As badly as she needed him caught, as totally as she had immersed herself in his case, she realized Bayard was right: the personal cost was too great. She didn't want back into a hell she'd spent months crawling out of.

Colenso touched her shoulder. She stared blankly into his concerned gaze, unaware until then that he had gotten up from his desk. "Stay there. I'll get you something to drink."

Minutes later he handed her a polystyrene cup of coffee. The hot liquid burned her mouth and was so sweet she could barely drink it.

Colenso propped himself on the edge of her desk as she sipped, his presence obscurely comforting because he blocked her off from the rest of the office, giving her time to recover. The last thing she needed was a cataloged report of an anxiety attack *in the office*. Bayard would have her out the door so fast she would be spinning.

Colenso studied the typed address label on the envelope, which was visible through the plastic. "If the card is from Lopez then it's manna from heaven. It could be the lead we've been waiting for."

But Colenso didn't think so.

The thought slid into her mind, as sharp and acid as the sugar-laced coffee, and suddenly Colenso's uncharacteristically PC behavior made sense. He was soothing her because he didn't believe the card was a serious threat.

* * *

Three days later, Bayard handed Taylor the forensics report on the envelope and the card. The envelope, the card, the ink and the stamp were all locally available items, most likely purchased in D.C. Whoever had sent the card had been professional enough to wear gloves, because the only identifiable prints besides Gail's and Taylor's had belonged to post office personnel. The postmark was local and the address was a computer-generated label that had been affixed to the envelope. The stamp showed no traces of saliva and because the envelope was of the self-sealing variety it hadn't yielded any, either, so there was no DNA.

Given that the envelope had been posted in D.C. on the same day Slater and the minor felons involved in the hostage situation had been sentenced, Bayard suspected that it was a hoax, most likely perpetrated by a family member or an associate of one of the felons. Without conclusive evidence of a death threat, he could no longer justify the around-the-clock security on her apartment or the escort to and from work, but she had options. She could scale down her hours until she felt better. If she wanted time off, she could have it on full pay. A holiday—a change of scene—could be just what she needed.

Taylor refused both offers point-blank. The "until she felt better" part had grated. She wasn't sick and she *needed* to work. The last thing she wanted was time alone. Without her job, she was an emotional amputee.

When she walked out of Bayard's office, the field room was abnormally quiet and no one glanced up, which was also unusual. She had known several of the agents for years, attended most of the departmental parties and done her share of hanging out at bars; the camaraderie had always been one of the best aspects of the job.

She had heard about the rumor that was circulating, that she had lost her grip, that someone down in records was running a book on the odds that she had mailed the card to herself.

Her stomach burned as she reached her desk. She checked her watch. It was after one, and she hadn't stopped for breakfast. Instead of sitting down, she shrugged into her coat and buttoned it against the wave of cold that was going to hit her the second she walked out of the building.

Colenso rocked back in his chair. "How did it go with Bayard?"

"The card was sent the same day Slater and his hired muscle were sentenced. He thinks it was one of them."

"Makes sense."

She hooked the strap of her handbag over one shoulder. "Want to go get some lunch?"

Colenso tapped his watch. "I ate an hour ago.

Besides, if I don't get these notes written up, Bayard's threatened to send me out with Tripp."

Taylor glanced across the office, more than willing for some light relief to stave off her own growing conviction that Bayard was right and that she really was losing her grip. Martin Tripp was sitting at his desk, staring at his computer screen as if it were about to suck him into cyberspace and he wouldn't mind the journey one little bit. Tripp, in his late forties, was a genius with computers and equipment, but he was also notorious for his bumbling in the field. Personally, Taylor thought he had a lot more potential than anyone had ever given him credit for. She glanced at Colenso with his sharp suit jacket and edgy haircut. At least Tripp had his ego under control. "He's not so bad."

Colenso glanced at Tripp and lifted a brow. "You've never been on a stakeout with him."

Rico Casale hunkered down on the roof of one of the older brownstones that lined the street just down from the Bureau's building. The brownstone was low enough that he got a good view of most of the street. With the aid of a pair of high-powered binoculars, he could just see the back entrance and the employee parking lot.

The roof of the brownstone also had the virtue of a water tower, a jumbled series of maintenance sheds and a waist-high parapet. It was cramped, and the parapet meant he couldn't use a tripod because the angle to the street below was too acute, but there was enough cover that he could remain hidden while he observed, even from buildings that overlooked his position. These days, after the Washington sniper, he couldn't be too careful. People were a lot more observant and a lot more suspicious. If he was spotted this close to the FBI building, it was game over.

A scattering of rain turned a miserable day even grimmer, but he was wrapped up warmly, with a padded coat, a woolen beanie pulled down low on his head and thick woolen mittens on his hands.

Crouching lower to avoid the worst of the rain and find an angle that would shield the lenses of his binoculars, he took time out to jerk the sheet of plastic he'd brought with him more securely over the rifle he had assembled more than an hour before.

Long minutes passed as he scrutinized the FBI building. He shifted, easing stiffened muscles and wiping moisture from his face. It was possible she wouldn't come out today, but she had yesterday and the day before. She might not eat at the same place or even walk in his direction, but so far she hadn't shown any signs of deviating from her pattern. He took a break to sip hot coffee from a thermos and checked the time. If she was going to eat lunch today, she was late.

A split second later, the door slid open and Taylor Jones stepped outside.

Tipping out the remains of his coffee, he slipped the binoculars into his knapsack, tugged the plastic sheet off the Remington and eased the butt of the rifle against his shoulder.

He swore beneath his breath. Jones had finally left for lunch, but today she had taken a route that angled away from his position, which meant he had to move, and fast.

With fingers stiffened by the icy wind, he disassembled the rifle and repacked the gun in a guitar case that had been customized to store the weapon. Seconds later, he slipped through the janitor's door and took the stairs to the ground floor.

He emerged out of the back entrance of the building, threaded his way down a service lane and out onto another, smaller street. Within minutes, his knapsack stowed in the trunk of his car, and his coat, beanie and mittens stripped off to reveal the business suit he was wearing beneath, he entered a second office building and took the lift to the sixth floor.

Within seconds of entering the room he had rented earlier in the week, he had reassembled the gun, locked it onto its tripod and trained it on the street below.

Taylor strolled into view, huddled against the wind. She disappeared momentarily beneath a shop awning, then reappeared, head down, walking directly into the crosshairs.

Four

Taylor paused by a Chinese food stall called Chen's, which was set up on a street corner just two blocks from the office. The stall was hemmed in by high-rises and situated in the protective lee of a large department store but, even so, the wind whipped her coat around her legs as she surveyed the stainless-steel bins of dishes.

Gray clouds were a solid mass above. In the few minutes it had taken her to walk from the office, the temperature had plummeted, the weather unseasonably cold for spring. The steady trickle of water from a gracefully weeping fountain set to one side of the department store didn't make her feel any warmer. "Nice day."

Chen shrugged. "Last I heard the forecast is for sleet."

A faint pattering of rain started as she ordered fried rice and spiced chicken. Huddling in closer beneath the small shelter, Taylor flipped up the collar on her coat and waited while he packaged her selection. The coat was pure wool, and lined. It would protect her for a while, but if it poured she was going to get soaked. "Sleet, great. I love cold—"

The raucous honking of a car horn cut her short. A taxi was stuck in traffic only feet away, slewed at an angle as a delivery truck double-parked. Wincing at the sustained assault on her ears, Taylor shifted to the other end of the counter, far enough that the steel wall of the take-out stand cut the direct blast of the horn.

Simultaneously, a tiny projectile sliced past Chen's head, bounced off the booth, ricocheted off the hot plate and embedded itself in the fountain. He blinked and went back to shoveling rice.

Taylor cocked her head to one side and stared at the punch mark in the back of the booth. It glinted in the dim light as if freshly made. She hadn't noticed it before and, cumulatively, she had spent a lot of hours staring at the back of Chen's take-out stand.

She continued to study the punch mark, then shook her head. The job *was* getting to her. To anyone else it would just be a dent; to her, the dent looked like it had been made by a bullet.

She dragged her gaze from the dented steel and

made herself watch the pedestrians hurrying by. Ordinary, everyday people: a businessman trying to talk into a cell phone; a woman struggling with an umbrella as the rain thickened and the wind turned gusty; a mother with two children in tow, all of them clutching bags filled with shopping.

The children, huddled close to their mother, and the nostalgia of gaily colored bags stuffed with bargains from the spring sales spun her back to her own childhood. Hot blue San Francisco skies, winters without snow, windblown beaches and walks in Golden Gate Park.

Looking back, the years she'd spent in a cramped apartment a stone's throw from the Pacific Ocean with her parents had seemed bright and happy, although she now knew that normality had been a sham.

Her father, Jack Jones, had always been an arresting, larger-than-life figure. When he'd been home from his "sales" trips, she had spent every spare second trailing after him. She could see why her mother, Dana, had fallen in love with him, and why she'd been so angry when she'd found out he was a cheap, two-bit con artist with a gambling addiction instead of the traveling salesman he had claimed.

The betrayal had cut deep. Dana had worked in international banking and her career had depended on a squeaky-clean reputation. She and Jack had fought for months. Then one day, Jack had slammed out of the apartment and had never come back. Two months later he had been killed in a hit-and-run accident.

The rain turned to sleet, stinging her cheek and sizzling off Chen's hot plate. Abruptly she grinned. At least she was alive and still kicking. Icy weather or not, she got a warm feeling inside every time she thought about the fact that not only had she escaped Lopez, but so had Rina. Now safely hidden on the Witness Security Program and settled into a relationship, Rina finally had a shot at happiness.

Brushing ice off her cheek, she finished the sentence the car horn had interrupted. "At least sleet makes us appreciate fine weather."

Chen fastened a lid on the fried rice and handed her the containers. "Hey, I could live with sunshine every day. It's good for business."

Still smiling, Taylor searched in her purse and counted change. Something zinged past her cheek. Frowning, she lifted a hand to her face. Her gaze caught on another dent in Chen's take-out stand. Adrenaline kicked. She was already moving when something punched into her back, shoving her forward. The containers of food spilled from her fingers. Blinking, she gripped the edge of the counter. The reason the dents looked so fresh and shiny was because they had just been made.

Chen's voice penetrated. "What's wrong? What's happened?"

Taylor felt like she had once when she'd come around from being knocked out, disoriented and a little shocky, only this time she hadn't been hit on the head. Her chest felt numb. "Call an ambulance. I've just been shot."

She was still standing, but her knees had turned to jelly and she was having trouble breathing. Disbelief gripped her.

The card. The jaguar's head.

Lopez, his voice flat. "I will kill you...it's only a matter of when."

Not when. Now.

"Get down...just in case—"

Chen was screaming. Around her, people were dropping to the pavement. The day was fading. Weirdly, she couldn't hear the traffic anymore. Funny, but she'd never thought it would feel like this, heat where she'd been hit, a cold numbness all around—a weird pastiche of sensations as muscles went into spasm and her legs folded.

The next bullet sliced a gash in Chen's arm and ended up in the bottom of the pool surrounding the fountain.

The sleet thickened, coating the sidewalk and turning the city gray. Chen pushed to his knees and peered over the top of his counter. People were still lying on the sidewalk. He could see the long dark hair and outflung arm of the woman he'd just served. After she'd fallen over the counter, she'd slid down onto the sidewalk and didn't appear to be moving.

In the distance sirens wailed. Someone must have called the police and, hopefully, an ambulance. He clutched his bleeding arm, wincing at the pain, his attention drawn to the sleet-covered outline of the woman's arm. She hadn't moved in a while. No matter how fast the ambulance came, he didn't think they were going to be in time.

Rico stepped out into the street, bracing himself against the icy wind. The guitar case bumped against his left thigh as he strode toward his car. A short, thickset man stepped out of a doorway, pausing to turn up the collar of his coat. The eye contact was brief and electric. Aldo Fabroni.

He ducked his head and walked on. As he strode down the street he could feel the older man's stare boring into his back. He swore beneath his breath and controlled the panicked impulse to break into a run. He couldn't get into his car, because that would give Aldo an opportunity to approach him and another point of reference to identify him, which meant he had to take the subway. He couldn't afford to stop a cab, not while he was carrying the gun and with a homicide one street over.

Rico couldn't believe it. He usually worked out of L.A., which was why he'd been chosen for this particular job. The client had wanted to make sure the hit was untraceable. In this business, secretive as it was, it was sometimes possible to trace the triggerman by asking around to find out who was available in the area to do the work. He had been the perfect choice for an East Coast job. Until Aldo.

He rounded a corner and stepped directly into the wind. Sleet pounded his face and froze his fingers. Shielding his eyes, he broke into a run, the ice-laden air shoving into his lungs hard enough to hurt. The sirens were closer.

As he dodged around pedestrians, he studied the street to orient himself. This wasn't his city, but he had done his homework. There was a subway entrance a block away.

Seconds later the subway sign came into view. When he reached the entrance, he slowed to a jog, grabbed the railing and slipped, almost losing his footing and the guitar case.

Breathing hard, he steadied himself and took the stairs as quickly as he could with the awkward weight of the case. A train pulled out, gathering speed, as he reached the platform.

He checked the displayed timetable. He was going to have to wait.

Clenching his jaw, he strode into the men's washroom, grabbed a wad of paper towels, dried his face and hair and wiped down his suit jacket. With any luck Aldo hadn't recognized him. If he ever asked him about it, Rico would simply say he had made a mistake; he hadn't been to D.C. in years.

When Rico exited the men's room, a familiar figure was staring at the timetable.

His stomach sank. He put on a smile. Finally, his acting classes were good for something. "Hey, *Aldo*. What are you doing here?"

"I could ask you the same thing." His attention dropped to the case. "No, don't tell me. You're in town for a concert."

Rico assessed the hard greed in Aldo's expression. He was a two-bit drug dealer and a fence, small potatoes all around, but he wasn't stupid. "How much?"

Aldo named a figure. Rico's stomach bottomed out.

Aldo grinned. "Don't worry. For that price your secret's safe with me."

Five

Steve Fischer stepped into the FBI building. It was just after four-thirty. The office was still open, but a lot of people had left early, eager to avoid the evening rush hour and worried that the escalating blizzard might create further delays.

Dusting sleet from his jacket, he stripped off his gloves, slipped them in his pocket and produced his ID. "Cold night."

The security guard checked his face against the photograph then waved him through. "Yes, sir."

He took the elevator, stepped out into the corridor and found the office he wanted. The door opened as he approached, which meant he didn't have to use his card and PIN number, which would record his presence in the office. He had a working agreement with the FBI, but Marc Bayard wouldn't tolerate interference in his investigation, old friendship or not. A woman and a man stepped out. Colenso and Burrows.

Colenso held the door. Burrows gave him a speculative look, but it was more female than curious. She had only recently transferred into D.C. and was still working out who was who, while Colenso had briefly met Steve during the hostage situation in Eureka last year.

The door closed behind him. Aside from a light in one of the end booths, the field room was empty. Walking through to an interview room, he took a seat and waited until the occupant of the booth left. Seconds later, the lights went out and the door clicked closed, signaling that he now had the office to himself.

Strolling to Taylor Jones's workstation, he sat down at her computer. The screen flickered the instant he touched the mouse. The computer hadn't been switched off, as he had expected. It had been in rest mode, which meant that when Taylor had left the building to get lunch, she had left the computer on, the system open. Frowning at the uncharacteristic sloppiness, Steve withdrew a disk and a flash card from an inside pocket of his jacket and plugged it into the USB port. The flash card was larger than normal, about the size of a pocket calculator.

He inserted the disk and waited for the program to install. Seconds later, he removed the disk, unplugged the flash card and slipped them both back into his jacket pocket. Taylor's security breach in leaving her computer on and unprotected while she was out of the building had just been solved. There was nothing to copy; her computer was clean. Someone had gotten there before him.

An hour later, he stepped into Taylor's apartment. Pocketing the duplicate master key he'd had made several weeks previously, he closed the door behind him and thumbed on a penlight. He didn't want to risk turning on a light in case Taylor's mother, Dana Jones, had caught an early flight and was already in town, although it was more than likely she would go directly to the hospital.

He moved soundlessly through the rooms in case one of Taylor's neighbors had caught the evening news and was nosy enough to check out who was in apartment 10A when the tenant was on the critical list.

The master bedroom was empty, the quilt a little wrinkled, as if she'd sat down on it that morning after the bed had been made. The quilt itself was plain, the bedroom furniture elegant but neat. No surprises there.

He moved through a second bedroom. The lack of luggage in the spare room confirmed that Dana Jones hadn't yet arrived. Given the weather conditions and the fact that even if she got a direct flight from San Francisco, it would take several hours to reach D.C., he didn't expect her to fly in until the morning.

The bathroom was cramped but spotless and contained the same clean, faintly sweet smell he had noticed in the bedroom and which he now identified as soap, not perfume. One towel was neatly draped over a towel rail.

Checking the luminous dial of his watch, he moved through to the sitting room. Like the rest of the apartment, the room was tidy, except for one corner, which was occupied by bookshelves jammed with reference books and a large computer desk awash with papers, notebooks and a stack of files. If he had needed further confirmation of what Taylor did with her spare time, apart from a rigorous fitness program, this was it. She worked.

And for the past few months, she had been busy. He'd had a tail on her ever since she had been discharged from the hospital after the hostage crisis in Eureka. Taylor's personal connection to Lopez, and the fact that, since Rina Morell had disappeared into the Witness Security Program, Taylor was Lopez's only link to his ex-wife, made her an automatic choice for surveillance. The fact that she had obsessively researched Lopez and the cabal, despite being first cautioned then pulled from the case, made her even more interesting. And now she knew about the book.

Locating the Internet files she'd searched had been easy. On a previous visit he had bugged her computer with a highly illegal piece of spyware designed to mimic the security system she used. His electronic friend recorded Taylor's online research and mailed to him the sites she had accessed and duplicates of any e-mail messages.

The microfiche material was something else entirely. Other than the time periods and the newspapers she had been researching—information that was noted on the register held at the front desk of the library—he had no idea what she was reading unless she created a computer file and e-mailed it to her work address.

Sitting down at the desk, he booted up the computer, inserted the disk and connected the flash card. A small window running percentages at the bottom of the screen indicated his copy program was complete. Removing the disk and flash card, he inserted a second disk into her drive. This one contained a powerful wipe program. Minutes later, her hard drive was clean.

Retrieving the disk, he took a small tool kit from his pocket, unscrewed the back plate of the CPU and attached a tiny, state-of-the-art transmitter, which was designed to look like part of the hard drive. FBI technicians would go over her computer with a fine-tooth comb, but until he activated satellite transmission, they were unlikely to locate it.

Six

Jack Jones was tall, about six-two, lean and rangy, with dark eyes and hair, courtesy of a Sioux grandfather. His hair was streaked with gray at the temples, just like it would be if he were alive, which Taylor knew wasn't possible. Jack Jones had been dead for more than twenty years.

She forced eyelids that felt like they'd been glued shut wider, so she could continue to study her dead father. The fact that he was standing just feet away, staring out of a window, convinced Taylor that the bullet that had punched through her back and sliced and diced at least one lung had, most likely, been fatal. If she was in Jack's company, she definitely hadn't gone to Heaven.

The only alternative to death was that she was alive and having a drug-induced vision, because to the best of her knowledge, Taylor didn't have a psychic bone in her body.

She turned her head and, like a switch flicking on, pain flared, burning in her chest and all down the back of her throat. She swallowed, trying to ease the dryness in her mouth, and the pain went ballistic.

A sharp click registered. Someone dressed in white bent over her. "She's awake and she's not supposed to be."

There was a second metallic clink, a cool sensation running up her right arm.

The next time she surfaced it was dark. A light glowed beside the bed, illuminating the fact that she was in a private room and her mother, Dana, was sitting beside the bed. Her chest still felt painful and tight; her throat was even sorer. A tube ran across her face: oxygen.

Dana's hand gripped hers. "Thank God. I thought I was going to lose you."

Taylor tried for a smile. Dana looked fragile, dark smudges under her eyes, the skin across her cheekbones finely drawn. "I'm hard to kill."

Although, if the way she felt now was any indication, she must have come close to dying. She was having trouble breathing. Speaking was even more difficult.

With an effort of will, she tried to remember what had happened, but her mind was a blank from the time she had consciously registered that she had been shot until she'd woken up and hallucinated that Jack Jones had been standing beside her bed. "Which hospital am I in?" There were wires and tubes everywhere. A shunt ran into her bandaged right wrist, and to her left she could hear the beep of a heart monitor.

"George Washington. They moved you out of ICU yesterday."

Yesterday. That meant at least a day had passed since she had last woken up. "How long since I was admitted?" She cleared her throat, suddenly ferociously thirsty.

"Two days." Dana leaned forward with a plastic cup and a straw. "You can have a few sips, but not too much. They don't want you throwing up in case you rupture your stitches. And don't worry about the back of your throat. The reason it's sore is because they've had a tube down there."

Ice-cold water filled her mouth then flowed down her throat. She winced at the rawness, took another sip and watched as Dana replaced the drink on her bedside table.

Two days. The amount of time that had passed explained why Dana looked so tired and rumpled; she would have caught a flight out yesterday. Dana had a key to Taylor's apartment but, knowing her mother, she would have bypassed the apartment and come straight to the hospital. She had probably slept here last night.

Dana's hand tightened around hers. "The bullet broke a rib and punctured the bottom lobe of your left lung. They've got you strapped up so the rib doesn't move. Luckily the bullet went all the way through so they didn't have to dig it out. They did keyhole surgery to repair the lung, but unfortunately, you had a reaction to one of the drugs they used, which is why you've been out for so long."

The sound of footsteps in the hall was followed by the glimpse of a woman carrying a brightly colored plastic bag. Taylor had a flashback of a woman with two children and other shoppers huddled against the cold. "Was anyone else hurt?"

"The guy who owns the take-out stand got grazed, but that was all."

Despite the fact that Chen had gotten hurt, relief channeled through her. There had been women and children on the street and at least three shots had been fired, maybe four if Chen's injury had happened after hers. "Did they get the shooter? Who's got the case?"

"The city police department picked it up, but when they realized you were an agent, they let the FBI step in and take over. And no, they haven't caught anyone yet."

A nurse stepped into the room, his gaze sharp as he took in the fact that she was awake. After a few routine questions, a check on her pulse and blood pressure and the drip feeding into her left arm, he made a note on the chart clipped on the end of her bed and left.

A metal trolley rattled in the corridor outside. With stiff movements, Dana got to her feet. "It's after eight. I need to get something to eat and freshen up. I'll be back in an hour or two. Is there anything you need?"

Taylor didn't know when she'd be able to wear them, but she needed some real clothes and some toiletry items. Her hair felt stiff, as if it hadn't been washed in days—which it hadn't—and her teeth felt fuzzy.

She gave Dana her list. "Have you talked to Bayard since you've been here?"

Dana's jaw firmed. She didn't like Marc Bayard or the FBI. Over the past few months Bayard had questioned her on a number of occasions about her involvement with Lopez and the fact that, years ago, she had been implicated in the theft of money from Lopez's account. Dana hadn't voluntarily had anything to do with either Lopez or the theft. Her association with Esther Morell had made her an unwitting pawn, but that hadn't made the interviews any less unpleasant. "Don't worry about Bayard, or your job. You don't have to go back after this."

Taylor's reaction was knee-jerk. Uh-uh. No way was she not going back.

Without her job she *would* die.

* * *

The next time she woke up Jack Jones was standing just inside the doorway, as large as life, a faithful rendition of the graying-at-the-temples version she'd seen at her bedside the previous day.

Whether it was the sedative effect of the painkillers or the possibility that she was hallucinating, Taylor didn't blink. She stared at his jaw and at eyes a lot like her own, and for a split second she was ten again and the loss was wrenching.

As a child, she had imagined Jack Jones walking back into her life in a dozen different ways. She and Dana would be told that there had been a mistake; he hadn't died, someone else had. Or, he had been revived in hospital—or even the morgue. Better still, his death, the funeral— the stark emptiness—had never happened. They had been part of a nightmare and one day she would wake up.

Years had passed; she hadn't woken up.

She met his gaze. The pressure banding her chest buttoncd off as she adjusted to the cold fact that Jack Jones was very much alive. That for over twenty years he had chosen to let her believe he was dead. "How did you get in here?"

"Taylor, I'm sorry—"

"How did you get in here?"

He lifted his shoulders. "I said I was your uncle."

She gasped for breath. The deep, gritty pain in

her chest edged through the haze of the painkiller. "Where did you go?"

Why did you do it? Why didn't you call? Ever?

Jack didn't confuse her question with the fact that she had woken up while he was in her room before. "Florida. The Keys. I've got a fish-and-dive charter business down there."

Another surge of emotion hit, this one more controllable. Years ago, after Jack had left, Dana had struggled to make ends meet. For a while they had been dirt-poor. The fact that her father had made a new life for himself in the sunny state of Florida didn't make being abandoned any easier to take. "Dana saw your body."

"That wasn't me. I was walking down the street when a guy got hit by a truck. I gave him first aid at the scene while we waited for the medics to arrive, but I couldn't find a pulse. His head was injured, his face practically gone. He was the same height and general coloring, so I swapped my wallet with his and walked away. I figured I was only going to get an opportunity like that once."

She locked on to the final part of Jack's statement, a cold, uneasy suspicion forming. "Why did you need another identity?"

"I'll get to that in a minute."

She studied his appearance. The haircut was cool and he was tanned. He was wearing expensive shoes and a quality coat. His hands were scarred and calloused, but if he worked with boats and fishing line, that was to be expected. Evidently, Jack Jones was doing all right. "How did you find out about me?"

He stepped farther into the room. "I've kept tabs on you. I knew you were an agent. I saw the late news the day you got shot and caught a flight out."

"Why?"

"I was worried about you. I didn't like the way the shooting panned out, so I checked with a contact."

The unexpected statement and the complete lack of expression that went with it made her stomach tighten. "What do you mean, you checked with a contact?"

His eyes were cold and very direct. "I used to be a hit man. That was the reason I left—not because I wanted to, but because I had to. I worked out of L.A., which is why I think I can help you now."

For a split second she didn't register any part of his statement other than the fact that her father used to kill for a living. Suddenly it all jelled: the gun collection, his disappearances. Thinking back, she had never entirely bought into the concept that he'd had a gambling addiction. "Did Dana know?"

"No."

She reached for breath. For the first time she had an insight into the way her mother must have felt when she'd found out the man she had married was a con artist, only he wasn't, he was worse than that. "Is Jack Jones even your name?"

"As a matter of fact, it is."

If that was the truth, he was lucky. Jones had to be as common as Smith. Together with Jack, his name was the identification equivalent of being invisible.

He checked the door again. "I don't have much time. The point is I think I can locate the shooter."

"How?"

"Contacts. Leverage."

Taylor felt herself go cold inside. "You're still in the game."

"No. I'm out, and it wasn't a game. I got caught up in it when I was a kid, then I met Dana and we had you. I tried to leave but changing careers wasn't an option."

He mentioned a couple of organized-crime high-flyers, one now deceased, another who had done time for what amounted to little more than a misdemeanor and was now back in business.

Taylor stared at the lean, hard planes of his face. So, okay, her father had been a hit man, working for a crime syndicate. It was difficult to take. She was in the business of shutting down people like him. "Who's your contact?"

He grinned quick and hard and for a moment she almost expected him to say, *That's my girl.* "Sorry."

"I could have you arrested and subpoenaed."

"And lose the only chance you've got at finding out who pulled the trigger? I don't think so."

The ache in her chest intensified. "What can you tell me?"

"I don't have a name yet. I know he's not local, and that he hasn't been in the game for long."

"Who hired him? Lopez?"

"Who else?"

Now it was real.

She had used Lopez's name to shock him, but he hadn't shown any reaction at all, which told her more than she wanted to know about her own father.

He checked his watch. "When you're discharged from here you need to get out of town, disappear for a while. Give me time to find him."

He pulled a business card from his wallet. "I know you won't want to contact me, but I'm going to leave this with you anyway." He crouched down by her bedside cabinet, took out her purse and slipped the card inside one of the side pockets.

He straightened, the movement fluid for a man in his fifties, but then, not much about Jack Jones looked either old or decrepit. He had a toughness, an edge she recognized, and the reality of what her father was finally sank in. "Did you ever kill anyone?"

The glance he gave her was sharp and utterly neutral. "Be in touch."

Seven

A week later, Taylor took a seat in Bayard's office. The fact that she had made it up the front steps of the building, albeit with Dana's help, was a major triumph given that she still felt as weak as a newborn baby.

Bayard shook Dana's hand, his expression controlled. Colenso and Janet Burrows, who had been assigned her case, looked uncomfortable, and Dana was distinctly unhappy. She had tried to convince Taylor to wait until she felt better, but Taylor had insisted on the meeting. She was the victim of a professional hit. After months of having her credibility questioned it was finally clear that she wasn't crazy and she wasn't paranoid. She had answered Colenso's and Burrows's questions, provided a statement and waited as long as she could. Now she needed answers. And she wanted back into the investigation.

Janet leaned forward and poured coffee from the tray set on Bayard's desk as Colenso ran through the ballistics report. Two slugs had been recovered, both from the fountain. The caliber of the bullets emphasized the fact that some kid high on meth with a Saturday-night special hadn't just wildly discharged a gun into lunchtime shoppers and randomly hit her in the back. The larger caliber was usually associated with hunting weapons and sniper rifles, a much more exclusive club of killers.

Janet offered Taylor coffee, but she refused. She didn't need food or drink. The way her heart was pounding, a shot of caffeine would finish her off.

Colenso slid a set of black-and-whites across the desk. A window in one of the photos was circled with black marker. An arrow indicated the trajectory.

Sixth floor, which would have given the shooter plenty of angle. "Have you got details of the tenant?"

Janet handed Bayard a cup, then set the coffeepot down. "The room was supposedly rented to an advertising firm. They never moved in. I checked the address and telephone number. The address was false, and the telephone was a cell phone that was only used for that one call."

Bayard opened the file in front of him. These

days he spent more time working budgets and politicians than he did taking part in investigations, which in Taylor's opinion was a criminal waste. In the intelligence world, Bayard was a shark. He also had a formidable knowledge of every agency the Bureau liaised with, and a prosecution rate second to none. When it came to cutting through red tape and getting results, Bayard reigned supreme. It had been his quick action and commitment to keeping his people safe that had gotten her out of Eureka alive. If she trusted anyone's opinion, it was his.

He slid a document across the desk. "We've gone over that room with a fine-tooth comb. So far, we have fifteen different sets of prints, but only three of them are traceable, and two of those belong to employees of the cleaning firm the building uses."

Taylor skimmed the top page, which was a list of National Crime Information Center fingerprint identification reports. The two cleaners were female, one with a conviction for shoplifting, the other for prostitution. The third file belonged to Pedro Alvarez, and outlined a ten-year-old conviction for car theft. According to the information, Alvarez was now twenty-seven, which would have made him seventeen at the time he was charged.

"We're talking to Alvarez."

But the chances that they were getting anything

were low. Taylor didn't need Bayard to tell her that the jump from teenage car theft to professional killing was huge. Which brought her back to the scenario that she had been shot by a professional, in which case the likelihood that he would have left any prints was close to zero.

She set the file down. "What about Lopez?"

The calling card had arrived the same week she had been shot. There was a direct connection. There was no way Bayard could dismiss it this time.

"We're doing everything we can at this point."

Her jaw compressed. "I can help. You need—"

"No." Bayard's expression was impassive.

She forced herself to calm down. "So where does that leave me?" He wanted her out of the office, on sick leave. It was even possible he would move her sideways in order to cut her ties to the Lopez case. Given what had happened, his logic was impeccable, but the thought of having to transfer out of D.C. made her head throb. She had been in line for a promotion. If she transferred to a field office, that opportunity would dissolve.

Dana touched her hand. "We're leaving. She's not supposed to get upset."

Taylor stared at Bayard's jaw. "I need to know about my job."

Colenso set down his coffee cup. The clink was oddly loud in the silence of the room. Janet looked embarrassed.

Bayard slid another document across the desk. "I'm sorry. We're running the paperwork now. The U.S. Attorney's office and the U.S. Marshal's office are both on my back. You're too valuable to the prosecution for Lopez's case to risk. They want you safe. All we need is your permission."

The paperwork was instantly recognizable. Witness Security.

Dana's hand tightened on hers. For that split second Taylor needed the anchor.

Lopez hadn't killed her, but he had come close. He had taken out her career.

Out on the sidewalk a freezing wind swirled, tugging at the lapels of her coat as Dana attempted to hail a cab. With every breath icy air stabbed into Taylor's lungs, cutting through the codeine and turning the low-key solo in her chest into a full-blown concerto.

Dana's expression was taut as another taxi cruised by. "Damn, why won't one stop? I don't want you out here."

Taylor's cell phone buzzed, a welcome interruption. She needed something to do besides dwell on the fact that this was the first time since the shooting that she had been out on a city street, stationary and exposed.

The voice was low, modulated and instantly recognizable. "Rina."

Mexico. Sun. Heat. Dry air that didn't hurt to breathe.

She hadn't ever seen a photo of the farmhouse Rina's partner, J. T. Wyatt, had bought. She wasn't even supposed to know where they were, but Rina had described the sprawling hacienda, mountains in the distance, a lush green river threading the dry landscape. It was a long way from cold weather and gray streets. "What's wrong?"

The only reason for Rina to ring was if something had changed. Technically, she wasn't supposed to ring at all.

"We're pregnant."

The day turned hazy. She caught snatches of Rina's voice. "Hadn't planned it… Had wanted to wait until Lopez was caught, but it happened, despite precautions—"

A baby.

Longing, unexpected and powerful, tightened the vise squeezing her chest. She blinked, cutting off the emotion. She didn't want to need that—not yet. What she needed was to be happy for Rina.

"Taylor, talk to me. Are you all right?"

"I'm fine." Under the circumstances. "I just lost my job."

Silence: no platitudes. Rina knew better.

Finally, Rina spoke. "Tell me what happened. I need to know everything."

Taylor's rendition was brief. If she drew it out,

she'd end up crying on the sidewalk, and she was tired of losing control, of wallowing in emotion.

A taxi swerved into the curb. Dana motioned her to get in.

Pain seared her chest, her back and all the way down her left leg as she climbed into the rear of the cab.

Rina's voice was urgent. "Are you sure it was Alex?"

Taylor rubbed at her temples. "It was a professional hit. The guy rented a room and waited."

"What was the payoff?"

Black humor surfaced. "You ask me that?"

"The calling card bothers me. Alex doesn't use gimmicks and he doesn't go in for revenge unless there's a payoff. So what was the payoff?"

She stared out the window of the cab. "Lopez wants me dead."

"Not enough. He doesn't waste time and he doesn't create unnecessary complications. Think about it, that's what you're good at. Maybe you're right, and Alex does want you dead, but it won't be personal. If you don't have something he wants, then you must know something."

Taylor stared at the weaving traffic and tried to think. Alex Lopez had waited more than two decades to obtain what he wanted from Rina. It hadn't been an act of revenge. He had been patient, methodical, efficient. He had waited behind the scenes, controlling her life, eventually marrying her. The payoff he had been after had been huge, an account number locked in Rina's mind worth billions of dollars.

"Maybe you're right." The only thing Taylor could be certain of was that she no longer saw Lopez clearly. Bayard had been right. She had lost her objectivity.

Weariness dragged at her, a cold sense of premonition. "It's no longer my problem. Bayard has the case."

"I know. He's good. I'm just worried," she said softly. "If it's not Alex, that means it's someone else. Watch your back."

Eight

A month later, her chest still healing, Taylor, now known as Taylor Jeffries, watched as a moving firm unloaded her furniture and carried it into a condominium in one of the beachside suburbs of Wilmington, North Carolina.

The condo had been an obvious choice. The security was good and it had a swimming pool. In order to help her damaged lung regain its normal capacity, she needed to do aerobic activity, but she wasn't allowed to jog yet. Aside from walking and the breathing exercises the physiotherapist had given her, all she was allowed to do was swim.

She stepped aside as two burly men maneuvered a couch through the front hallway, and watched as they unpacked furniture and possessions she hadn't seen since the morning of the shooting.

Aside from the loss of her job, the WITSEC placement meant separation from Dana until Lopez was caught and it was safe for Taylor to resume her normal life. Dana had also had the option of a WITSEC placement, but she had chosen to stay in San Francisco. According to the FBI report, the attack on Taylor had been viable because of Taylor's routine. The risk that Lopez, or one of his people, would make a second attempt now that Taylor was protected by WITSEC was minimal. From Dana's point of view, if remaining outside the Witness Security program posed a threat to Taylor's security, she would go, gladly, but until then they could leave her life the hell alone.

For Taylor, there had only been one option, but walking away from the commitment she'd made to the Bureau, the years of specialized training and the knowledge that her skills could make a difference, had hurt. Every day she checked the papers and the Internet for career options. Enforcement of any kind was out, and she had signed an agreement to stay away from anything that made her publicly visible or was even remotely life threatening. She was supposed to "blend," but she couldn't see herself fitting into retail work or an office job.

When the movers had gone, she walked through the apartment: two bedrooms, two bathrooms—one an en suite—a large sitting room and dining area and a compact kitchen. The front of the apartment opened onto a small, sun-drenched balcony that framed a breathtaking view of the coastline.

She made her bed, unpacked her cases, then started on the sitting room. The movers had unpacked the computer and placed it on her desk, which was situated in an alcove.

Anticipation hummed through her as she booted up the computer. She clicked on an icon and her filing system opened up. She stared at the directory. It was empty.

She clicked back to the desktop and tried again. All of the programs were still there and the computer itself was functioning perfectly, but the files were gone.

The movers had assembled her desk and placed the computer on it, but they hadn't connected it up or switched anything on, so there was no way they could have wiped the files. It was possible whoever had emptied her apartment had damaged the hard drive, but she didn't think so. The hard drive had simply been cleaned of all the content she'd saved, which meant someone had gotten into the system and wiped the files.

Dana had used her apartment until Bayard had transferred her to a hotel closer to the hospital, but she traveled with her own laptop; she didn't ever use Taylor's computer. According to Bayard, her apartment had been locked and under surveillance. Nothing had been touched until the movers had arrived.

It was possible that Colenso or Janet had seen the files and uploaded them, and maybe even searched through her computer, but not likely. They had kept her in the loop every step of the way, and there was nothing on her home computer that couldn't be obtained from her work computer.

If they had decided that any of the files on her PC contained anything sensitive, they would have had to go through a legal process to impound the PC, then document the removal of the information. Even if that had happened, which was unlikely because she would have to have been informed, they would have taken only the files that were sensitive. Wiping everything didn't make sense, unless whoever had done it had been operating clandestinely, in a hurry, and had used a comprehensive wipe program.

Skin crawling, she began opening the boxes of books and files stacked against the bookshelf. The movers had offered to fill the shelves for her, but she'd insisted on doing the job herself.

She emptied one box, then another. Reference books spilled across the floor. Ripping open a third box, she pulled out more books. The fourth box contained a set of bookends, ornaments and sporting trophies from her school years, all wrapped in bubble wrap. At the bottom was the carved wooden box she kept her disks in.

Tearing the bubble wrap off the box, she opened it up, expecting it to be empty. The disks were still there.

Pushing to her feet, she checked the desk drawers, then walked through to the spare bedroom and opened the boxes stored in there. She found a few more books, her collection of CDs, vases and photographs, but there was no sign of her notes and files. Whoever had gone through her desk and computer had taken every disk, every file and loose piece of paper. They had been thorough; the only thing they had missed had been the box of disks, because it looked more like an ornament than a storage box.

She would call her WITSEC contact and get him to check with Colenso. She didn't think Colenso would have any answers, but he needed to know that her apartment had been broken into and that information had been stolen.

She stared at the computer keyboard. Movers at each end had handled it. In any case, in the few seconds she had used the keyboard and the mouse, she had probably obliterated any prints that might have been left behind, but there was always the possibility that she could pick up a partial, or even a whole print on one of the keys.

Walking through to the spare room, she found a box filled with FBI memorabilia. Among the contents was a fingerprinting kit she'd used when she'd completed a course in evidence collection.

Setting out spare bedsheets on the carpet to protect it from the fine graphite dust, she dusted the surfaces of the computer and the desk. An hour later she had transferred a number of prints to strips of clear sticky tape and smoothed the tape onto plastic sheets, sealing the prints in.

Most of the prints had been obtained from the sides of the monitor, hard drive and the desk, which indicated they probably belonged to the movers. The keyboard and the mouse had given her a small number of well-defined prints, but Taylor was almost certain they were all her own. Aside from the keys she knew she had touched, the keyboard had been clean when there should have been prints on every key, which meant whoever had used her computer had wiped it down.

When she was finished, she labeled and dated the prints and placed them in an envelope. She would express them to Pete Burdett, her contact at WITSEC, in the morning, with a note to forward them on to Colenso so they could run the prints through AFIS and NCIC.

She carried the sheets through to the laundry then wiped the computer and the desk down with a damp cloth. Now that she had collected the prints, her prime concern was to obliterate the touch of whoever had broken into her apartment.

The fact that the theft had happened weeks ago should have blunted the shock, but the clinical manner in which the information had been stolen, and the time it had taken for her to realize a crime had been committed creeped her out. In all likelihood, they had searched through her things to make sure they had gotten everything. The fact that they hadn't found the disks was sheer luck.

Walking through to the kitchen, she washed her hands, which were coated with a fine film of black graphite. When she'd dried off, she searched in the cupboard for the coffeepot and the fresh grounds she'd brought with her on the trip down.

She measured the coffee, then searched for a mug while the filter machine gurgled and spit.

Unable to wait for the machine to finish dripping, she removed the carafe and poured coffee into a mug, ignoring the burning smell as liquid splashed onto the hot plate. After replacing the carafe, she carried the mug out onto the balcony.

Holding the mug with both hands, she lifted the coffee to her lips and sipped. The hot, sharp taste filled her mouth. There was no sugar, milk or cream, but it didn't matter. It was the familiarity of the taste, and the comfort of the ritual she craved right now.

The sun dazzled her eyes as she stared at the unfamiliar view and tried to relax. She was hundreds of miles from D.C. and her old life, about as far from Eureka and the ordeal with Lopez as she could get without leaving the country. But, suddenly, Wilmington, North Carolina, didn't seem far enough.

Nine

Two days later, Taylor got a call from Burdett to inform her that Colenso had checked out the prints and come up blank. Colenso had also gone to her previous apartment, but with two sets of movers and a cleaning firm through in as many weeks, evidence collection hadn't been viable.

Burdett cleared his throat. "Are you sure someone tampered with your computer? Maybe it was a virus."

Taylor's jaw tightened. "Is that what Colenso said?"

"He thought it was a possibility."

"The last time I used my computer was the night before I got shot. It was working perfectly then. If I'd had a virus, I would have known about it."

"Maybe it's a new one, and you got unlucky. Have you had your computer checked out?"

"I've checked it myself. My computer security is very good. The program doesn't register an intrusion."

Seconds later, Taylor hung up and stared at the slice of beach she could see from her kitchen window.

Instead of working the case, Colenso seemed more interested in implying that she was paranoid and closing down what could have been a valuable lead. It didn't make sense, when the theft of information connected with the Lopez case and linked so closely with the shooting of an agent researching that case should have guaranteed it a high priority.

Maybe Burdett had relayed the message to her in an insensitive way, but Taylor didn't think so. Pete Burdett was a professional. If Colenso had been actively pursuing an investigation, he would have said so.

Collecting the keys to the apartment, Taylor slipped dark glasses onto the bridge of her nose, locked up and started her daily progress toward the beach. She called it progress, because the gentle stroll didn't qualify as walking. Every time she reverted to her normal stride, her chest tightened up and she was reminded that her lung, although mostly healed, still wasn't operating at full capacity.

Closer to the water, the view wasn't as idyllic. The beach was crowded with tourists and the wind had turned easterly, making the sea choppy and turbid. Removing her sandals, she strolled below the line of dried seaweed and shells that delineated the high-tide mark and began following the gentle curve of the bay, working through the breathing exercises designed to expand her lung capacity.

Half an hour later, she stopped at a beachside café, bought a soda and sat at a shaded table, sipping the icy drink while she got her breath back. The café was at the edge of a crowded marketplace, filled with stalls selling local produce and handmade crafts. Idly, Taylor watched people strolling from stall to stall. A young woman wearing a bikini, a bright blue muslin sarong around her waist; a couple pausing by a hot-dog stand, the man tall and lean with glasses, his dark hair close cropped, the woman carefree in a red ankle-length dress, her hair tumbled around her shoulders.

Her eye attracted by the vibrant red, she automatically continued to watch the woman in the ankle-length dress, now on her own.

A tall man with glasses.

She searched the line of stalls, but the man she had thought was with the woman had already moved out of view. Leaving the drink on the table, she threaded through the crowd, moving in the direction he had gone. The odds were it hadn't been the man she'd noticed in the library studying a microfilm—it was crazy to think that he could be— but something about him had struck a chord.

She caught a glimpse of a dark head, the glint of spectacles. She rounded a stall, moving into a new lane of the market that was crowded with shoppers and rank upon rank of colorful sarongs fluttering in the breeze. She broke into a jog. If the man had been strolling, he should have been visible. It was possible he had doubled back, but she didn't think so, because she had been careful to check either side of the lane.

Gasping, her chest burning, she stopped at the edge of the market. A movement off to her right jerked her head around. Her guy had just crossed the road. She watched as he disappeared into the shaded entrance of a shop.

Her hand automatically grasping for a gun that wasn't there, she crossed the road, ignoring a blaring horn. Instead of entering the shop, she rounded the corner in time to see the man climb into a vehicle at the end of the street. He had gone into the shop then exited by a side door. She caught a glimpse of the dark sedan as he accelerated through an intersection, but she was too distant to establish the make of the vehicle or the number plate.

Heart pounding, she leaned against a wall and waited for her breathing to stabilize. She hadn't seen him head-on, but she was sure it was the man she had noticed in the library in D.C. the week before she had gotten shot.

Offhand, Taylor couldn't think of any other

reason for him to be in Wilmington…other than to finish the job he had started in D.C.

Just how he had found her was an interesting question. WITSEC was supposed to be foolproof.

An hour later, she was seated in the U.S. Marshal's office in downtown Wilmington. Burdett had filed a report and she had worked up an Identi-Kit, which they had run through their computer system without a conclusive result. A call had been put through to Colenso, who was in a meeting. He would return the call as soon as he was free. Burdett had authorized around-the-clock security for her apartment. In the meantime, he advised her to go home and stay inside until he contacted her.

Burdett rang back later that afternoon.

Taylor grabbed the phone. "What have you got?"

"Nothing yet. Colenso's got his people looking into it."

Her fingers tightened on the receiver. The words carried an unexpected sting. "Colenso's people" meant Colenso had gotten the job she had been in line for. "I need to talk to Colenso. I saw the guy. *I can describe him.*"

"We have the description. Everything's taken care of." Burdett's voice was flat. She was an ex-agent recovering from a near-fatal shooting. The WITSEC placement was an adjustment. They would post security around her apartment for a couple of days and ask the Wilmington PD to keep an eye out for the man she had described. If there was genuine cause for alarm, they would move her to another location, but at this stage, they would follow procedure.

Taylor stared at the phone after Burdett had hung up.

If there was genuine cause for alarm.

Colenso didn't believe her. Neither did Burdett.

Something was wrong. Burdett had been polite, but he had treated her as if she was paranoid and overanxious.

The attitude was staggering. She was used to instant credibility. She wasn't an agent any longer, but that didn't mean her expertise and investigative savvy had evaporated overnight.

She couldn't understand why Colenso wasn't interested. Twice, she had supplied him with information, and both times he had ignored her. Granted, she hadn't seen the man's face. It was possible she had made a mistake, and that there was a reasonable explanation as to why he had been in such a hurry.

She paced the sitting room, avoiding the area in front of the patio. Seaview Apartments was surrounded by eight-foot-high masonry walls, but suddenly, the large picture windows and sliding doors felt open and exposed. It was secure from the street, but not from neighboring buildings.

Walking through to her bedroom, she opened the drawer of her bedside table and took out the handgun and shoulder holster she kept there. She found the magazine for the Glock in a box in her wardrobe, checked the load and slotted the clip home.

Slipping the shoulder holster on was like sliding back into her old persona. Shrugging into a light cotton jacket that was loose enough to cover the bulge of the weapon, she found her purse and searched for the business card Jack Jones had slipped into a side pocket.

She studied the card, then replaced it. Her mind made up, she collected fresh underwear and toiletries, and slipped the items into her handbag. She would be away a minimum of three nights, but she didn't want to carry too much with her in case Burdett's security picked up on the fact that she was leaving town. She could buy whatever she needed when she got to Key Largo.

Locking the apartment, she walked in the direction of the nearest shopping center, which was less than two blocks away. Burdett's security detail was easy to spot, an unmarked car parked across the road from the entrance to Seaview Apartments.

She found a cash machine and withdrew the maximum her account would allow, then walked into the nearest rental car agency. Maybe it was paranoid to avoid using her credit cards, but after today, she was officially paranoid.

Twenty minutes later, after handing over more than half of her cash, she drove an SUV out onto U.S. 17 and headed south.

She drove until she was bleary eyed, checking the rearview mirror frequently and making stops in smaller towns, just to confuse anyone who might be following her. Burdett wouldn't be happy when he found out she'd gone, but for the first time in weeks Taylor finally felt in control.

Just short of midnight, she booked into a motel in Jacksonville. After sending out for pizza, she had a shower and dropped into bed.

She arrived in Key Largo late the following afternoon. Driving to a mall, she walked into a discount clothing store, purchased fresh underwear, a pair of loose white cotton pants and a fresh tank top. After paying for the items, she walked back into the changing room, removed the tags, changed into the fresh clothing and placed the worn outfit in the plastic bag. After driving all day, she needed a shower, but that would have to wait.

Parking at the marina noted on Jack Jones's business card, she took a few moments to stretch and cool off then walked into the office and made some inquiries.

An obliging receptionist indicated the pamphlet that advertised her father's charter service and offered to take a booking. Refusing the offer,

Taylor picked up the pamphlet and followed the directions to his mooring.

At first glance, dressed in a colorful loose shirt and board shorts, a straw hat pulled down over his forehead, she didn't recognize Jack Jones. When he saw her, he dropped the cloth he'd been using to clean chrome fittings on the flying bridge of a gleaming launch, climbed down a ladder and stepped up onto the dock. "What's happened?"

No preliminaries, just cut to the chase. Taylor's throat tightened at his instant concern. The reaction caught her by surprise. "A man I'd noticed at a library I'd been using to research Lopez in D.C. turned up in Wilmington."

His gaze sharpened. "Bayard didn't take care of it?"

"I wouldn't be here if he had."

If the comment stung, he didn't show it, but then she had already seen an example of his mental toughness in the hospital.

His gaze moved slightly downward, subtly letting her know that he knew she was armed. He jerked his head in the direction of the launch. "You'd better come on board."

She followed him into a sleek, roomy cabin and watched as he made coffee. He handed her a mug. She added powdered creamer and sugar from the containers on the bench and sat down on one of the leather banquettes on either side of a polished mahogany table.

She caught Jack staring at her as she drank, the first break in that tough facade she'd seen. He looked older than he had in Washington, rumpled and tired after a day out on the ocean, and suddenly the link between them hit her.

She had always had trouble with emotions. When she chose someone, she was fiercely loyal, and she didn't let go, no matter what. Jack Jones had been the exception to the rule: she had been forced to let him go. Now she had to adjust to the fact that he was alive, and he was nothing like she remembered.

He sipped his coffee. "So, who is this guy?"

"He's not Bureau and he can't be working for the U.S. Marshal's office, because he was in the picture before the shooting." She watched a gull settle onto a wharf piling. "Unless they've had me tailed since Eureka."

She'd gone over the reasons why the U.S. Marshal's office would allocate a chunk of their annual budget to surveiling her until she was tired of thinking about it. The U.S. Marshals had their own very specific agenda. In Lopez's case, they were solely concerned with apprehending him so he could stand trial. It was a stretch to believe that they had been watching her on the off chance that Lopez would try to make contact.

"That brings us back to Lopez." He reached

down into a cabinet slotted beneath a padded window seat and pulled out a notebook and a pen. "Describe the guy who was following you."

She gave him the details. "I could help you find him."

"No."

The answer didn't surprise her. Jack Jones had been a part of a criminal underworld, she had been an agent; he couldn't work with her breathing down his neck. But she couldn't let go of the fact that the man who had followed her could be a bona fide lead in the Lopez case. "You'll need my cell phone number."

His expression didn't change as he wrote the number down, but the tension was palpable. Taylor couldn't help but be aware that asking Jack Jones for help—giving him her number—strengthened a link she'd spent years rejecting.

"Have you got a place to stay?" His expression was cool and direct, the message blunt. He didn't want the risk of her staying with him.

"Not yet." She pushed to her feet and adjusted the strap of her handbag over one shoulder. "I'll book into a motel in town, then head back to Wilmington in the morning."

Steve Fischer stepped down off the pier onto a moored yacht as Taylor walked past, his focus sharpening as he studied her expression.

Something had changed.

Keeping his head down so the bill of his ball cap shaded his face, he continued to study her through dark glasses, then thumbed the speed dial on his cell phone and lifted it to his ear. "You pick up the tail. There's something else I have to do here. And be careful—she's armed."

Keeping an eye on the launch Taylor had just spent the past half hour in, he settled down to wait.

Ten

Instead of repeating the two-day drive back to Wilmington, Taylor made arrangements to leave the car at the Miami airport and caught a flight out the following afternoon. She had driven to the Keys so that Burdett, or anyone else who might be following her, wouldn't have the easy convenience of a paper trail to follow. Now that she'd concluded her business, the fact that her name would register on a flight manifest was no longer a problem.

When she stepped into her apartment, her answering machine was flashing and her phone was ringing. It was Burdett, and he wasn't happy. She hadn't informed them that she was leaving town after he had authorized extra protection. He was more than happy to supply the protection—they were there to support her—but she had to cooperate.

Taylor understood Burdett's view perfectly, but that didn't change her reality.

After a restless night, she showered and dressed, shrugged into the shoulder holster and slipped on a fresh jacket. Checking the load on the Glock, she placed it in the holster.

She made coffee, then grimaced when she discovered the milk had gone sour. Emptying the milk into the sink, she spooned sugar into her cup instead and drank the coffee black while she did an inventory of the cupboards. She was reluctant to leave the apartment complex, but she was almost out of food, which meant she had to shop.

After loading laundry into the washing machine and discovering that she didn't have washing powder, either, she added that to her list, locked the apartment and strolled to the front gate. One of Burdett's men waved at her as she stepped out onto the sidewalk and relief channeled through her. Despite Burdett's annoyance, he hadn't canceled the security detail.

She waved back and kept walking, but her response to Burdett's security had made up her mind. Wilmington was supposed to be her refuge, but not any longer. Somehow, despite all the precautions, her security *had* been compromised. When Burdett had calmed down she would request a new placement, and tighter security. If Burdett didn't listen, she would call Bayard and keep calling until she got results.

The beach was still crowded, the roads crammed with tanned couples holding hands, kids wearing fluorescent shorts and eating ice cream, but Taylor couldn't relax. There were plenty of tall, dark men around, but none wearing spectacles. She studied faces, but dark glasses distorted appearance to a degree that she had to accept that even if she looked directly at the man who had been following her, she wouldn't recognize him.

She walked into the nearest mall, found a supermarket and bought the few items she needed. Without a car, she couldn't carry much so she kept her purchases to basics: fresh milk, salad vegetables, wholegrain bread and washing powder. There was no point in loading up with food when she would be leaving Wilmington.

When she stepped out of the mall, she slipped dark glasses on, studied the queue of tourists lined up waiting for cabs and decided she would get home faster walking. Crossing the road, she threaded her way through a parking lot. As she stepped onto the sidewalk, light flashed from one of the apartment balconies overhanging the street. A flicker of movement drew her eye, another flash, and for a disorienting moment she was transported to a cold, gray street in D.C., ice and rain forming a misty murk, and shiny dents in stainless steel.

She was already moving when lettuce and whole-grain bread exploded and, for the second time in less than two months, she hit the sidewalk.

The Glock in one hand and dragging her handbag, which contained her cell phone, she crawled behind the nearest cover, a shiny black convertible. Her right forearm was burning where the bullet must have grazed her. Blood had already soaked her jacket sleeve and was steadily dripping, making her grip on the gun slippery.

A metallic pop split the air and a sideview mirror shattered. Her arms jerked up, shielding her face, but it was too late. Her skin stung where shards of glass had either cut her or become embedded.

Long seconds passed while she waited for the next shot. When it didn't come, she risked checking out the direction the shots had originated from. Above street level, floor space was mostly given over to apartments with balconies, and in the balmy weather a lot of doors and windows were open. The flash of light she'd seen had most likely come from a telescopic sight. She knew the general location, but she couldn't pinpoint the exact balcony.

Staying low, she fumbled in her bag, found her cell phone and dialed emergency services. Normally she would have the local police department on speed dial, but with a new identity, and living in a strange city, she hadn't thought she would need that particular number.

The operator picked up and began taking details. Blood dripped from her wrist, soaking into her clothes and forming a small, viscous puddle on the asphalt as she answered questions.

The operator's voice was soothing. "Stay calm, ma'am. We'll have someone with you shortly."

"I am calm." But she wasn't. Her voice sounded hollow, as if she were talking into a drum, and adrenaline kept kicking through in spurts, making her shake.

A horrified gasp jerked her head up. She registered the wide-eyed stare of a slim, tanned woman wearing tennis whites.

Unclenching her teeth, she motioned for the woman to get down. "It's okay. I've been shot, but I think he's gone."

But it wasn't okay. Whoever had shot her had wanted to hit her. They had fired at least twice.

She dialed Burdett, then hung up when she spotted one of his men crouched behind a car near the entrance of the parking lot, talking into a radio. She had been aware that he had followed her, keeping a discreet distance, but she hadn't seen him since she had entered the mall.

The woman, who was now huddled down by the back wheel of the car, stared blankly at her face. Taylor didn't bother checking. She could feel the stiffening of her skin where the blood from the cuts had dried. If her face looked anything like her arm, she was a mess.

Across the parking lot, she could see people strolling in the sun and loading groceries into their cars. Seconds later, the sound of a siren cut the air. The medics took a little longer, which was a crying shame.

It was weird, but in contrast to being shot in the chest, the shallow crease across her forearm hurt like hell.

Eleven

Cold Peak was a long way from Wilmington, North Carolina, both geographically and psychologically. The town was small to middling, with a population of twelve thousand that included the outlying farming district. It was cool, despite the fact that it was still technically summer, and the whole beach-resort thing that Wilmington had had going on just didn't exist in landlocked Cold Peak.

The peak for which the town was named hung suspended in the distance, almost blotted out by the bony line of the Green Mountains, its main distinguishing feature a broad, steep face popular with rock climbers. A few miles north, a ski resort attracted a steady stream of tourists in winter and provided Cold Peak with its main source of revenue.

Taylor depressed the button on the garage remote and parked the secondhand SUV she'd bought the day after she had moved in. The SUV was both sleek and serviceable, with multipurpose tires for off-road use and four-wheel drive—something she was going to need, because before the end of the summer, she intended to climb Cold Peak. Right after that she was going to get a ski rack fitted to the roof of the SUV.

Easing tired shoulder muscles that had stiffened up after a strenuous session at the gym, she unlocked her front door and stepped inside.

This time, instead of an apartment, she had opted for a house—the first house she had ever rented. The fifties bungalow had three bedrooms and a sunroom and was a regular piece of suburban paradise, complete with its neatly cared for front yard, and a barbecue area out the back. To go with the respectable facade of the house and SUV, she even had a job as a personal trainer at the Cold Peak gym.

It was a job Taylor had never envisioned having but which, weirdly enough, she was qualified to do. Over her years in the Bureau, she had accumulated all of the required medical passes. She also had a degree in physical education, which she'd gained at college while she'd been studying criminology. At the time, she hadn't ever thought of becoming a personal trainer; she had done the papers purely out of interest.

Dropping her purse on her bed, she changed into jogging clothes—dark blue track pants and a white tank—locked the house, zipped the key into her track-pants pocket and started out slowly, enjoying the warmth spreading through her muscles and the calmness that came when her body settled into a steady rhythm. She still struggled with the distances she had used to run, and her lung still threw some phantom pains at her but, combined with her regular exercise routine, she was getting there.

She reached the end of the block, crossed the road and, out of habit, began studying houses and vehicles, checking out who was around her and what made them tick. One of the best indicators of personality she had found was the vehicles people drove.

A car nailed three key areas: socioeconomic class, what the person liked to do in their spare time *and* personality. Houses did also, to a degree, but sometimes people rented, so that didn't express their true socioeconomic status or personality.

Her neighbor, Letitia Clayton, dressed like a sixties flower fresh out of Woodstock, but the Buick she drove told another story—old money and a solid portfolio of shares cushioning her retirement. Mr. Scanlon across the road was the complete opposite. Early sixties, balding, with weight issues. He drove a Corvette. In his case, the contrast between his vehicle and his house, which was badly in need of roof maintenance and a coat of paint, pointed out priorities that were markedly different from Letty's. Scanlon might not make his mortgage payment, but that wasn't going to worry him, because he had sunk all of his money into a car that would hold its value. If he had to make a quick getaway, he wasn't leaving the majority of his investment behind.

She rounded a corner and jogged into a street with a solid family feel. Some of the homes had swing sets out front, and the glint of swimming pools was visible in a number of backyards. She studied a two-story weatherboard house with a neat square of lawn out front, her attention drawn by the vehicle parked in the driveway. The gunmetal gray four-wheel-drive truck had tight suspension and off-road tires, and was as different from the mom-and-pop sedans visible in the neighboring driveways as a mountain lion from a bunch of tabby cats. A spattering of mud over the wheel arches indicated that it was used for the purpose for which it had been designed.

A loud detonation, followed by a high-pitched shriek, sounded off to the left. A split second later, Taylor's shoulder hit ground that was as iron hard as the sidewalk. She rolled out of bare, exposing sunlight, into the shadow of a hedge, wincing as a shaft of pain shot up one ankle. Another shriek, this time of laughter, and a second shot, made her flinch.

A breathless giggle came from behind the hedge, followed by the sound of feet pounding on grass. Pulse still hammering, she lifted her head. *Kids.* Playing with cap guns.

Since the shooting in Wilmington and another round of follow-up therapy, she had made gains. Bayard had been right about her obsession with Lopez; not having to deal with the case on a daily basis had improved her life. She was sleeping better and she had gotten past the anxiety attacks— mostly. She no longer considered that she had a phobia for needles and briefcases. The sound of gunshots, however...

Rolling over, she pushed into a sitting position and gingerly rotated her foot.

"Are you all right?"

She hadn't been aware of anyone behind her, but she instantly recognized the voice. Steve Fischer from the gym. He'd started a couple of weeks after her, taking care of the weights and running the training program for Cold Peak's power-lifting team.

He crouched down beside her. "Looks like you've hurt your ankle."

As she probed at the bone, she caught the sharp scent of fresh sweat. He was dressed in track pants and a washed-out gray tank top. If he had just been for a run, that would explain why he'd come up behind her so fast. "I'm fine, it's just a twist."

This close, Fischer seemed a lot larger and edgier. His hair was dark and clipped close, his face tanned, with clean-cut cheekbones and a tough jaw. His eyes were close to black, which pointed to some kind of Hispanic or Native American heritage. He also had a couple of interesting scars, one across the bridge of his nose, one on his jaw. For the first time she noticed he had a pierced ear but no earring.

"It got ripped out at football practice. I decided it was a liability."

And she just bet he hadn't needed the prop of an earring, anyway.

She felt herself grow warm that he'd noticed her looking. Football. That figured. And it would explain the scars.

"Give me your hand."

He pulled her to her feet. She tested her weight on the ankle, wobbling slightly. He steadied her. The touch was firm and impersonal, but with the heat of his palm burning through the damp cotton of her tank at the small of her back, suddenly it was hard to reestablish that original low-key impression. Fischer might be a businessman who had recently moved to Cold Peak for the climbing, but he smelled like a man and, standing this close, she was reminded that he was taller than her by several inches.

Still uncomfortably warm and aware that Fischer was watching her, she hopped away a half step and put weight on the foot. It was tender but nothing to make any fuss about. Ice packs and a quiet evening and she would be fit for work in the morning.

"Are you okay to walk, or do you need a ride?"

A graphic, flagrantly sexual image of Fischer naked and on top flashed through her mind and Taylor almost choked. The last date she'd had had been months before she'd been assigned to the Lopez investigation, and it had been a lot longer than that since she'd let anyone get close enough for intimacy. "It's okay, I live just down the road."

His gaze connected with hers for a split second and the fiction that Fischer was low-key, maybe even boring, vaporized. The look was blunt and sharply male, and the faint suspicion that he had deliberately phrased his offer of a ride in an ambiguous way grew stronger.

"See you at work tomorrow."

Dazed, she watched as he crossed the road and walked into the house opposite. The four-wheel-drive truck she had been studying just before she'd panicked and hit the dirt belonged to Fischer. The vehicle was large and uncompromisingly male—like Fischer.

Shaking her head, she limped past his house. She must be slipping. She couldn't understand how she could have missed that about him.

* * *

Letitia Clayton was snipping at her roses as Taylor walked past. Letty was gray haired, thin and birdlike, with large, worried eyes. A medallion swung from a gold chain around her neck, and she was wearing what looked suspiciously like a tie-dyed skirt. The remnants of sixties flower power aside, Taylor wasn't fooled. On the only occasion she had been in Letty's house, the sitting room coffee table had contained a neat stack of business publications. Beneath the charm and the "sweet old lady" facade, Letty was a Wall Street shark.

She waved. "You haven't seen Buster, have you?"

Taylor resisted the urge to glance at her front gate. She had already spotted a tuft of fur, which indicated that Buster, a large tabby cat with white paws, was lurking beneath the thick arch of wisteria that hung over her front gate.

"I think he's in my front yard." Lately, Buster had been spending his days sleeping on the deck just off her sunroom. A couple of times, he had even managed to get inside the house in the evening and make himself at home on her bed.

"I don't know what's wrong with that cat, the last few days. I've hardly seen him. Such a worry when I'm packing to go on holiday this week."

Bright blue eyes fastened on hers, and the light-bulb finally went on. Letty wanted her to look after the cat.

The shears nibbled their way through another rosebush. "I was hoping that, since he's spending so much time at your place, you wouldn't mind feeding Buster and keeping an eye on the house while I go and stay with my son in Boston. I've had the holiday planned for a month, but with all the burglaries, I'm on the verge of canceling. I couldn't go if I wasn't convinced Buster and the house were safe."

A sense of resignation filled Taylor as she noted that Buster was now cleaning himself on her deck.

"Don't worry about the food, I'll have that delivered, and you won't need to check my mailbox. I've stopped the newspaper, and I'll arrange for the post office to hold my mail until I get back."

Taylor frowned as she closed her front gate behind her.

A series of burglaries, targeting houses that were empty while the occupants were away on holiday, had been making headlines in Cold Peak for the past couple of weeks. Appliances were taken, and in a couple of instances pets had disappeared and hadn't been recovered.

The mini crime wave had shaken the residents, and it was a sharp reminder that quiet, sleepy Cold Peak wasn't as safe or innocuous as it seemed.

Twelve

Cold Peak boasted three computer shops/Internet cafés. During her lunch hour, Taylor strolled to the closest one.

When she stepped through the door, a lean, dark-haired kid with glasses and a name tag with *Neil* printed on it unfolded himself from behind a computer screen.

"I need a new security suite for my computer." She gave him the make and model, and watched as he pulled a box off the shelf behind him.

The packaging was familiar. "I already have that one."

"Have you been updating it?"

"Every week. It didn't do the job."

His eyes glinted. He moved farther along the shelf and retrieved a box from a locked cabinet.

"This is what you need. It's expensive, but it's worth it. I use it myself."

She paid for the program and completed the rest of her shopping, adding in a can of tuna and an extra carton of milk for Buster.

When she got home that evening there was an entire box of cat food on her front step with a delivery docket from one of the supermarkets. She glanced over at Letty's house, but the place looked closed up.

She picked up the carton, unlocked the door and walked inside. Letty hadn't said exactly when she was going, just that she would be away for a few days, but it looked like she had already left.

Buster materialized from beneath the wisteria and glided in the door behind her, his attention on the box of cat food.

He ate a whole can in one sitting. Taylor hadn't yet tried to pick him up, but he looked like he weighed about twenty pounds and none of it was fat. His paws were large, the claws, when he extended them, like razor-sharp hooks. One ear had a notch chewed out of it and at some stage he'd gotten a gouge across the nose. Beneath his fur, he no doubt had any number of old wounds. Cute he might be, but in cat terms, Buster was the equivalent of a badass.

Taylor missed out on her usual run in favor of doing some yoga. It gave her a chance to rest her ankle and, if she was honest, to avoid the possibility of another one-on-one with Fischer.

After showering, she made herself a salad and put a potato in the oven to bake. Periodically, she checked on Letty's house, which was partly visible through her kitchen window. As she dressed the salad, Taylor noticed that sometime in the past few minutes the curtains had been closed, which meant Letty was home after all, and had probably decided to have an early night.

After dinner, she carried her purchase through into the sunroom. After uninstalling her previous security suite, she slid the new disk in and started the installation process. Buster ambled into the room and sat staring out of the French doors at Letty's house. He hadn't shown any propensity to leave, and Taylor was reluctant to shoo him out just yet. If she was looking after him for the next week, he might as well make himself at home.

When the download was complete, she pressed a button and initiated the program, then watched as it processed the operating files on her computer. A report flashed up on the screen. One program had compromised her system.

She studied the file name highlighted. It looked like her old security system, but it couldn't be. She had uninstalled the old system before she had installed the new one.

She copied the highlighted file to a Zip drive,

and placed the Zip in her bag. She would take it into the computer shop during her lunch break and ask Neil to take a look at it.

On impulse, she found the box containing her disks, slipped the disks into an envelope and propped the envelope beside her purse. She would get Neil to copy the disks for her before she risked downloading them onto her computer. After almost losing her research on Lopez, she wasn't taking any more chances.

Just before going to bed, she picked Buster up and took him out onto the deck. The moon was up and almost full, casting a silvery light over Letty's house, which was still in utter darkness. Repressing a shiver at the cool bite in the air, she closed the door behind her so Buster couldn't scoot back inside and carried him across to the hedge, intending to drop him over. Just before she reached the hedge, Buster went rigid. A split second later, he exploded out of her arms and disappeared beneath a thick clump of hydrangeas.

Clutching her arm where his claws had dug in, she walked back into the house, ran the tap over the kitchen sink and cleaned the scratches. Dabbing her arm dry with a paper towel, she walked back outside, this time with a flashlight. She didn't know if Letty had a cat door or if she routinely put Buster outside at night, but she was betting that he normally slept inside, in which case, she wasn't comfortable with Buster being locked outside all night.

Crouching down, she directed the beam beneath the hydrangeas, but the foliage was too dense for it to penetrate more than a few feet. After searching along the thick border of shrubs that edged the backyard, Taylor decided to try another tack. For all she knew, Buster had slipped back through the hedge onto Letty's property and, if there was a cat door, was already safely tucked up inside.

Flicking the flashlight off, she strolled through her front yard, out onto the sidewalk and carefully opened Letty's front gate so the latch wouldn't creak. Moonlight flooded the front yard as she walked up the neat path.

The gracious lines of the house looked faintly creepy by night. The verandas were thickly twined by gnarled stems of wisteria and climbing roses, and towering oaks and elms plunged the sides of the house and the backyard into dense shadow.

Flicking the flashlight back on, but taking care to cover most of the beam with her fingers so that only a narrow slit of light glowed through, she checked the doors and windows. If Letty didn't have a cat door, it was possible she left a window open wide enough for Buster to get in, although with the burglaries, that wasn't likely.

She circled the house then returned to the rear porch, which was roomy enough to accommodate a set of wicker furniture and an assortment of plants. After establishing that Buster wasn't under the couch or either of the chairs, or crouching in the thick jungle of potted plants, she stepped back out onto the lawn, flicked the flashlight off and waited for her night vision to improve. She checked the luminous dial of her watch. Twenty minutes had passed since Buster had bolted. There was no way he could have gotten inside Letty's house, which meant he was either still on the loose outside or he had sneaked back into her place.

A faint rustling in the trees off to her left kicked her pulse up a notch. Cursing herself for not thinking to carry a weapon, Taylor flicked the flashlight on and flooded the area beneath an ancient oak with light. Aside from a clump of lilies, the area was bare of everything but dried leaves and a few scattered acorns. She shifted the beam sideways as something small and shadowy streaked up the trunk of the oak. Her stomach muscles unclenched. A squirrel.

Keeping the flashlight on but directing the beam away from the windows of the house in case she woke Letty, she walked through to the front yard. The squirrel hadn't made a sound when it had bolted up the trunk of the tree. Maybe her mind was playing tricks on her, but for a few brief moments the old paranoia had flooded back and she had been certain someone, not something, had been there.

After the shadowed dimness of the backyard,

the combination of moonlight and street lighting was almost ludicrously bright. Letting the gate snick shut behind her, Taylor quickened her pace. Paranoid or not, checking Letty's house over had reminded her that she had left the door to the sunroom partially open. If there was someone creeping around, they had had free access to her house for the past few minutes.

She checked the kitchen and the sitting room. Everything appeared to be as she'd left it, but the tingling feeling at her nape was still there. Keeping her tread silent, she walked through to her bedroom, placed the flashlight on the bed and retrieved her gun from the closet. Snapping the clip in place, she checked the two spare rooms, then ghosted through the rest of the house, opening doors and checking cupboards.

A sound in the direction of the sunroom froze her in place. Even though the sound had most likely been made by Buster sneaking back inside, she held the gun in a two-handed grip as she paced silently down the hall.

When she stepped into the sunroom, a furry head popped up from behind her computer monitor. Round green eyes stared at her like miniature lamps. Her gaze dropped. The source of the noise was obvious in the pens scattered across her keyboard. Buster must have knocked the jar of pens over when he had jumped up on the desk.

She closed the sunroom door and locked it before he could get out again and set the gun down on the desk. Buster was wedged in behind the monitor. If he hadn't looked up, she wouldn't have seen him at all, which was probably the point. He was hiding.

Walking through to the kitchen, she rinsed and dried her forearm again, then got the first aid box down from the top shelf in her pantry and dabbed her arm with antiseptic. Normally, the small pinpricks Buster's claws had made wouldn't have registered, but they had punctured the still-tender scar tissue from the bullet crease, which accounted for the extra zing.

She packed the first aid box away, and made herself a cup of chamomile tea. While she waited for the tea to steep, she stared out the window at Letty's house. The moon was still high, glinting off the windows and the bleached weatherboards. She noticed one of the curtains in the upstairs bedroom was now partially open, which indicated that she had disturbed Letty. In all probability, Letty had checked out of her window, recognized her in the bright moonlight and gone back to bed.

Carrying the tea through to the sunroom, she sat down and sipped and tried to coax Buster out from behind the computer.

The silence in the house was profound. She checked her wristwatch, surprised to see that it was close on midnight. Cold pushed through the glass doors, raising gooseflesh on her arms and reminding her of the moment she had stared into the darkness, certain something had been there. A faint shudder went down her spine and she drew the curtains, blocking out the night.

She'd had enough of darkness and creepy old houses. The paranoia and the scar on her forearm were both reminders she could have done without.

She was safe in Cold Peak. After Wilmington, Burdett had taken extra precautions. No one knew where she was, not even Dana.

No one had followed her.

Thirteen

Neil opened the rogue computer file and studied it for long seconds, blue eyes unblinking behind thick-lensed glasses. "I can tell you what it's not, and that's a security program, although it's dressed up to look like one."

He reached for the can of soda sitting beside the scrunched-up wrapper of the burger he'd just eaten for lunch and gulped a mouthful as he continued to read. "Cool." He gave her an apologetic look. "Whoever wrote this was smart. It's designed to mimic the security suite it bypassed." He grinned. "Smart, but not smart enough."

He finished the drink, crumpled the can and tossed it into the trash can beneath the counter. "Looks like it was installed about six months ago and it's been sending stuff to this address." He pointed at a row of code.

"You mean dialing out?"

"Not on its own, because then you'd know. It just sends while you're online."

"Can you locate the server?"

"Leave it with me, I'll see what I can do. Meanwhile…" He rummaged in a drawer and pulled out a disk. "I'm guessing that you're going to have trouble removing that sucker, so run this through your machine. It's a program I designed to uninstall hostile software."

She slipped the disk in her purse, then pulled out two twenties.

He looked faintly embarrassed. "You don't have to pay me. I don't even know if I can find the server."

And obtaining the name of the server probably wouldn't give her anything extra to go on. Even if she could get the server to hand over the personal details of the account, the chances were that whoever had registered it had given a false name and paid cash. But, blind alley or not, right now, she didn't have anything else to go on.

She put the bills down on the counter. "You'll probably have to do it in your spare time, so it's not fair if I don't pay. If you can locate the server, I'll pay a bonus."

Slipping the disks he had copied for her into her purse, she drove back to work, making a stop at her bank on the way. Aside from renting a safe-deposit box to keep her personal papers and the disks safe, she now had decisions to make regarding the money from the sale of her apartment in D.C. At the moment it was sitting in an account, but she was seriously considering buying a house in Cold Peak and she needed to check out the viability of the investment.

After signing up for a safe-deposit box and securing the disks, she requested information on mortgage rates. When she stepped out of the interview room, a familiar set of shoulders sent a mild shock through her system. Fischer, dressed in faded jeans and a white T-shirt that clung across his chest, was just finishing up with a bank teller. The bank was close to the gym, so she shouldn't be surprised to see Fischer here.

He arrived at the door a split second before she did and waited for her to walk through ahead of him.

"How's the ankle?"

She was aware of his focus on her legs and the fact that he was enjoying the view afforded by the short sundress she was wearing. "It's fine."

"If you want a lift back to work, I'm on my way there now."

She spotted his truck, which was parked in the space directly behind her SUV, and the tension in her stomach tightened another notch. She was almost certain he knew he had parked behind her vehicle, because her SUV was parked at the gym every day she worked.

Reaching into her handbag, she pulled out a set of keys. "It's okay, I've got my car."

He shrugged and slipped dark glasses on the bridge of his nose. "It was worth a try. I'll see you back at work."

As she slid into the driver's seat, she caught a glimpse of the truck in the rearview mirror. Taking her time, acutely aware of Fischer behind her, she fitted her key in the ignition and latched her seat belt, waiting for him to pull out first. When he didn't, she realized he was waiting for her, which meant he would be tailing her all the way back to the gym.

Jaw tight, she put the car in gear, signaled and pulled out, trying to concentrate on traffic as Fischer nosed in behind her. Minutes later, she parked in the private lot behind the gym and tried to ignore the fact that Fischer, just two spaces down, was already out of his truck.

Collecting her bag, she locked the SUV and strolled toward the back door of the gym. Fischer hold the door, letting her precede him into the building. The act was polite and any number of men would do exactly the same thing, but with Fischer it felt different. He wanted to make her aware of him, and he had succeeded.

What she was feeling for Fischer didn't make any kind of sense. For weeks she had been *immune.* Now, suddenly, she was turned-on.

The only explanation she could come up with was that *she* had changed, not Fischer. Her biological clock was ticking, courtesy of the attempts on her life, and Fischer had just happened to walk into the frame.

Despite the hormones, the timing was wrong. The place was wrong. Until Lopez was caught, everything was wrong.

When she got home that evening, Letty's house was still closed up, the curtains drawn, and Buster was lying on Taylor's sundeck. Hooking the strap of her purse over her shoulder, she walked down the neatly kept path and knocked on Letty's front door. She waited a couple of minutes, then knocked again.

Just to double-check, she called out then walked around the back. When she tried the back door, that was locked, too. She checked the garage, which was also locked, but when she looked in the window, the Buick was still there.

Frowning, she studied the car. Letty drove everywhere in it. If she had caught a flight out, though, it made sense that she would have gotten a taxi to the airport, because long-term parking was expensive. Either that, or her son had driven from Boston to pick her up.

Feeling uneasy, because she had assumed Letty would fill her in on when she was leaving and when she was due back, and leave a contact number just in case something went wrong, she walked back to her house.

Changing into track pants and a crop top, she went out for her evening jog. When she got home there was a truck with C. K. Hansen Lawn Mowing printed on the side parked in Letty's driveway and she could hear a lawn mower. Walking around to the rear of the house, she waved at the man pushing the mower until he cut the engine. "Did you know Mrs. Clayton's away on holiday?"

The guy, presumably C. K. Hansen, took off a ball cap to reveal a shaved head that went with the steel earrings punched through both ears. He wiped the sweat off his face. "It's okay, she paid me in advance."

Which meant she had taken the time to make arrangements with her lawn-mowing service but not with Taylor. "Did she tell you when she's due back?"

He shrugged. "The next time I'm scheduled to mow the lawn is two weeks from now, if that helps."

After dinner, Taylor ran the program Neil had given her to wipe the spyware that had been posing as her old security suite. When her computer was clean, she reinstalled the files she'd saved to disk, then began reviewing the information she still had on the Lopez case. Both Burdett and Bayard would go nuts if they found out she had retained her microfilm and Internet files—in effect, everything the FBI had had on Lopez up until the time she had left.

The room was dim, the computer screen glowing in the dark, before she finished reading the material. Sitting back in the chair, she stretched the kinks out of her neck and shoulders. She had read every word, and some things twice, and she kept coming back to the same conclusion. Since Slater's arrest the previous year, the only breaks in the case had been the two attempts on her life. Apart from that, the Lopez case was as cold as her own shootings appeared to be.

The fact that the D.C. police department had offloaded her case on the Bureau didn't mean a thing, either, other than that the FBI had put their hand up for the job. With hundreds of unsolved homicides every year, a nonfatal shooting wasn't that big a deal. An overworked detective would have taken the break for what it was and handed over the paperwork before the case could get pushed back at him.

Smothering a yawn, she closed the file. Buster, who had spent most of the evening behind the monitor, was sitting on the floor, staring through the glass doors at Letty's house. Shutting down the computer, she pulled the curtains, blocking the view. Without Letty's presence, the old villa wasn't nearly so appealing, and she could do without the reminder about how she'd overreacted the night before.

Fourteen

She called on Neil during her lunch hour. He had managed to track down the server that hosted the account the spyware had been mailing information to, but when he'd failed the security questions relating to the account, the program had tossed him out and now refused to allow him access.

Taylor studied the low-key graphics of the server, a midblue background and a message stating that the user was in breach of the security requirements.

Neil hit a button and the message dissolved. He shrugged. "For what it's worth, I looked up a physical address for the server. It's based in D.C."

Despite the fact that a lot of servers had their offices based in the capital city, the mention of D.C. sent an unpleasant ripple down her spine. Taylor handed Neil another twenty. "What you've done is great. If I need any more help, I'll let you know."

The last thing she wanted was Neil walking into a dangerous situation. Most servers had prominent logos and advertising. According to Neil, this one hadn't had anything displayed except the basic log-in menu, then the message locking him out, which was curious in itself. She would pass the information on to Burdett to hand to Colenso although, based on past performance, she wasn't confident Colenso would follow up on the lead.

A lunchtime yoga class was just finishing when Taylor strolled into the gym.

Mandy, a water bottle dangling from long, elegant fingers, joined her at the front counter. "I just got you a date."

Taylor almost dropped the file for her one-o'clock appointment.

Mandy grinned. "You can thank me later. It's a double, with me and Dane tomorrow night." She nodded in the direction of the weights. "You're with Fischer."

Taylor glanced across the width of the gym where Dane was talking with Fischer. No prizes for guessing what they were discussing. A split second later Fischer's gaze locked with hers and sheer panic hit. Biological clock ticking or not, she wasn't ready.

Friday night. That was tomorrow.

* * *

The date was simple, pizza then a nightclub, which meant casual with glitz. In theory that should have been easy, and normally it would have been, but the thought of a date with Fischer terrified her on a basic level.

She'd dated plenty of tough, physical guys, but she had never had such a straightforward physical and emotional reaction to a man before. Aside from that, he *intrigued* her.

For the first time in her life she understood how women became entangled in relationships they weren't sure they wanted. With Fischer, nothing was predictable and she wasn't in control.

After feeding Buster, she showered and changed, keeping it simple—loose hair, black pants and a shell-pink halter top that looked good with her tan. She kept the jewelry low-key and the makeup to a minimum and stepped into heels that pushed her height to six feet. She wouldn't quite be eyeballing Fischer, but close enough. The effect was elegant, feminine and reserved. She had agreed to the date, but she wasn't about to serve herself up on a plate. If she gave Fischer an inch he *would* take the mile.

Checking the load on the Glock, she slipped it into her handbag, collected a cashmere wrap and strolled to the curb to wait. She didn't feel comfortable standing out on the street with the neighbors' curtains twitching, but she didn't want Fischer on her doorstep or inside her house. Within seconds, Fischer pulled up, climbed from the truck and came around to open the passenger-side door. Dressed in dark, close-fitting pants and a shirt made of some light, gauzy fabric, the dangerous, male edge she'd glimpsed was accentuated in a subtle way. The clothing was expensive, but in no way did it make him look soft. She checked his pierced ear, which still lacked the vanity of an earring. Getting into the truck, she decided she would have been disappointed if he'd given in to the cliché.

Friday nights in Cold Peak were reassuringly like Friday nights in any town. The cafés and bars were overflowing, the streets filled with couples strolling. Schoolkids were out in force in their trucks and cars, blasting everyone within a mile radius with their stereos.

The pizza café was cheerful and bustling, with bright red tablecloths and ultraslim waitresses wrapped in long black aprons. After they'd ordered they sat back, conversation stifled by the volume of noise and the music pounding from the club next door.

When the bill arrived, Fischer took charge of it.

Fischer's gaze connected with hers. "Where I come from, the man always pays for the lady."

The waitress was already at the counter, swiping the card. If she wanted to cancel the transaction, she would have to make a scene. "Where exactly is that?"

"Louisiana."

Suddenly, Fischer fell into context. Taylor had once spent a week in New Orleans and when she was there the qualities that set Southerners apart had struck her forcibly. The frank enjoyment of the rituals of courtship—the blunt appreciation of sex—and the slow, relaxed approach that made Southerners appear lazy when they were anything but.

When the check was settled they strolled next door to the nightclub. Seconds later they were caught up in the crush of the dance floor. As Taylor threaded her way into a gap on the floor, a couple moved back, almost hitting her. Fischer's arm curled around her waist, the heat of his palm burning through the silk of her halter as he jerked her against his chest.

He released her almost instantly, but not before Taylor registered the fact that he was aroused and didn't seem bothered that she knew it. The moment threw her straight back to the encounter outside the bank, when he'd made no bones about the fact that he found her attractive.

The music changed, a slower, bluesy number. The dance floor emptied out a little, leaving more room. Taylor took a deep breath and went into Fischer's arms, keeping her distance. The hold was loose and unthreatening; she'd danced this way hundreds of times before.

The music cycled back into a disco beat. Mandy waved at her from the edge of the dance floor, where she and Dane had retreated in favor of edging closer to the bar. Taylor waved back, taking the opportunity to step away from Fischer and fill her lungs with oxygen. Automatically, she scanned the occupants of the club. The drab lines of a dark suit jacket and the neatly trimmed back of a male head, quickly swamped by bright T-shirts and sequined tops, made her stiffen.

"What is it?"

Taylor studied the jostling crowd, her stomach tight, her heart pounding from more than just exertion. "I thought I just saw someone I knew."

It hadn't been the tall guy with glasses, or Lopez. She would have *known* if it had been Lopez.

Fifteen

Taylor stared at the swirling crowd. "I need to leave."

She could have made a mistake. It was more than likely the man she had seen sidling through the crowded nightclub had been familiar on a professional level, not a personal one. Maybe an agent or a narcotics cop working Cold Peak's nightclub scene.

When Fischer's fingers closed on hers, she didn't argue. After a quick detour to let Mandy and Dane know they were leaving, they threaded their way outside.

Fischer released her the second they stepped outside. Taylor positioned her handbag to give her easier access to the gun if she needed it. She skimmed the crowded café tables set out on the sidewalk and the groups of teenagers spilling out onto the street, but there was no sign of the man she'd seen in the nightclub.

They turned a corner and strolled toward Fischer's truck, footsteps echoing in the empty street. With every step the sound of the nightclub receded, but Taylor couldn't relax. For a split second the man she'd glimpsed *had* seemed familiar.

Maybe what she was feeling was just another stage of paranoia. But with her track record, she couldn't afford to make assumptions.

A buzzing sound broke the silence. Fischer flipped his phone open and set it against his ear.

A monosyllabic reply later and he slipped the phone back in his pocket. "Sorry about that. Business."

At eleven o'clock at night? "I thought your business was personal training."

He shrugged. "I don't spend all of my time in gyms."

The sound of a window closing in one of the apartments overhead made the skin at her nape tighten. Both times she had been shot it had been from apartment buildings. The ones in Cold Peak weren't as high or as elaborate as either of the buildings in Washington or Wilmington had been, but they were high enough to do the job.

She felt warmth down her back as Fischer moved closer, his proximity distracting.

"Anything wrong?"

She scanned the apartment block. Four up, six across. Twenty-four balconies. Her attention dropped to the parking area out front and the service alley to one side, both of which were well lit. Common sense told her that if there was a shooter, he would be opening a window to get a clear shot, not closing it. "Nothing. I just like to watch my back."

"Anything to do with this?"

His fingers brushed the scar just below her shoulder blade and adrenaline surged for the second time that evening. The scar was still ultra-sensitive, but that didn't explain the intensity of her reaction, or the sudden conviction that he knew it was a bullet wound. She stepped away, reestablishing her personal space. "It's nothing. I was in the wrong place at the wrong time."

Fischer's truck pulled up at the curb outside her front gate. The light she'd left on in the kitchen glowed warmly, but that wasn't what compelled her attention. Beneath the glare of street lighting the pale glow of paper strewn on the sidewalk in front of Letty's gate was clearly visible.

Taylor climbed out of the truck and walked over to examine the litter, which turned out to be a collection of envelopes and advertising flyers which had obviously dropped out of Letty's mailbox. A breeze must have blown the mail across the sidewalk.

Looping the strap of her handbag over one shoulder, she gathered up the papers. When she straightened, she noticed one of the curtains had been partially pulled aside, leaving a gap of a few inches. The previous day, when she had walked around the house to speak to Hansen, the curtains had been pulled.

Shoving the mail down in a pile beneath the mailbox, she glanced at Fischer, who had stepped out of the truck. "Something's wrong. Wait here."

She extracted the Glock from her purse, no longer concerned with hiding her enforcement background. The metallic snap as she chambered a round was preternaturally loud as she strode down the front path. Surveying the blank windows and the shadowed areas to either side of the house, she stepped up onto the porch and tried the door. It was locked. A faint scraping sound jerked her head around. Fischer had followed her. She caught the gleam of a key in his hand.

"It was under a pot plant. People are predictable."

Not always, she thought grimly, as he stepped past her, unlocked the door and pushed it open in one smooth motion.

Glock still in a two-handed grip, she stepped past Fischer and stumbled to a halt as the stench hit her in a wave. Cold light from the streetlamps washed across the hall. Letty was lying crumpled on the hall runner, one side of her head oddly misshapen.

With her hand clamped over her nose and mouth, she crouched down to get a closer look at the wound and the dark stain on the carpet, then rose to her feet and backed out of the hallway onto the front step, taking care not to touch anything.

Judging from the lack of blood, Letty had died instantly. The fact that the blood was dried meant she had been dead for some time, at least a couple of days. In all likelihood she had died the day Buster had moved into Taylor's place, which meant her body had been here when Taylor had done her nighttime circuit of the house.

The implications began to pile up. If Letty had been dead that long, that meant someone else had moved the curtains, and not just on one occasion but over a period of time. The cold-blooded nature of a murderer who had either stayed in the house, or returned after committing the crime, not once, but on at least two occasions, added a level of calculation to the crime that made her feel queasy.

She reached for her cell phone, but Fischer was already calling the cops. Gulping in fresh air, she stepped back into the house.

Fischer's hand clamped around her arm, halting her before she got more than a half step into the hall. "I'll go first."

She considered arguing, then decided against it.

Fischer was physically fit, with a cold toughness that was becoming more and more evident. He didn't have a gun or her enforcement expertise but, if the murderer was still inside the house, she couldn't ask for better backup.

Flattening herself against the wall, she let Fischer glide past. A thin flicker of light indicated that he had a penlight, which meant they wouldn't need to risk switching on lights and thereby compromising any prints left on the light switches. Cold Peak's finest would have a fit when they found out they had walked through their crime scene, but after what had happened in Wilmington—even though the M.O. was totally different— Taylor needed to know if Letty's killing could in any way be related to the two attempts on her life.

Keeping one hand clamped over her nose and mouth, she followed in Fischer's silent wake and began a systematic check of the house. The sitting room was a mess, the television, VCR and stereo gone. Within seconds she had established that the spare room downstairs and the upstairs bedrooms were undisturbed, which made sense if this had been a simple appliance theft. The bedrooms were filled with heavy, old-fashioned furniture; there wasn't a piece of digital equipment in sight.

Aside from the sitting room, the kitchen was the only room that wasn't as neat as a pin. The remains of a meal and a number of dirty plates and utensils littered the table and the kitchen counter was covered in dishes that had been washed but not put away.

The scene in the kitchen didn't make sense. From the partially filled sink and the already cleaned dishes stacked in a drainer, it looked like Letty had finished her evening meal and had been in the process of drying and putting away dishes, which didn't explain why a fresh mess had been made.

Unless the killer had decided to help himself to a meal from the leavings in Letty's fridge.

As repulsive as the thought was, if that was the case, it was manna from heaven for the Cold Peak PD. Lifting prints off the crockery and cutlery would be child's play.

When Fischer jerked his head toward the door, Taylor followed him out. As she skirted Letty's body she noticed a kitchen towel lying on the hall floor and the picture of what had happened became clear. Letty must have been in the kitchen drying dishes when the doorbell had rung. She had opened the front door with a towel in her hand; the thief had hit her on the head, then walked inside. He had stolen the TV, VCR and the stereo, then helped himself to a meal.

The assault appeared to be a straightforward blow to the head with a blunt instrument, no exotic weapons, no weird aberrations, just old-fashioned brute force mixed with a dose of miscalculation that had shunted the Cold Peak appliance thefts into the murder category. Although that didn't explain why the killer had come back to the house later. Revisiting the scene of the crime wasn't the kind of behavior practiced by appliance thieves, unless there was more to steal. That clearly hadn't been the case here because, aside from the sitting room, the rest of the house appeared to be intact and the Buick was still parked in the garage.

Cold congealed in her stomach when she realized that the killer must have been in residence when she had walked around Letty's house in the dark. With Letty dead and the house securely locked, that was the only explanation for the curtains that had moved. It also pointed to the fact that the killer had either stayed there for at least two days or else come back again at intervals, which posed the burning question: Why?

Apart from that aberration, it seemed cut-and-dried that Letty had been just one more victim in the rash of appliance thefts in Cold Peak, only this time she'd had the misfortune to be at home when the perpetrator had called.

Taylor gulped a mouthful of fresh air as she stepped outside and relief hit her in a surge. Maybe relief was an odd emotion to feel when her next-door neighbor had been brutally murdered, but the nature of the crime underlined the fact that the murder couldn't have had anything to do with her.

Fischer folded his phone closed and slipped it into his jeans pocket. "Are you all right?"

"Not entirely."

Letty had deserved to live out her final years in peace and dignity. Instead she had been struck down, her body left sprawled on her hall floor, and all for a couple of thousand dollars' worth of secondhand goods that she could have replaced with an insurance claim.

What had happened hadn't been particularly gruesome or even shocking, but the fact that she had known and liked Letty made the murder *personal*. The conversations over the fence and the quiet presence of the older lady had helped anchor Taylor in Cold Peak when she hadn't been certain she would be able to settle anywhere.

The distant sound of a siren cut through the night air. Seconds later a cruiser parked outside Letty's gate.

Fischer leaned in close. His breath feathered her cheek, and for a crazy moment she thought he was going to kiss her, until she met the remote flatness in his eyes.

"Give me the gun." In a slick movement he loosened her fingers and slipped the gun into the waistband at the back of his pants, letting his shirt cover the bulge it made.

The easy way he'd disarmed her and the smooth way he'd concealed the gun sent a ripple of unease through Taylor. But then it wasn't the first time Fischer had surprised her. "You look like you know your way around weapons."

"I was brought up on a farm, plus I used to shoot as a sport."

His arm came around her waist as he urged her down the path toward the open gate. The second the heat of his palm burned through the silk of her top, her body reacted, shudders rolling through her in uncontrollable bursts. She hadn't realized how cold she'd become walking through the dark rooms of Letty's house.

The doors of the cruiser slammed and two uniforms appeared. The officers introduced themselves as Driscoll and Hart. Driscoll produced a notebook and began asking questions, while Hart retrieved a flashlight from the cruiser and went to have a look inside the house.

Taylor leaned against the bonnet of the cruiser, folding her arms across her chest to preserve warmth. Seconds later, Fischer, who had taken time out to lock the truck and stow the gun, draped a leather jacket he must have grabbed from behind the seat around her shoulders.

Fingers closing on the lapels, she hugged it around her, luxuriating in the soft leather and wallowing in the pooling warmth. Within seconds the deep shudders had stopped, although she was aware that she had been suffering from reaction as much as the cold. Trying to decide whether or not a hit man had moved in next door for the specific purpose of killing her didn't make for a warm, fuzzy feeling.

Hart came back, looking queasy. He reached into the cruiser, grabbed the radio hand piece, confirmed the homicide and popped the trunk. Within minutes, Letty's house and the backyard were sealed off with crime-scene tape and a second police vehicle, this one unmarked, had arrived.

Driscoll continued the interview, wanting names and contact details and a record of where they'd been that evening, along with the exact times, if they could supply them.

Fischer leaned against the side of the cruiser, his expression unreadable as he waited out Driscoll's process. "You're going to be looking at a time frame outside of the last twenty-four hours. She looks like she's been dead a couple of days."

"I'd go for three," Taylor said flatly. "I haven't seen Letty since I talked to her late Tuesday afternoon."

Driscoll swore and yelled for Hart. When Hart backed up what Fischer had just said, he made a note and started all over again, increasing the scope of his questions.

Taylor stared at the clean line of Fischer's jaw and his level, dark gaze as he answered the new raft of questions. Most men would be shaken by finding the victim of a homicide, but not Fischer. The cops even responded to him, which wasn't always the case. When Fischer had seen Letty's body, he had quietly assumed control, calling the Cold Peak PD, then insisting on taking point when they'd searched the house. He had also had the presence of mind to conceal her weapon. The action, protective as it had been, could have landed him in hot water. If the Cold Peak police had searched her handbag and found the weapon, she would have been able to pull some strings and smooth out the situation. If Fischer had been searched, he could have been arrested for carrying concealed. It was even possible he could have been held on suspicion of murder, despite the fact that a gun hadn't been used to kill Letty.

Within minutes an ambulance arrived, followed by a news van. The reporter, a cocky young guy in jeans, lifted his camera. Taylor turned so he couldn't catch more than the back of her head.

A plainclothes detective replaced Driscoll. Muir was older, with the calm, patient expression and the worn-down demeanor of a cop who had been in the job a lot longer than he'd bargained for. When Muir had finished taking their statements, Fischer indicated they should sit in the truck. Taylor was more than happy to comply. Even though it was still technically summer, the temperature had plummeted.

Fischer started the engine and turned on the heater, although as lightly dressed as he was in jeans and a shirt, he didn't appear to feel the cold.

Taylor watched as the coroner went into the house, followed by the evidence techs who had been cooling their heels for the past half hour, waiting for him to arrive. Technically, they couldn't start work until Letty was officially pronounced dead. A small crowd, comprised mostly of residents looking shell-shocked and wary, had gathered. She recognized Mr. Scanlon from across the road; Beth Graham, another neighbor; one of Letty's bridge cronies.

At one in the morning the ambulance crew emerged from the house with Letty's body zipped into a body bag. The stretcher was slotted into the rear of the ambulance and they left with lights flashing, but this time, no siren. Over the next few minutes the crowd quietly dispersed. The evidence team packed up and left, followed by the two uniformed cops.

Muir took time out to stop by the truck and update them. As far as the police were concerned, the discovery that Letty's television, VCR and stereo were gone made the motivation for the crime cut-and-dried. It seemed clear that the killer hadn't expected Letty to be home, probably because he'd had prior information that she was going away on vacation. He had pressed the doorbell as a precaution then had been surprised when Letty had opened the door.

Despite the fatality, the M.O. for the theft was familiar. More than half of the appliance thefts in Cold Peak had been from addresses where the occupants were away on vacation. That meant that whoever was committing the crimes had a system for finding out who was leaving town. Letty hadn't had time to cancel her mail—or else she had forgotten that detail—but she had canceled her regular newspaper delivery. It was possible the thief had checked with the news agency and, when Letty had stopped the paper, moved in. Unfortunately, the theif had been a day early.

To Taylor's mind, that didn't answer all of the questions. The Cold Peak appliance thefts had been slick, which suggested that the perpetrator had kept risks to a minimum, although that didn't rule out the idiot factor. A lot of crimes were solved through stupid mistakes, miscalculation and sheer panic on the part of the perp.

When Muir had gone, Fischer opened the glove compartment and handed her the Glock. "When was the last time you used the gun?"

"About six months ago." Before she'd become a walking target.

"If you're going to carry a weapon, you need to shoot regularly. There's a shooting range just out of town. If you're interested, I'll take you Monday afternoon."

He had a point. The biggest problem with

handguns was losing proficiency through lack of practice. To be confident and accurate you had to practice regularly, something she hadn't considered, and should have.

"Okay." A shooting range she could handle. It was less like a date; it was home territory. With a practiced movement, she ejected the clip and stowed both the gun and the magazine in her handbag. "You haven't asked me why I'm carrying a gun."

His expression was unreadable. "I could say that I assumed the scar on your back was the reason, but the fact is I know who you are."

Shock reverberated through Taylor. Suddenly, the way he'd stood back when she'd first gone in the door of Letty's house made sense. Most men would have assumed a protective role and muscled her aside, and Fischer fitted that mold. She hadn't fixed on his behavior at the time because her need to find out exactly what had happened had been too urgent. "What do you mean you know who I am?"

"You're a distinctive-looking woman. I was in D.C. when you got shot."

The story hadn't been front-page news but, according to Bayard, one of the major tabloids *had* gotten hold of her photo. The story had also aired on local television and radio stations. There had always been a risk that the publicity surrounding her shooting would compromise her security. It was a miracle that someone hadn't recognized her sooner. "How long have you known?"

"I recognized you the first day."

Her jaw tightened. "I need to know if you've told anyone."

His expression turned from guarded to remote. "First off, I don't make a habit of endangering federal officers. Secondly, given what happened, it's an easy bet you're on Witness Security."

She stared at the line of his profile, every cell on high alert. "You said you had a business. What is it?"

"I'm an ex Navy SEAL. I run a security business out of D.C. These days I'm not required there all the time. It gives me the latitude to pursue a few personal goals."

The second he said ex Navy SEAL, the final piece in the puzzle that was Steve Fischer slotted into place. When they'd searched Letty's house he had reminded her of a cop, but a SEAL made even more sense, and it explained the pull of attraction. She had always gravitated toward dangerous, physical guys, and that was exactly what Fischer was. His background as a SEAL also explained why he'd chosen a place like Cold Peak as an alternative to D.C. The outdoor focus in Cold Peak, with the rock climbing and the skiing, and the physicality of the job at the gym, would fit perfectly with his training ethics. "What kind of security firm do you run?"

He reached into the glove compartment and handed her a business card. She studied the card in the glow of the streetlamp. She didn't know the firm, which was based out of Georgetown, but she hadn't expected to. Not that the details made much difference. As solid as Fischer seemed, that didn't change the fact that she was compromised.

She pushed her door open, bracing herself against the wash of cool air. "Thanks for the date."

She had inserted her house key in the lock when Fischer walked down her front path.

"You might need this." He handed her her cashmere scarf, which she must have left in his truck. "If you don't want to stay the night here you can come back to my place. Or I can book you a motel for the night."

She took the wrap, pushed the door open and flicked on the hall light. "Thanks, but no thanks. I'll be fine." The fact that he knew her real identity was just one more reason not to take him up on the offer.

"I'll give you my phone number, and my cell. Just in case."

She watched as he wrote the details on the back of another one of his business cards and slipped it into her handbag. When she turned to go inside, the warm weight around her shoulders registered. Shrugging out of the jacket, she handed it to him. "You'd better have this."

"That wasn't what I wanted."

The blunt statement sent a raw flash of heat through her. "There's no point."

Instead of taking the jacket, his fingers threaded with hers. She had plenty of time to pull back, but the plain fact was she didn't want to.

A hot pulse of adrenaline went through her. *Three days.* It wasn't long enough. She didn't know enough about him—

Distantly, she was aware that both the jacket and her handbag had slipped to the ground. Her palms slid over his chest, bunched in the fabric of his shirt. His hands settled at her waist. A half step back and her spine connected with the cold line of the doorjamb. A split second later his mouth came down on hers. The first touch of his lips shivered through her and she wrapped her arms around his neck and gave in to the uncomplicated need to be held. It had been years since she'd felt female and wanted, years since she'd felt so needy.

He lifted his head, dark eyes glittering. "If you want me to leave we need to stop now."

She stared at the taut lines of his face, the stubble that made his jaw even tougher, and regret pulled at her.

He said something low and graphic. His breath washed over her throat. His teeth fastened on the lobe of one ear and a sharp shudder jerked through her.

In an abrupt movement, he released his hold and

stepped back, stooping to pick up the jacket. "I'll see you on Monday."

Her legs distinctly wobbly, she watched as he walked down the path and climbed into his truck. When the sound of the engine faded, she closed the door and tried to get her breath, and her sanity, back. Not only was her WITSEC placement blown for the second time, but sometime between last Tuesday and two minutes ago she had fallen for Steve Fischer.

The fact that she had let it happen didn't make sense. Somewhere inside her there was a benchmark that was carved in stone about loyalty, honor and honesty. She applied it to herself and to other people. Fischer had already lied to her, even if only by omission.

Then there was the whole can of worms about trust. She didn't trust easily, but once she did, that was it—she gave her all. She had trusted a total of three people in her life: her father, her mother and Rina.

Jack Jones had failed her. Maybe that was why she'd become such a difficult sell in the relationship game. Every time she had entered into a relationship with a man she had expected to be betrayed, and she had cut it off before that could happen. The strategy was simple, effective and safe, and it kept her lonely most of the time.

Lately, she'd been lonelier and more isolated

than normal. Maybe that had made her more vulnerable, but it wasn't a reason to consider sleeping with a man she barely knew—let alone trusted.

Sixteen

The Cold Peak Shooting range was situated five miles out of town, backing onto an old quarry and surrounded by silent woods and acres of rolling farmland.

Taylor watched as Fischer put on a set of ear protectors and safety glasses, focused, aimed, then squeezed the trigger in controlled bursts. The target was set at thirty feet.

Taylor slipped on her own ear protectors as noise filled the booth. Fischer's gun was a Bernadelli Practical, a sporting pistol specifically designed for target shooting. As sporting weapons went, it wasn't fancy or top-of-the-line, but the Bernadelli came in two calibers, the lower a twelve shot, the higher, sixteen shots. Fischer had the larger caliber.

"Nice shooting." The center of the target had turned into a ragged hole.

He inserted a second magazine. "I used to shoot competitively for my sports club. One year I almost made the Olympics."

The words were stated casually. No fanfare, no emotion. "What happened?"

He lifted the pistol, emptied the clip, then ejected the magazine. "Competing conflicted with work. I had to make a choice. I chose the job."

Taylor stepped up to the mark. Since they'd started shooting, she had hit the target but, unlike Fischer, she wasn't drilling the center. In the old days, that lack would have worried her and she would have put in extra time practicing until her aim was perfect. It was an indication of just how much she had changed that, unlike Fischer, perfection was no longer her goal. The competitive edge that had driven her all through her years with the Bureau had dissolved along with her job. If she could consistently hit the target, she was happy, because it meant that if she did have to use the gun she could make a body shot with reasonable accuracy.

Another emptied clip later, Fischer checked his watch. "Time's up."

Taylor glanced at her own watch, surprised to see that they'd spent more than their allotted half hour. Despite the fact that it was Monday, the range was busy. One of Cold Peak's tourist attractions was fishing and game hunting. Most of the slots were booked out to clients from a popular hunting lodge situated less than a mile away.

Outside, the sky was cold and gray and the wind was blowing from the north, sending leaves rattling across the parking lot. Rain scattered as they made a beeline for Fischer's truck. Ducking her head, Taylor quickened her step. Simultaneously, something zinged past her head. Time froze. She could hear the detonations of rounds being fired on the shooting range. One of the detonations echoed, sharper, out of sync with the rest. Adrenaline pumped. A split second later she was flat on the pavement.

Fischer crouched beside her. She sucked in a breath and wondered if she was going crazy. "Someone just fired a shot. A rifle."

Long seconds passed while she waited for a second shot. When it didn't come, Fischer handed her the keys to the truck. "Get behind the truck and stay down, I'll be back in a few minutes."

He extracted the Bernadelli from his gear bag, shoved a magazine into the breech and melted into the screen of shrubs that formed a decorative border around the parking lot.

Keeping low, the Glock gripped in her hand, Taylor took up a position behind the truck. Given that the shooting-club building formed a barrier, the only possible location for a sniper was a hill to the left of the shooting range where the ground rose steeply.

Long minutes passed while she studied mowed fields bordered by a pine forest. Her palms began to sting and the fact that the Glock was slippery with blood registered. She must have skinned her palms when she'd hit the sidewalk. Wiping the excess blood on her jeans, she readjusted her grip.

Rain was falling steadily now, pulling a misty gray curtain over the hills and soaking her hair and clothes. The background noise of cars on the main road into town registered, but beyond that the only sound was the wind gusting through the treetops and the flat detonation of shots being fired in the shooting range.

She checked her watch. Fifteen minutes had passed, but it felt longer. In that time no one had entered the parking lot or left, and no one inside the shooting range appeared to realize that a rogue shot had been fired.

A flickering movement drew her attention. She tensed then relaxed when Fischer detached himself from the dense shade of a clump of trees and loped across the parking lot. She was wet, but he was wetter.

Fischer collected his gear bag and stowed it in the large lockable box he kept in the rear of the truck. "I found a casing and some trampled ground on the edge of the pines." He took the brass casing from his pocket. "Looks like a .302 caliber, which is a hunting rifle. It could have been a stray shot from a hunter, although no one should be hunting this close to town."

Taylor examined the casing, her tension returning full force as she climbed into the passenger seat and Fischer pulled out of the parking lot. Fischer hadn't found anyone, but he must have come close, because whoever it was had finally made a mistake and left the casing behind.

Fischer extracted a towel from behind the driver's seat and passed it to her. When she'd blotted the water from her face and hair, she handed the towel back.

"You need those hands bandaged."

"I'll clean them up when I get home."

Right after that, she was leaving town.

Someone had just taken a shot at her, and the near miss had cleared her mind. She wasn't paranoid, and she wasn't wrong. Maybe it *had* just been a kid fooling around with his dad's gun at the wrong end of the range, or a hunter getting in some free target practice, but she'd stopped believing in fairy tales and happy endings months ago.

Setting the Glock down on the floor, she buckled herself in. She noticed Fischer had placed his gun down on the floor without removing the clip, keeping the weapon within easy reach, and the tension in her stomach increased. If Fischer believed there wasn't a problem, he would have disarmed the gun and packed it away and told her to do the same. It was unlikely to happen, but if the highway patrol pulled them over and found they were traveling with loaded weapons, regardless of who they were, they would both be arrested.

Minutes later, Fischer pulled over onto a grassy verge and cut the engine. Opening the glove compartment, he pulled out a first aid kit and levered off the lid. "Let me have a look at those hands."

She studied the metal first aid box as he swabbed her palms with disinfectant then smeared on antiseptic cream. "That looks military."

His gaze connected with hers. "The quartermaster liked me."

She glanced away from taut cheekbones and tanned olive skin. If the quartermaster had been female, she was willing to bet it had been a whole lot more than liking. "I bet you outranked him."

He motioned her to hold out her hands while he taped on wound dressings. He hadn't answered her question, but the suspicion that he had held some kind of command grew stronger.

It was possible that the fact that he was so close-mouthed was a carryover from his time in the SEAL teams. He could also be an accomplished liar.

He could be married.

She would be crazy not to consider the idea. She hadn't seen any indication that he wore a wedding ring, but some men didn't. "So what was your rank? Lieutenant?"

This close, his eyes were flecked with gold. She hadn't noticed that last night, but then she had been more concerned with controlling her reactions than cataloging physical details.

"Lieutenant commander. How come you know so much?"

"I used to date a SEAL."

"Now you're pissing me off."

As he replaced the first aid kit in the glove compartment, Taylor had to wonder just how annoyed he was. Despite her effort at cold analysis, and distance, she was hoping that he was big on understatement. "Hey, Fischer...thanks."

"The name's Steve, not Fischer." He leaned across and brushed her mouth with his.

The kiss threw her off balance. When he would have pulled back, she cupped his neck and held him there, leaning into the kiss, part curiosity, part experiment. He adjusted the angle, her head tilted back and the pressure firmed. His tongue in her mouth sent a bolt of heat straight to her loins. Taylor's heart slammed in her chest. It was sex, pure and simple, she decided...but that didn't explain why Fischer was so damned irresistible.

His mouth lifted and sank back onto hers and the half-formed notion of pushing free receded.

Not for the first time she wondered what it would be like to stretch out in a bed with Fischer, to spend an entire night with him.

Not that she would allow that to happen.

For now, she would enjoy the fantasy and the kiss, secure in the knowledge that after today she wouldn't ever see him again.

The rain had stopped by the time Fischer dropped her off at her house, and watery sunlight warmed an afternoon that had become distinctly chilly.

Fischer had offered to call the police, but she had turned him down. Even with the evidence of the casing, there wasn't much the Cold Peak PD could do. Unless she broke WITSEC and supplied them with her real identity, the supposition that the shot had been aimed at her wouldn't be taken seriously. Also, any approach to the Cold Peak police would generate a report that could reach Burdett. As it stood, she had half expected a response from Burdett over Letty's murder. If her new name appeared in the police database again, her placement would be officially blown. Burdett would be knocking on her door within hours, and she wasn't sure she wanted that.

Despite WITSEC's protection, her security had been breached—twice. She couldn't think of any other way for the leak to happen but through WITSEC. This time, she intended to take care of her own security.

* * *

Taylor strode through to the bedroom, placed the Glock on her bedside table, grabbed fresh underwear and a black T-shirt and jeans, then quickly showered and changed. Hair hanging in a wet curtain down her back, she shrugged into the shoulder rig, which disappeared against the black fabric of the tee, holstered the gun and pulled on a dark jacket.

Pulling suitcases from her closet, she packed. Within minutes she had everything she needed. Zipping the bags closed, she carried them out to the SUV and stored them in the rear storage compartment. With her bedroom stripped, she walked through to the kitchen, her mind running over lists—what she needed to take, what had to be left…when, and if, to call Burdett. If she walked out on WITSEC she would be on her own, and effectively on the run from Lopez.

Shoving basic food items—bread, butter, cereal and cheese—into an unused trash sack, she made another trip to the garage and wedged the food in the trunk, beside the cases.

Walking quickly through the house, she gathered the few personal possessions she couldn't bear to leave behind—jewelry, family photos and an antique sampler that had belonged to her grandmother. There wasn't time, but she didn't know if she would ever see any of her possessions again.

When the items were safely stored in the backseat of the SUV, she walked through to the sunroom and stopped, for long seconds unable to comprehend what *wasn't* there. *Her computer.*

Her stomach hollowed out. She went hot then cold and for a dizzying moment she thought she was going to throw up. The last time she'd had a break-in, she hadn't been aware of it for weeks and all the thief had taken was information.

This time he had taken the entire computer.

Glock held in a two-handed grip, she systematically searched the house, then the grounds. The only evidence of the break-in was the damaged lock on the sunroom doors.

Her computer had gone, but it was an expensive model and clearly visible on the desk in the sunroom. If the appliance thief had been in Letty's house, he would have seen the computer. She had checked and nothing else had been stolen, but then the thief hadn't had much time, just the hour or so she had been away with Fischer.

It was possible the theft was just a lousy coincidence and unconnected to the Lopez case. As determined as she was to get out of Cold Peak, she couldn't allow herself to give way to panic. She needed to report the theft, because any evidence collected could provide the break the police needed to catch Letty's killer. If she did nothing else before she left town, she had do that.

Instead of dialing the police, she found the card Fischer had given her and dialed his home number.

He picked up almost immediately. "What's happened?"

"Someone's been in the house." Her throat closed up and for long seconds she had difficulty speaking at all. "My computer's gone."

"I'm on my way." The phone clicked, disconnecting the call.

She dialed Muir's cell. The conversation was equally brief; Muir would be there in five. Hanging up, she walked out to the SUV, stowed her jacket and the holstered gun, then walked back to the kitchen and filled the kettle with water. She was neither thirsty nor hungry, but she needed the physical activity. Over the passage of years, she'd studied and walked into countless crime scenes, some of them disturbing enough to give her nightmares. By comparison, the theft of her computer was innocuous, but it didn't feel that way.

Her hands shook as she plugged the kettle in. The distress was irrational, *but they had taken the box.*

Whoever had stolen the computer must have watched her from Letty's house and had seen her store disks in the box. Maybe they hadn't wanted the information. Maybe they had just taken the box because it was attractive, or they had decided it might have contained programs they could sell. But the fact that the information she'd hidden had been targeted had shaken her.

She heard Fischer's truck pull up at the curb. Setting the mugs down on the counter, she walked through to unlock the front door.

Fischer's expression was calm. "Have you touched anything?"

"Not in the sunroom. As soon as I saw the computer was gone, I backed out of the room."

"Have you rung Muir?"

"He's on his way."

Fischer stepped into the hall. "You've checked the house?"

"It's clear."

"I'll take a look anyway."

Walking through to the kitchen, Taylor ignored the boiled water, found the coffee in the pantry and spooned it into the filter. They were going to need coffee, and a lot of it. Once Muir and his evidence techs arrived, the investigative process would take at least one, maybe two hours. She would be lucky to get out of town before nightfall.

Seventeen

It was dark by the time Muir and his people wrapped up the investigation. The interviews had been brief, because Taylor didn't have anything more to tell them than that her computer and a box of disks had been stolen. The fact that her television and DVD player hadn't been taken had been noted and seemed to support the theory that Taylor had arrived back home and disturbed the thief. When he had realized she was back, he had cut and run.

The theory was plausible and chilling, because the thief could have been in the house while she was taking a shower. The only problem with Muir's scenario was that neither Fischer nor Taylor could recall seeing a vehicle parked close to her place. There had been odd cars dotted through the neighborhood as they'd driven in, but nothing of any size, and definitely no vans or trucks.

Muir hadn't been put off. At this point they were assuming the robbery had been perpetrated by the same guy who had robbed Letty's house and killed her. He had spent time in Letty's house, scoping out Taylor's place, therefore he must have had a vehicle parked somewhere. It was even possible he was a resident in this part of town and locals were used to seeing his vehicle.

The evidence techs left first, followed a few minutes later by Muir. After collecting the coffee mugs, Taylor rinsed them in the sink, then stacked them in the dishwasher. As she loaded the carafe she noticed one of Buster's dishes in the rack and comprehension hit. She hadn't seen Buster since she had gotten home. She had been so absorbed with the events at the shooting range, then the break-in, that she had completely forgotten about him.

"What's wrong?"

"Buster." When Steve frowned, she added, "Letty's cat." Although, he was her cat now and already she had lost him.

"I've got a flashlight in the truck. I'll take a look out back."

Grabbing her own flashlight from the pantry, Taylor walked down the back passage, stepped out the door and began calling. To her left, thick trees pressed in on the narrow, grassed space. To her right, Letty's house was bone white and elegant in the moonlight. The thought that Buster, who had probably been scared by the thief, was hiding somewhere on Letty's property sent a shiver down her spine, although she didn't think that was likely. She didn't know much about animals, but she was willing to bet Buster wouldn't go near the house, which to his acute senses must still be laden with the scent of death.

She crouched low, sending the flashlight beam skimming at ground level, picking out the woody stems of the hydrangeas and rhododendrons against the boundary fence. Eyes gleamed. Something small and fast flitted sideways and streaked up the side of a tree trunk. Another squirrel.

Following the squirrel with the beam of the flashlight, she searched the branches of a spreading oak. She'd assumed, because Buster was sturdily built, he preferred to stay at ground level, but if he were frightened enough, he would climb.

The beam of Fischer's flashlight swept the side of the yard that bordered Letty's place. They double-checked the backyard, then either side of the house. While Taylor walked along the street, calling, Fischer did another circuit of the house then checked Letty's backyard. When Taylor came up blank, she searched the house, checking under beds and in closets. Buster was gone, far enough that he hadn't responded to repeated calling. She was packed and ready to go, and she had done all she could to make sure Letty's killer was caught, but she couldn't leave Cold Peak without making sure Buster was safe.

Taylor was setting a dish of tuna and a bowl of water on the deck when Fischer materialized out of the darkness. As she straightened, he pulled her into his arms, the hold loose and meant for comfort, and she learned something more about Fischer. He was definitely comfortable with women.

She tilted her head back and stared into his eyes. "You've been married."

"Briefly. A long time ago."

"What happened?"

He released her and stepped back, and she drew in some much-needed air.

"The job."

It was the answer she had expected. Beneath the surface cool, Fischer had a ruthless streak. She was willing to bet that when it had come to his marriage he hadn't given an inch.

He propped himself against the deck railing and crossed his arms over his chest. "You're staying at my place tonight. Or I sleep here."

From the point of view of security, Fischer's offer made sense, but for a brief moment she felt herded. "All right. Let's make it your house. I'll take my car and meet you there." That way Fischer wouldn't find out that she was already packed and ready to leave. In the morning all she would have to do was find Buster, and drive.

* * *

The weather had closed in again by the time Taylor pulled out of her driveway. Instead of turning left and heading for Fischer's house, she took a right and drove into town. Minutes later, after threading through the complex weave of inner suburbs, and keeping an eye on her rearvision mirror, she doubled back and parked beside Fischer's truck.

If anyone had been tailing her, the steadily drumming rain and reduced visibility should have forced them in close enough that she would have spotted them.

The rain thickened as she sat in the driver's seat, watching the road to see if anyone cruised past. When the street remained empty, she collected her overnight bag, locked the SUV and walked inside.

Fischer's house was neat, but spartan: stained wood floors, basic furniture, a television and a stereo. The only luxury was the bed in the master bedroom, which was king-size. In terms of stamping his personality on his home, Fischer had succeeded in creating a blank page.

Fischer indicated that she should take the bed.

"You don't have to give up your bed." She dropped her bag beside the couch to underline her point.

Feeling edgy after the drive around town, her nerves strung tight by the fact that she was forced to spend another night in Cold Peak, she followed Fischer into the kitchen. He had already started to assemble dinner: two steaks ready for the grill, fresh bread rolls he must have bought earlier in the day and a salad. With a kitchen towel slung over one shoulder, he was an odd juxtaposition of domestic and dangerous.

He opened the fridge door. "Beer or soda? Sorry, I don't have wine."

She blinked, abruptly disoriented. A drink before dinner. It was a civilized ritual, something taken for granted in any number of households, and it hammered home how far she'd stepped away from normality. "Soda. Thanks."

He took a frosted can from the fridge, ripped the tab and poured sparkling lemonade into a glass. While she sipped, she listened to the rain and watched Fischer cook and periodically take a pull from a beer. The label was Jax. The only touch of the South she'd seen so far in his house.

He slid steaks onto warmed plates then rinsed the pan, his movements economical and ordered as if nothing dangerous or unusual had happened that day, and suddenly the reason Fischer had gotten beneath her skin hit her.

He made her feel safe. Not sexually or emotionally, but in every other way that mattered.

In the middle of the chaos that was her life, he was as solid and dependable as the proverbial rock.

Nothing appeared to shake him. As hard as she'd fought against trusting anyone, on a primitive, instinctive level she trusted Fischer, and with good reason, because every time she'd called on him, he had come through.

"What's wrong?"

"Nothing." Everything. She was in love with him.

In retrospect it hadn't been a sudden process. She had seen him on a daily basis for weeks and steadily grown into the emotions. The day she had gone jogging and had finally registered Fischer on a sexual level, the attraction had blindsided her. From that point on, she had been gone.

His gaze sharpened. "Something's changed."

He took the glass of soda from her hands and set it down on the counter. She registered his intent a split second before his head dipped and his mouth settled on hers. The hungry pressure of the kiss sent a raw shudder through her. Fischer had been polite, the perfect host, but she had no illusions that he would play the gentleman when it came to sex. Safe haven or not, he had never made any bones about the fact that he wanted her.

Fischer lifted his mouth, his gaze searching. "I hadn't meant for this to happen. It's your call."

She hooked her fingers in his shirt and pulled him close. "Don't give me time to think." If she had time she would say no, because doing this was crazy. She had to leave, and sleeping with Fischer was going to make walking away even more difficult.

He stepped in close, crowding her against the counter. "What made you change your mind?"

"Don't ask." She cupped his face and kissed him back, imprinting the scent and taste of him, the hard warmth of muscle. She didn't want to talk, didn't want to examine—not when she would lose him tomorrow.

Long, drugging minutes later, his hands, settled at her waist, swept upward, peeling her limp T-Shirt from her arms. Cold air raised goose bumps. A split second later his mouth fastened over one breast through the fabric of her bra and the stirring ache in her belly sharpened.

Rain pounded on the windows, the cold from outside at odds with the heat flushing her skin. She felt the release as her jeans were unfastened, Fischer's hands working her jeans and panties down, the rush of cool air against her skin. His hands closed on her bottom and she wound her arms around his neck as he lifted her onto the counter. Seconds later, he shoved deep.

Shock reverberated as she registered the drag of the condom. She hadn't seen him sheathe himself and she hadn't given a thought to protection, but Fischer had; he must have had the condom in his jeans pocket.

Her fingers dug into his shoulders as he continued to thrust. The hot, stirring ache started again and her belly clenched. She lifted her head, Fischer's eyes locked with hers and sultry heat exploded in the room.

For long seconds she simply hung on, her head buried against his shoulder while she adjusted to the feel of him.

A small shiver went through her as he finally withdrew and carried her through to the bedroom. Rain pounded on the windows, filling the room with a damp chill, as he set her on her feet, unhooked her bra, discarded it then peeled out of his clothes.

She pulled back the bedcovers and slid between the sheets. Lamplight slid over his broad, tanned back as he smoothed on another condom, then joined her in bed, the heat of his body burning away the chill.

She wound her arms around his neck and settled against him. "What about dinner?"

His gaze locked with hers and heat swept through her again.

"Later."

When she woke, it was still raining and the wind was gusting powerfully enough to make the windows shake. Light from the sitting room filtered down the hall, dimly illuminating the room, although she didn't need light to know that Fischer—*Steve*—was awake.

Her palm slid over his chest, enjoying the feel of hard muscle and damp skin. His hand closed over hers. Her eyes flipped open and she logged the fact that he was watching her.

"So what made you notice me? Up until a few days ago I was the invisible man."

She smothered a yawn. With light gleaming off broad shoulders, a five-o'clock shadow roughening his jaw, she wondered that she had ever not noticed him. "Your truck."

"If I'd known that I would have taken it to work earlier."

She propped herself up on one elbow. "You can tell what people are really like by the vehicle they drive. For example, Dane looks great—the tan, the ponytail—but he drives a *hatchback*."

His expression was bemused. "What's wrong with hatchbacks?"

"They're short. Cut off."

Fischer wound a finger in her hair and tugged. "Back to the truck."

She shifted closer, her thigh sliding between his. "If anyone had asked me, I would have had you pegged for a station wagon or an SUV. Something manly but practical." She ran a finger down his chest. "Instead you had a four-wheel-drive muscle truck with mud spattered on the wheel arches."

"The mud counted?"

She smothered a yawn. "It meant you went off road."

"You are kidding."

"Nope."

He pulled her close, his fingers sliding through her hair. "You drive an SUV. What does that mean?"

"The SUV doesn't count."

"Because it goes with the new identity." His teeth closed over one lobe and a shiver went down her spine.

She let out a breath, the tension in the pit of her stomach growing. "That's right."

"What if my truck was a cover?"

She slid a hand beneath the sheet, found his penis and gently squeezed. "Trust me, it isn't."

Eighteen

Morning sunlight beamed across the front of Taylor's house as she unlocked the door and stepped into the hallway. Moving quickly, she walked through the rooms, checking closets and cupboards, just in case Buster had somehow managed to conceal himself and was trapped inside. When she'd ascertained that the house was empty, she began searching outside. Fischer had left for work at his usual time. When he realized she wasn't coming in, he would come looking for her. By her calculation she had until eight-thirty, maximum.

Calling softly, she searched underneath the house and the deck, then started on the backyard. The empty tuna dish on the deck indicated that Buster had come back to eat—either that, or the dish had been emptied by one of the neighboring cats.

A sharp wail, like the sound of a crying baby, jerked her head up. At the rear of the yard, just beyond the fence, she caught a glimpse of tabby markings and a fluffy white paw.

Heart pounding, because she had never heard an animal utter a sound like that, she climbed the fence into the overgrown reserve that backed onto her property, pushed through thick undergrowth and finally emerged in a clearing. She searched the area directly behind her house then began to walk, still calling. The ground sloped gently toward a drain, the surface lumpy and uneven where water had flowed over the ground, flattening grass and scouring the dirt. Mounds of leaves, shaken loose in the storm, lay in thick drifts.

Something pale gleamed at the edge of the clearing. She walked toward the flash of color, calling Buster's name, then froze, as the peculiar arrangement of light and shadow suddenly made sense. The outline of a body, partially covered with leaves and dirt, was just barely discernible.

Stepping closer, she studied the head. He was male and Caucasian, with a patch of shaved scalp punctured by two neat, round holes. The glint of a steel earring made him instantly recognizable: Hansen. The last time she had seen him alive, he had been mowing Letty's lawn.

She retraced her steps so she didn't disturb the

crime scene any more than she already had. Clambering over the fence, she pushed through shrubs, stopping short before she stepped out onto the open, exposed area of her lawn.

Muir had thought that the appliance thief might have a connection to the newsagents or the post office, but a lawn-mowing service was even better. Hansen had regularly traveled around quiet neighborhoods, talking to residents and neighbors; he would have been notified when clients were away on vacation.

From memory his truck had been covered, not open, and it had been *backed* into Letty's driveway. In retrospect that hadn't been necessary when all he'd had to do was unload a lawn mower and an edge trimmer. But if Hansen had been concerned with loading appliances, backing in made perfect sense.

If she wasn't mistaken, Cold Peak's appliance thief was now lying in a shallow grave at the edge of the park with a double tap to the back of his head. In contrast to Letty's murder, the execution-style killing of the lawn contractor was both professional and chilling. Muir had been satisfied that Letty's death was linked to the thefts, but that theory might not fly now that Hansen had wound up dead.

For the first time in months her mind was sharp and clear. The shot fired at the shooting range, the theft of her computer and two distinctly different murders happening right next door suddenly made sense. Neither murder was the result of miscalculation or coincidence; they formed part of a pattern. A lethal pattern that had almost snared her for the third time.

She had been the killer's focus all along. He had targeted Letty's house as a soft option for getting close, moved in and waited to set up a shot, but Hansen had broken in, disturbing him and discovering Letty's body.

At a guess, the killer had marched Hansen out of the house at gunpoint, made him climb the fence into the reserve then had shot him. That scenario explained why the killer had returned to Letty's house, despite the greater risk of discovery after not one killing, but two. It would have taken time to bury Hansen and he would also have had to dispose of the getaway van with the stolen appliances. It also explained why he had taken the added risk of stealing her computer. In a creative twist, he had decided to use the spate of computer and appliance thefts to cover his real target, which had been the disks.

And there was only one logical reason for him to want the disks. Rina had been right when she had stated that Taylor must have something that Lopez wanted. Somewhere in the torrent of material on Lopez there was information that was important.

She stared at Letty's house. He wasn't there now. With crime-scene tape making the house conspicuous—and a second body—it was no longer a safe haven. But that didn't mean he wasn't close.

Leaves shivered. Buster materialized at the edge of the lawn, half-hidden by shadows, his normally greenish eyes dilated and black.

He stared at her blankly for a few seconds, then began to keen, the sound high pitched and eerie. Her heart squeezed tight. She finally understood what had been happening. Buster had been spooked for a couple of days before Letty had been killed. With his acute senses, he had known it was no longer safe. He would also have known Letty was dead the night Taylor had tried to take him back, which explained why he had recoiled and bolted. Then, just when he thought he was safe, the killer had broken into her house.

Scooping Buster up, she carried him inside and through to the kitchen. Setting him down, she reached for a can of tuna, opened it and emptied it into a dish.

While Buster was eating, she walked through to her bedroom and grabbed an oversize shirt and a dark blue ball cap off a hook in the closet. Coiling her hair up, she jammed the cap down tight then shrugged into the shirt. The shirt made her figure shapeless and the cap hid her hair and shaded her face.

Walking back into the kitchen, she scooped Buster up and carried him out to the car, sliding in beside him and closing the door before he could lunge through. If he got away now, she would never have another chance to catch him, and she owed it to Letty to make sure Buster was safe.

Putting the SUV in gear, she reversed out of the garage and onto the road. The street looked normal, a quiet backwater. Just across the road Scanlon was washing his Corvette. Farther down, an elderly lady was walking her Corgi. Neither were candidates for espionage and murder, but somebody was. They had been operating within yards of her, and she had missed them.

She reached for her cell phone and called the Cold Peak PD as she drove.

Dispatch picked up the call. She reported the body, supplied the address, then hung up.

With a jerky movement, she depressed the accelerator. By the time she reached the first intersection, Buster was howling and had somehow managed to entangle himself with her feet and the accelerator.

After installing Buster in a cattery on the outskirts of town, and paying two weeks in advance, Taylor drove back into Cold Peak, taking a circuitous route. When she was satisfied that she hadn't been followed, she parked the SUV on a small side street and walked through a mall. Sliding dark glasses onto the bridge of her nose, she crossed the road and walked into the bank. It was nine o'clock and the branch had just opened, so the likelihood that anyone from the gym would be inside was slim. She needed cash, but that would have to wait. Time was running out, and she wasn't about to expose herself any more than was necessary by standing at the main counter or an ATM.

Stopping at the information counter, she produced her safe-deposit box key, then waited until a bank officer was available to take her through to the vault.

Minutes later, she slipped the disks containing copies of the Lopez research files into her bag, along with an envelope containing a set of fake identity papers she had used on and off for operations over the past two years: a birth certificate, driver's license, bank account and credit card.

Colenso had requested the return of the papers when her resignation from the Bureau had become effective. Normally, Taylor would have complied without a thought, but a bullet in the back had changed her priorities. She had balanced the ethics of retaining a second identity against her life and told Colenso the ID had been stolen along with the rest of her papers and files.

Slipping the safe-deposit key into a side pocket of her purse, she strolled out to the main reception area. This early, the bank was quiet. A woman was making a deposit at one of the teller's booths. To one side, behind a screen of opaque glass, a couple were in conversation with a banker. The main street came into view through the wide expanse of glass windows and doors.

She froze in midstep. *Fischer.*

He was standing just outside the bank, talking with another man. The stranger turned slightly. Shock reverberated through her. He was wearing dark glasses, not spectacles, but she recognized him. The first time she had seen him had been months ago in the library in D.C., the second time on the beach in Wilmington.

Nineteen

She was already shuffling back. Fischer had his back turned to her. He hadn't seen her, but all his companion had to do was turn his head and he would.

The inquiries clerk, a pretty blonde in her early forties, lifted a brow and mouthed, *Someone you don't want to see?*

As understatements went, that one was huge. She had dated Fischer; she had *slept* with him. She had wanted more, but it was now clear that Fischer never had.

Despite Burdett's extra precautions, Fischer and his friend had followed her from Wilmington. They had kept her under surveillance. Fischer had even gone as far as moving into her place of work and renting a house just down the road.

Not all of the facts stacked up. The attempt on her

life didn't fit with Fischer taking the time to get close to her. If he had been paid to kill her, the equation was as simple as it had been in D.C.: one good shot and problem solved. If he had wanted information, he could have made his move weeks ago.

Only one thing was certain—whoever Fischer worked for, and whatever he was doing in Cold Peak, he wasn't here for the rock climbing.

She met the woman's concerned face. "He's an ex-boyfriend. He doesn't like taking no for an answer."

The woman was careful not to look at the two men, who must have still been in plain view. "Do you want to call the police?"

The thought was tempting but dangerous when her first, last and only priority had to be to get out of town. By now Muir would have found Hansen. When dispatch replayed the tape of her phone call, he would recognize her voice. His next move would be to find her. "It's okay, he's not violent, just persistent."

Fischer and his friend would have been caught on the bank's security cameras. All she had to do was advise Burdett and he could pick them up, although she was aware that it wouldn't be that easy. Fischer and his buddy were professionals. Once they realized she had left town, they wouldn't stay in Cold Peak long. "Is there a back door I can use?"

"Sorry. That's off-limits to everyone but staff." The woman walked around from behind her desk, opened the door to an interview room and peered inside. "There's no one in here. If you want, you can sit down for a few minutes and I'll let you know when the coast is clear."

Taylor set down her bag, took a chair and checked her watch, her urgency to leave town mounting. By now Muir would have discovered that she wasn't at work. He could even have put an APB out on her car, which meant she needed to be gone. It would take her twenty minutes to make it to the nearest town large enough to have an ATM and a rental-car agency so she could ditch the SUV. It would take a further hour to hit a city with a large enough population that she could disappear. Vermont was pretty, but it was definitely rural, a perfect place to be trapped on narrow country lanes.

She checked her watch again. It didn't make the time go any faster, but it helped keep her mind off the mind-numbing emptiness of the mistake she'd made in sleeping with Fischer.

It was a fact that Fischer had followed her and watched her. Now she had to consider that he had murdered both Letty and Hansen, *and* stolen her computer. His sidekick had probably broken into her house and taken the computer while they were at the shooting range.

The logic was inescapable. Even the timing of

the gunshot that had narrowly missed her made sense. They had had the computer and the disks, therefore she was now expendable.

It seemed fair to assume the shooter had been the guy with the glasses. Fischer had probably phoned him while he was out of Taylor's hearing, made sure he had the disks and given him their current location at the shooting range.

The reason he hadn't removed the clip from the Bernadelli now also made sense. At the time she had thought he was on edge because of the possible threat to her, but it was more straightforward than that. There was no way a trained professional like Fischer would disarm himself while traveling in the presence of someone who was armed.

The door opened and the woman popped her head inside. "I checked down the street. They're both gone."

Taylor let out a breath. "Thanks. You saved my life."

Twenty minutes out of town, she turned down a side road and pulled over in a shady spot where her vehicle wouldn't be visible from the highway.

She picked up her cell phone, found the speed dial for Dana's number, and stopped. She needed to calm down, to *think*.

Dana wasn't safe. Taylor needed to talk to her, to get her out of San Francisco as soon as possible, but she had to assume that Lopez had both Dana's cell phone and her home and work numbers tapped. After what had happened in Cold Peak, he would also have Taylor's under active surveillance. She couldn't afford to call Dana.

They would be waiting for her to do just that.

She turned the cell phone off, put the car in gear and headed back toward the highway.

She would buy another cell phone when she changed vehicles, but even then she couldn't afford to make the call herself. She would have to find another way.

Twenty

Steve caught the urgency of the traffic on the police band the second he climbed into his truck. A body had been found on the reserve behind Taylor's place. Muir and the evidence techs were already there; the coroner was on his way.

Slamming the truck into gear, he pulled out onto Cold Peak's main road. The gender of the body hadn't been specified and there was no reason to assume that it was Taylor, but after more than twelve years working undercover operations, he was short on optimism. And Taylor hadn't turned up at the gym.

He braked for an intersection. While he waited for the lights to change, he picked up his cell phone and called the gym. Mandy answered. Taylor still hadn't come in, and she hadn't phoned.

When he arrived at Taylor's house, several police cruisers were parked along the road. A news van was just nosing into a space across the street and a group of bystanders and neighbors were gathering on the sidewalk. An ambulance was standing by.

Driscoll was on guard at the front gate, his face green.

"Male or female?"

For a split second, Driscoll didn't respond. "Male."

Some of his tension dissolved. "I need to talk to Muir."

Driscoll was reluctant, but Steve was banking on the fact that because he had called in Letty's murder, Muir would see him. The second killing had raised the stakes. Driscoll had to know that if Steve had information that would help with the inquiry and he blocked him, Muir would go ballistic.

Driscoll spoke into his radio. A split second later, he jerked his head. "You can go in."

Muir glanced up as he walked toward the house. Steve reached into his pocket, slowly, because Muir looked pissed and Hart looked almost as green as Driscoll, and produced his ID.

Muir glanced at Steve, his expression mild, considering the information on the ID. "Now what does the death of an elderly lady and a lawn-mowing contractor have to do with the CIA?"

Steve supplied him with a copy of the letter that went with the ID. It didn't contain much more than a list of the agencies that had agreed to cooperate with his investigation, but it was written on Office of the Director of National Intelligence letterhead and signed off by Saunders.

Muir took his time reading it. "I'm going to need a copy of this."

"Be my guest." He nodded toward the backyard. "Has the body been identified?"

Briefly, Muir filled him in on the details. Hansen had been dead for two, maybe three days. He had been on their list of suspects for the appliance thefts and they'd had an APB out on his truck ever since his girlfriend had called the previous night to say that he had gone missing.

"Who found the body?"

"An anonymous female caller, but my money's on your girlfriend."

"Mind if I take a look in the house?"

Muir still didn't look happy. "Hart goes with you. The body is out-of-bounds."

Hart led the way into the house.

As Steve passed the sunroom with its empty computer desk, he took his cell phone out of his pocket, stabbed the speed dial, spoke briefly then hung up. Taylor must have come back here shortly after he had left for work to look for the cat, found the body, reported it and left town. He was willing to bet that she had also found the cat, which meant her first stop would be a cattery.

He noticed that the photos in the sitting room were gone, along with a sampler that had been on the wall. Apart from taking these few personal items, it appeared that she had packed just the necessities.

When he walked out of the bedroom, Hart was waiting in the hall. "Where's the body?"

Hart looked wary. "Over the fence in the adjoining park."

"Mind if I take a look from the backyard?"

"Just as long as you don't go over the fence. After the rain last night, the evidence techs are going crazy trying to find anything but mud."

Steve stepped out of the back door just as Muir cleared the two ambulance officers carrying a stretcher and a body bag to hand the equipment over the fence. "How did he die?"

Hart watched in mute fascination as two uniformed officers disappeared with the stretcher into the overgrown reserve. "Two in the back of the head. That's a first for Cold Peak."

The tension in Steve's stomach intensified. The sniper who had shot Taylor in D.C. had fired at least four rounds and only one of them had hit the target. The attempt in Wilmington had been a clear shot from an apartment window that had also been bungled, leaving Taylor with a grazed arm. This guy had made sure.

The shooting was different; connected, but different. Maybe it was simply that the killing had been so neatly executed; no mess on either Letty or Taylor's properties, no sloppy marksmanship, just bad luck that Taylor had climbed over the fence and gone looking for her cat.

A burst of static erupted out of Hart's radio. "It's Harris. They've found the truck. It's in a ravine on Herbert Pierce's place, just off Highway 103. There's a television and a VCR in the rear."

Muir swore. "Tell Harris not to touch a thing and don't let *anyone* near it."

Muir issued orders, but Steve already knew the truck was another dead end. He'd been trailing this guy for months. If Muir thought he would find anything to hang a case on in the ravine, he was going to be disappointed. The only piece of information that was of real interest to him was that Harris hadn't reported another body.

Just after twelve, Taylor used the new cell phone she had bought in Springfield, a town thirty minutes south of Cold Peak, and dialed Jack Jones's number.

He picked up almost immediately. "What's wrong?"

The sound of her father's voice loosened off some of her tension. At this time of day he could have been out on his launch with clients and out of cell phone range, and right now every second counted. "I've left the Witness Security program. I need your help."

"Where are you?"

"Nowhere yet, I'm driving. Don't worry, I'm safe. There's something I need you to do. It's important."

There was a brief silence. He said something sharp and succinct. "Dana."

Relief made her feel weak. The conversation had been conducted in a weird short code, but they were on the same wavelength.

"Why didn't they go for Dana before?"

"Because they had a line on me. Now that's gone."

There was a dull clunk, as though he'd set a plate down. "What happened?"

Briefly, she filled him in on the murders, the shot that had narrowly missed her and the fact that she had been followed to Cold Peak.

"Damn it. *Where are you?*"

"That's not important. All I need is for you to get Dana out of San Francisco and keep her safe."

"She isn't going to like it."

"She'll understand. You're the only one I trust to do it."

There was a tense silence. She heard background noises, the sound of canned laughter. She had a sudden mental picture of her father watching TV while he ate lunch alone and she experienced an unexpected, vivid sense of connection. Jack

Jones hadn't lived the life she'd wanted him to live, but he was *alive* and, right now, he was the only person she trusted to help her.

"I'll get a flight out this afternoon. As it happens, I was on my way to the West Coast. I've got a lead on the hit man and a contact who's willing to talk."

"Forget the hit man. Just get Dana out."

At ten o'clock Taylor turned into a popular motel chain just off Highway 91 on the outskirts of Northampton, Massachusetts. She paid for a room with cash and parked the rental she'd picked up in Springfield outside the unit.

The motel room was sparse but comfortable. After depositing a change of clothes and toiletries in the bedroom, she dialed Burdett.

He picked up immediately, despite the fact that it was late, and he wasn't happy. He'd had the Cold Peak PD, the FBI and the Attorney General's office in his ear and he wanted her back in protective custody, ASAP.

Cutting him short, Taylor supplied the address of the bank, and the time and date Fischer and his sidekick had been outside, talking. "If you get hold of the bank's front door and ATM security camera tapes, you should be able to get clear footage of two men who followed me to Cold Peak. One of them, the guy with the glasses, was in Wilmington. I'll be in touch."

Twenty-One

Taylor strolled through a mall, a shopping bag filled with a few necessities—milk, fresh fruit, decent coffee and a blond wig. She'd only slept a couple of hours, but despite that she felt alert and in control.

She was supposed to have felt this way in the Witness Security program but that hadn't happened. She'd thought long and hard about exactly why the program had failed her. The problem could be as simple as the publicity surrounding her shooting in D.C. making her too visible. Either that, or someone powerful enough to circumvent WITSEC had betrayed her.

She was betting on the second option. A mole who had eluded protection had disrupted the Morell/Lopez investigation. It was an uncomfortable notion to think that she had been personally targeted by the mole, but given that the information she'd had stored on the disks had pertained solely to the Lopez investigation, she had to consider it.

The way she saw it she had two options. She could disappear, renege on her agreement to testify against Lopez and start a new life with a false identity, or she could find out who wanted her dead—and why—and stop them.

With the contacts she had, and with Jack's help, she could arrange a false identity. But if she took that route, Dana would have to come with her, which would mean a huge disruption in a life that had already been derailed by the Chavez cartel. It would also mean taking the coward's way out. After all she and Dana had been through, after all the effort she'd put into catching Lopez, she was damned if she would roll over now.

She turned down the street that led to her motel, her gaze watchful. Despite her tiredness, her stride was loose and her chest felt close to normal. The hours she'd spent at the gym and jogging around the streets of Cold Peak had paid off.

When she reached her motel unit, she unpacked the groceries, had breakfast, pinned up her hair and tried on the wig. With her hair color changed from dark brown to honey-blond, she looked radically different. Satisfied, she changed clothes, collected the bag of disks and her purse, locked the unit and walked back to the mall, which had an Internet café.

She hired a computer for the morning, sat down and placed the stack of disks beside the hard drive.

There were twenty in all. Setting the disks in order of date, she inserted the first one and began to read. By the time she inserted the second disk, the noise of people checking mail and transacting business at the counter had faded and she was once more hotwired into the world that Lopez had locked her out of.

As she worked, she made brief notes about the interweaving threads of the Chavez cartel and the wild card of the Nazi cabal that, according to Slater, had backed Alex Lopez. She had every confidence that if she searched long enough, she would find what it was that had pushed Lopez's buttons.

At eleven she stopped to stretch her legs and iron the cricks out of her neck and shoulder, then paid for the afternoon. The café was open until late, which suited her. If she had to stay until closing, she would.

She slipped in another disk and the cadences of the investigation began to flow, the strange coincidences and seemingly unrelated incidents forming a pattern that had implications beyond the investigation into the Chavez cartel.

She took a break from the screen to read the notes she'd made about the *Nordika* dive tragedy and Tito Mendoza, and suddenly the pattern made sense.

There was a book. It was the last piece of information she had found while she was working on the case. Just days after e-mailing the file to her work computer, she had been shot.

Maybe she was stretching things too far, but she didn't think so. When she had read the Mendoza article months ago, she had connected it with Lopez, because Slater had said Lopez had made a trip to Bogotá to retrieve a book from a safe-deposit box. What she hadn't focused on were the implications behind what the book Mendoza had had in his possession contained: names, dates, blood types and numbers tattooed onto German ex-nationals.

If the articles about Stefan le Clerc were correct, SS officers had hijacked the *Nordika* and used it to transport so-called genetically superior children and a cargo of looted art and gold bullion to South America. If any of the SS officers were still alive, they would be elderly. The children would now be past middle age.

There were no actual estimates of the value of the art and gold bullion, but the le Clerc article suggested that it was enormous. More than enough to bankroll a new life in the United States and to form the financial base of an exclusive club based on a shared past and genetic heritage.

And what better way to control the members of the cabal than through a book that had the potential not only to expose individual members but the entire cabal?

According to Slater, the cabal was ordered, secretive and primarily in the business of making money through shareholdings in large corporations and manipulating lucrative defense contracts. The reason the CIA were involved in the investigation was clear. The cabal's activities weren't confined to the United States: they had political and terrorist affiliations and operated on a global scale. If Slater's information was correct, their influence extended all the way to the White House, and the list of crimes perpetrated by members of the cabal included conspiracy and high treason.

Tito Mendoza, a hit man, had gotten hold of the book right about the time the navy divers had disappeared. The close timing with the naval tragedy was what had drawn her attention to the news report about Mendoza in the first place. At a gut level, she had been certain that Mendoza and the book were linked to the *Nordika* dive tragedy.

She inserted the disk with the article about the missing divers. Partway down the second page, the name of the SEAL team leader caught her eye: *Todd Fischer.*

She stared at the name for long seconds, transfixed. She hadn't paid the actual members of the dive team much attention before, because she had been focused on Lopez and the cabal.

Pulse racing, she scrolled down the page. Todd Fischer's next of kin were listed. His wife, Eleanor May Fischer.

His son, Steven John Fischer.

She searched through her disks and inserted one that had a grainy photograph of Todd Fischer. The family resemblance was clear. Steve was taller, his skin and hair a little darker, but he looked enough like Todd that the relationship was in no doubt.

She went online and searched "Steve Fischer." A number of hits came up, among them an article with a photograph of Lieutenant Commander Steve Fischer accepting a trophy on behalf of his naval shooting team. There were a number of official records cataloging medals and awards for tours of duty in the Middle East, and one brief article from an in-house naval magazine outlining Fischer's secondment to the office of the Director of National Intelligence in a special projects role, reporting directly to Rear Admiral John M. Saunders.

The report was more than a year old, and in that time he hadn't changed much, except his job.

She already knew he had followed her to both Wilmington and Cold Peak. He wasn't Bureau. It was possible he was operating under the umbrella of the CIA. The office of the Director of National Intelligence oversaw the entire intelligence community and it had a wide reach. Special Projects threw it even wider.

The reason Fischer had focused on her was clear. He had known she was being hunted. He had had her watched in D.C. Given that he had known she was researching Lopez and the cabal, the spyware on her computer had likely been his. Every time she had e-mailed files to her work address, he had received a copy. He had kept close but not too close, staking her out while she acted as a sacrificial goat. That wasn't the act of a man falling in love, or even in lust. It was the act of a cold-blooded professional. It didn't explain why he had risked his cover by getting so personally close to her, but she was certain there had been a net gain involved.

He was good; he had fooled her. He had watched her and moved in close; he had even slept with her. He was on his own private mission, hunting his father's killers.

The government was paying him, but she was willing to bet that he would do it for free.

Twenty-Two

Dana Jones stamped a deposit book, slipped it across the counter, smiled at the client and checked her watch. Half an hour until her lunch break. The next customer wanted to cash in traveler's checks. Tapping a key, she shuffled through the menu, found the requisite program, then entered the amount. Sliding a form from beneath the counter, she filled out the check details and the amount, routinely advising the customer of the cost of the transaction. Her hand was steady and her voice was smooth, but that didn't change the fact that the transaction was an unwelcome reminder of her time in international banking. She no longer had a hankering for high finance, and the way she felt dealing with a minor two-bit transaction like this was the reason why.

She had gotten burned so badly that even if anyone in international banking would give her a job, she wouldn't take it.

She slipped the form across the counter for a signature, stamped it, then handed over the cash and smiled politely as the next customer stepped up to the counter.

Her smile froze. She went hot then cold, then calmly put the Closed sign on her counter, picked up her purse and walked out of the office.

Jack Jones.

Memories pushed at her, a few bright and burning, most tarnished and edged with anger. Their relationship had worn her out and taken her youth, but even so, when she'd gotten the news that he was dead, she had *grieved*. She had stood at her husband's grave, shattered at the utter finality of his death. She had even prayed for him.

She tapped in the exit code on the door that led to the staff parking lot. The lock disengaged and she was outside, enveloped in steamy heat and the smell of melting tar. She blinked, adjusting to the harsh light and discordant sounds of traffic after the dim, muted coolness of the bank. The fact that she was close to tears shook her and, briefly, she wondered if she could have made a mistake. Maybe it hadn't been Jack, just someone who looked like him?

It had been Jack. She had met his gaze for a split

second and she'd seen the recognition in his eyes. He'd had plenty of time to look at her before she'd seen him, plenty of time to turn on his heel, walk out of the bank and leave her in peace.

Her eyes stung and the parking lot swam, a mishmash of glittering cars, flashing mirrors and shimmering heat. Quickening her step, she wiped beneath her eyes with her fingertips, careful not to smudge her mascara.

She reached into her purse and found her car keys.

Hard fingers closed on one arm. "Dana."

Jerking free, she spun, her handbag swinging, even though she knew this wasn't a mugging.

He blocked the blow with ease, but instead of trying to physically detain her again, he bent down and retrieved the keys she must have dropped.

Dana stared at her car keys now dangling from Jack's fingers. "What do you want?"

"Taylor sent me."

Dana stared at his jaw. The fact that Taylor knew her father was alive was a shock, but that was a minor point. If Taylor had contacted Jack Jones that could mean only one thing: trouble. "Where is she?"

"I don't know."

Wrong answer. "You expect me to fall for that?"

"She called last night." Briefly, he repeated the conversation.

Dana weighed the information against what she knew about Taylor and WITSEC. Jack Jones was a con man, a gambler and a liar; he was going to have to try harder if he was going to convince her that Taylor had left WITSEC. "If there was a problem, she would have rung me herself."

"She didn't want to tip Lopez off."

Dana felt all the blood drain from her face. If she had one nightmare in this life, it was Alex Lopez. Just the mention of his name made her feel physically sick. Twenty-three years ago, he had walked into her life and taken it over. Through those years the only thing that had kept Dana sane had been the need to keep Taylor safe and as untouched by Lopez's twisted world as possible. But, like a poisonous vine, Lopez had stuck to them. No matter how hard they tried to cut loose, he never let go.

"Dana—"

Her jaw clenched. "Give me my keys."

"I can't let you take your car."

"You can't stop me. I've got a spare set."

He swore beneath his breath, and she had time to notice that decades might have passed, but some things never changed. Jack Jones was lean and handsome, younger than he had any right to look, and without the lines of strain she knew were etched on her face. He barely showed any signs of going gray, just a touch at the temples. Dana had to keep a regular salon appointment to keep her hair honey-blond; otherwise she would look exactly like her mother had at fifty-five, tired and ten years older than she really was.

She unclenched her jaw. It was tempting to argue—*she wanted to argue*—but she wasn't stupid. If Taylor had sent him, there was a problem, and Taylor's life was too important to risk. "How is she? Is she all right?"

For the first time he seemed to be at a loss, and that more than anything else convinced her. "I don't know. She didn't talk for long. She's not exactly comfortable with the relationship."

She stared at Jack's face, his eyes, looking for a chink that would tell her that he was lying, that this was all some crazy scam. "When did she find out that you were still alive?"

"I visited her in the hospital in D.C."

Finally, something that made sense. Taylor's shooting had been reported in a number of papers, which explained how Jack had been able to make contact. "If I can't take the car, what happens to it? When this is all over, I'm going to need that car."

"I've taken care of it." He jerked his head in the direction of a truck double-parked to one side of the parking lot. "They're going to store the car for you." He dug in his pocket and pulled out a business card for a well-known storage firm.

Dana stared at the vehicle he'd indicated. Without the glasses she normally wore for driving, her distance vision was blurred and indistinct, but she could make out the lettering. There were two men sitting in the cab, which gave credence to his story, since one guy couldn't drive both vehicles.

She studied the card, buying a little more time. The fact that Jack had taken time out to make arrangements for her car was sobering. If Taylor had rung him last night and he'd had to fly in from the East Coast, he hadn't had much time. "What about my job? If I walk out now, I could get fired."

His expression didn't change. "Take sick leave."

Dana's jaw tightened. She knew a doctor in the Mission district. For a price, he would give her a medical certificate. It wasn't the first time she'd had to use him. When Taylor had gone missing last year she had needed time off work to search. She had paid Gomez for the certificate, but in retrospect, she hadn't needed to. Any legitimate doctor would have given her time off work. She let out a breath. "I don't know if I believe you, but I'll come with you—for now. Just…don't touch me."

Fifteen minutes later, after walking a circuitous route around the financial district and into the trendy Embarcadero Center, Jack ushered her into a rental car. After another few minutes of driving around side streets, he finally took an exit out of town and headed across the Bay Bridge.

Dana stared at the brassy strip of sea visible

between the network of steel struts and cables. "You're going the wrong way. I live south of the Mission district."

"I can't take you there."

She studied his profile and suddenly panicked. They were heading in the opposite direction she wanted to go, and it was happening too fast. "Turn the car around. I need clothes and toiletries. It won't take more than a few minutes."

When he didn't respond, she gripped his arm and yanked. "Turn the car."

Jack swerved and straightened. The squeal of tires was punctuated by honking.

He shook her grip off. "I'm not turning back. You need to get out of town. Now."

The cold remoteness of his expression shocked her to her core. The entire time they had been married, she had never backed down. He had always been the soft one, the one who had walked out the door. "How would you know?"

"Because Lopez had men closing in on you. You've got to listen to me, Dana. I wasn't a gambler or a con artist. I was a hit man. That's why I had to leave."

She blinked, concentrating on the one fact she could absorb. "How do you know Lopez had men closing in on me?"

"Because I saw one out on the street, and I'm

certain the parking lot was watched. And, honey, if I had been given the job, that's exactly what I would have done."

Twenty-Three

Two days later

Taylor cruised through the quiet suburb of Woodside just outside Washington, D.C. At seven o'clock in the evening, it was close on dark and most houses had their lights on. According to the staff register still stapled in the back of her address book, Martin Tripp lived at 87 Renner Drive.

She needed access to the Bureau's files and getting that was going to be difficult. If she wanted to get into the system, she was going to have to break into it. She'd gone over her options and decided she had only one: Martin Tripp.

Tripp's entire life was the computer and the Bureau. He was single and he lived on his own. She was willing to bet that he worked at home and that when he logged on, with no one in the house to compromise his security, he stayed logged on for convenience.

The house number eighty-five flashed in her headlights, a two-story weatherboard house with an immaculate front yard. Taylor braked, slowing to a crawl. Eighty-seven was a similar style of house, matching several others in the shady, tree-lined street, although Tripp's had no upper story. Wraparound verandas and an overgrown garden completed what was, even with the dimming light, a bedraggled picture. She noticed that the property was unfenced and situated on a corner. The lack of a fence and the extra street frontage would give her several points of entry to choose from.

Taylor turned the corner, made a slow circuit of the block until she was back on Renner Drive, then did another drive-by from the opposite direction.

This time she caught a glimpse of Tripp's car parked beneath a carport. A run-of-the-mill, silvery-gray sedan. No surprises there.

The car and the house were a lot like Tripp. There was definitely potential, if only he could pull his head out of cyberspace. She was willing to bet he was online now. In fact, she was banking on that—and the knowledge that Tripp hated cooking and regularly ate out.

She circled the block again, and this time parked several doors down. Checking the fit of her wig, she got out, shrugged into a small backpack and began walking. The evening was chilly and she was dressed for jogging, which instantly helped her blend. She had noticed several joggers while she'd been driving around the neighborhood. The back-pack wasn't out of place, either. It was a dark blue sports pack that matched the blue track pants and jacket she was wearing. If anyone noticed her at all, shc would bc just another ultracoordinated jogger taking advantage of the crisp autumn evening.

As she approached Tripp's place, keeping to the opposite side of the street, she studied the sur-rounding properties, looking for signs of dogs and nosy neighbors. A dog had barked farther along the street, but so far that was the only one. She checked her watch. All of the front yards were empty, which she had expected. It was almost seven-thirty. Most people would be either eating dinner or watching television.

She walked to the end of the street, crossed the road and strolled back, this time on Tripp's side of the road. As she passed Tripp's front gate, the porch light flicked on and the front door popped open. Keeping her gaze forward, she squashed the urge to speed up. She had caught a clear glimpse of Tripp, but his vision would havc bccn hindcrcd by the flooding porch light. If he had registered her at all, he would have seen a blond female out walking.

Rounding the corner, she stopped, shrugged out

of the backpack, extracted her phone from a side pocket and pretended to make a call while she studied the layout of Tripp's place and waited for him to leave. The perimeter of his yard was planted with an array of unkempt shrubs, punctuated by a large oak. A garage was situated to one side of the house. There was also a garden shed.

Headlights swept the front lawn as he backed out of his driveway. Seconds later, as Tripp accelerated down the road, the house was plunged into gloom.

Taylor noted the time he'd left and slipped the pack onto her back. Tonight she was just doing a reconnaissance, and timing Tripp to get an idea of how long it took him to get dinner.

After doing a circuit of the grounds, she checked out the garden shed and found that not only was it unlocked, it contained an assortment of junk, including an old wooden toolbox. Walking around to the front of the house, she flicked on a penlight and shone the beam through finely etched glass into a nicely proportioned hallway. A peeling sticker on the glass panel of the front door indicated that he had an alarm system. She could make out a discreet box mounted on the wall. A small, glowing light at the base of the box indicated the alarm was active.

Proceeding cautiously, she moved around the house, checking doors and windows to see if every window was wired. If it was an old house and the system hadn't been installed by Tripp, chances were good that not every window had been connected. The classic was to skip bathroom windows, especially if the window was high and tiny, or louvers had been installed.

Tripp didn't have louvers, but he did have a small bathroom window set high in the wall. She risked flicking the penlight on again.

The window wasn't sitting flush with the frame.

Shrugging out of the pack, she extracted a pair of latex gloves, pulled them on and reached up to try the window. It swung smoothly open.

Heart pounding, Taylor stared at the gap. It wasn't a casement window—that would have been too easy. It was a flip-up style, old-fashioned and tiny, and the reason it was unsecured was immediately evident—the sliding screw that locked it was missing. It had probably fallen into the garden and Tripp hadn't bothered to either look for it or purchase a replacement. The gap was small, about eight inches. It would be a tight squeeze, but providing she could maneuver her head through, she could make it.

She checked the luminous dial of her watch. Tripp had been gone ten minutes. If she allowed him half an hour, maximum, to collect his dinner and get back home, that would give her a clear quarter of an hour inside.

This wasn't part of her plan. She had intended to break into the house by cutting a square of glass out of a French door or a windowpane and crawling through, thereby bypassing the need to open the window or the door. The method was crude. The vibration could trigger the alarm anyway and the biggest downside was the fact that Tripp would know he'd had a break-in. This way, he didn't have to know. When she weighed the benefits of ditching her original plan, with its inbuilt margin for safety in knowing how long Tripp was likely to be out, and the benefits of concealing the break-in, there was no contest.

Removing the wig, which would be pulled off when she went through the window, she stowed it in the backpack and collected the toolbox from the garden shed. The shed was festooned with cobwebs, emphasizing the fact that Tripp had no interest in his yard. The dust-coated toolbox, which was empty, indicated he was even less of a handyman.

Seconds later, she had the toolbox propped on its end for maximum height and positioned beneath the window. Leaning her pack beside the box and holding the flashlight in one hand, she stepped up, gripping the window frame to keep her steady as she positioned her head inside the window and slowly straightened. The frame scraped her back as she pushed forward and up, fitting one shoulder through, then the other. Her hair, which had been clipped close to her head beneath the wig, collapsed around her face. Tiny clicking sounds indicated that clips had fallen into the bath, which was directly below the window. She would have to remember to collect them before she left.

Slipping the rubber thong at the base of her penlight over one wrist, she braced both palms on the windowsill and surged upward until her torso was through.

Flicking on the penlight, she checked out the bathroom. It was surprisingly upmarket, nicely tiled in neutral beige, with a glassed-in shower and a separate bath. Leaving the penlight turned on, but letting it dangle from her wrist, she twisted and attempted to ease one leg through.

After overbalancing and almost losing her grip on the sill, she decided there was no way she could climb through the window. It simply wasn't wide enough for the maneuver. The only way forward was to continue on in a controlled dive, headfirst, into the bath, using her hands to cushion her fall.

Leaning forward, she slid her palms down the tiled wall, her stomach muscles protesting as she gradually wriggled her torso over the sill. She inched forward, her jaw clenched as her hair slid across her face, impeding her vision. Abruptly, her center of gravity shifted. Hands flailing, she caught the sides of the bath and managed to slow the momentum. An ungraceful sprawl later, her shins burning after being scraped across the edge of the sill, she pulled herself out of the bath. She was in.

Reaching up, Taylor pulled the window closed and collected the hairpins that had landed in the bath. Satisfied that the bathroom didn't show any signs of her entry, she padded down the hall, switching her penlight off because Tripp had left the lights on. As she stepped into the sitting room, the cozy warmth of central heating made her realize just how cold she'd gotten standing out on the street.

The house was large and airy and, despite the neglect of the garden, was furnished in surprisingly good taste. Golden light from strategically placed lamps flowed over dark leather couches. A faded Turkish rug took center stage on the floor and bookshelves gleamed with what looked like genuine leather-bound books. Signs of Tripp's occupancy were visible in a folded newspaper and a mug left sitting on a coffee table.

Her heart sped up when she noticed that one corner of the sitting room was devoted to a large antique walnut desk and a computer, and that the computer was switched on.

Padding across thick carpet, she pulled out Tripp's chair and sat down. The second she moved the mouse the screen saver flicked off, revealing text. Her heart skipped a beat when she realized that Tripp hadn't even bothered to exit the file he'd been reading.

Scrolling down the page, she skimmed the content. Tripp was working the Chavez case, which made sense. Thousands of documents had been generated about the cartel and Chavez over the years and Tripp, with his love of computers and research and his lack of a social life, was uniquely fitted out to sift through and evaluate the information. This particular file contained recently compiled material on Marco Chavez, Alex Lopez's father, and the cabal connection, supplied by a previously undisclosed South American source. Taylor frowned as she stared at a name she recognized but hadn't expected to see: Edward Dennison, a former FBI agent…who had worked for Lopez.

She checked her watch. She had five minutes, maximum, left.

Hitting the print button, she continued reading while pages fed out. Combined with Dennison's statements about the nature of the cabal, she found documentation detailing Marco Chavez's links with Nazi war criminals, backed up by a report that stated Chavez had harbored German nationals after the end of the Second World War. Most of that documentation had been generated over twenty years ago, when the Navy SEAL team diving on the wreck of the *Nordika* had disappeared. The naval operation itself was dismissed as a bungled, illegal mission. The accepted conclusion was that the SEAL team had gone AWOL, probably with a lifetime's supply of cocaine.

But there were no supporting documents to give credence to the theory. A notation on the file referred to a classified naval file. In other words, the investigation had been locked down, with no access for civilians or civilian agencies.

The sound of a vehicle accelerating down the street jerked her head up. When the vehicle slowed, she got to her feet and collected the printed-out pages of the file. Pages were still feeding out. She checked the page number. Another seven to go. Heart pounding, she debated whether to cancel the print job or wait on the last sheets. The vehicle slowed further, then accelerated as it turned the corner.

Pulse still pounding, she checked her watch. Two minutes, then she was out.

She clicked to the file directory and typed in a search request using her name.

A list of hits came up, most of which she recognized and had read. She selected the one new file that had been added and hit the print button. As pages began to feed out, she skimmed the file from the screen, a report of her own shooting in D.C.

A bolded statement caught her eye. According to a series of surveillance reports, Taylor had made suspected connections with Lopez on two occasions.

She went hot, then cold, utterly rejecting the

words. At no point in the investigation had she ever been compromised. If surveillance reports had been compiled, they were fictional.

She scrolled through the file. The reports themselves weren't included, which meant she couldn't obtain the name of the agent who had done the surveillance. The fact that the reports weren't attached to the file wasn't unusual. If the document was compromising for the agent involved, especially for an interdepartmental investigation, it would be classified. Bayard, and maybe Colenso, would have access, but she doubted anyone else in the department would have.

The final page contained a brief summary, signed off by Colenso. The content was clear and concise. Given the evidence and her connections, Colenso concluded that it was possible she was the mole.

The sound of a vehicle slowing penetrated. She glanced at her watch. She had been staring at the screen for a lot longer than the two minutes she had given herself. She was out of time.

Headlights flashed through the windows. Closing the file, she reinstated the file Tripp had been reading, her fingers fumbling slightly on the mouse in her haste to scroll back to the correct page.

A car door slammed. Heart pounding, she activated the screen saver, grabbed the printed pages of the file and walked quickly down the hall. There was no time to climb out the bathroom window. She would have to position herself in one of the back bedrooms, wait until Tripp disabled the alarm system, then unlock a door and slip out before he could reinstate the alarm.

The sound of Tripp's step was clear as she turned into a bedroom that had a set of French doors opening out onto a small patio. The room was obviously Tripp's.

Walking quickly to the French doors, she opened the drapes and pulled the security bolts.

Closing her eyes so her night vision would be better when she stepped outside, she waited for Tripp to open the front door. The second she heard the faint click of a key in the dead bolt, she turned the key in the lock. Stepping outside, she drew the drapes to conceal the fact that when she closed it the door was going to be unlocked.

With any luck Tripp would think he'd simply forgotten to lock up.

Stepping with care on slippery, moss-encrusted pavement, Taylor worked her way around the side of the house. Seconds later, she collected her backpack and the toolbox from beneath the bathroom window. Returning the box to the garden shed, she pushed through the perimeter plantings and stepped out onto the sidewalk.

It was fully dark now, with a thin sickle of moon climbing slowly in a sky hazed by mist and smoke.

Cold night air penetrated the fabric of her track-suit as she loped across the road. Craning over her shoulder, she glanced at Tripp's house. The kitchen light was on, which meant he had probably walked directly to the kitchen counter and not into the sitting room.

Retrieving her car keys from a zip pocket in her track pants, she deactivated the lock on her car and shrugged smoothly out of her pack. Opening the driver's-side door, she slung the pack on the passenger seat, started the car, did a U-turn so she didn't have to drive past Tripp's house and headed for her motel.

Martin Tripp pushed the computer keyboard forward, making room for steaming hot containers of Beef Rendang and rice. Returning to the kitchen, he collected the glass of water he'd filled and a silver fork and cloth napkin. The food was takeout and he'd hardly notice what he was eating once he became absorbed in his work, but the food *was* high-quality takeout, and he didn't like eating with plastic forks.

Shifting the mouse to bring up his screen, he sat down.

The seat was warm.

Frowning, he rose to his feet and placed his palm on the nubby fabric. It was definitely warm.

A second problem registered. His printer was

making a humming noise. The cooling fan was working, which indicated it had just been used.

He hadn't used the printer at all today.

Reaching down, he located his briefcase, which was lodged beneath the desk. Placing it on the seat, he entered the combination and extracted the weapon he always kept there.

The gun in hand, he stared around his warmly lit lounge, a sense of unease growing. He lived quietly and very privately. He doubted that any of his neighbors even realized he was an FBI agent, which suited him. If people knew what he did for a living they would annoy him with concerns about break-ins and expect him to check their alarm systems, which had happened at the last place he'd rented.

He did a slow circuit of the sitting room, his nostrils flaring as he caught an unfamiliar scent. It didn't appear that anything had been taken, but someone had been in his house, using his computer. If he wasn't mistaken, that someone had been female.

When he reached his bedroom, a faint gap in the curtains made all the hairs at his nape stand on end. Stepping forward, he yanked the curtains wide, then used a hank of curtain fabric to depress the handle so that he wouldn't spoil any prints. The unlocked door swung open.

"Clever girl."

But not clever enough. She had gotten into his

house, probably through the bathroom window, which he hadn't gotten around to repairing yet, and so bypassing his alarm system, but she hadn't been able to get out without leaving a door unlocked.

Stepping outside, he walked around the house then checked the sidewalk, studying the vehicles parked outside neighboring houses. He didn't expect to find her. Taylor—and he was certain it was Taylor Jones—was long gone.

Walking back inside, he picked up the phone and made a call. It was a call he didn't want to make because it exposed his own incompetence. He was the one who had left his computer on, unsecured, and dialed into the Bureau network.

Colenso's answering machine picked up, which figured. Colenso had an active social life. It was likely he was eating out or had female company.

Tripp made a second call. Bayard picked up on the second ring, which Tripp had expected. One of the things that had persuaded Tripp to stay with the FBI when he could have taken easier and more lucrative positions in several other government agencies was Bayard's example. He had worked his way up through the ranks and he knew the Bureau inside out. In contrast to Colenso, who lived for the more dangerous aspects of the job, Bayard was subtle and intelligent. Those qualities would take him to the top, and Tripp would be right behind him.

Briefly, Tripp related what had happened. Taylor had to be stopped. He might be perceived to be a bungler in the field, but he had never flinched from doing what needed to be done.

Twenty-Four

Taylor closed the door of her motel unit, walked through to the bedroom and began to pack.

She had been shot at three times, once almost fatally, because she had information or evidence that could break the case open. Now she had an additional problem. There was only one reason for a set of bogus surveillance reports to be produced. She had been set up to take the fall for the real mole. With her out of the way, he could continue undetected.

And whoever the real mole was, he wanted Taylor dead before she worked out what was happening and exposed him.

She walked into the bathroom, emptied the bathroom cabinet and packed the items in her case. Zipping the case closed, she carried it out to the car. It only took a matter of seconds to collect the food she'd bought from the kitchen. Within minutes she had checked out and was once again back on the road.

She could have stayed the night, but she no longer felt safe in D.C. She had taken an unconscionable risk breaking into Tripp's house, especially in light of the fact that someone within the Bureau had set her up and was now systematically hunting her down.

It crossed her mind that the mole could be Tripp...or Colenso or even Janet Burrows. It could be any of a hundred agents who had worked some aspect of the Lopez case. The only certainty was that it was someone Bayard believed, when he didn't believe her, because that kind of surveillance could only be sanctioned at the highest level.

When she reached Dulles airport she called Jack and relayed the information she had just discovered. Dana came on the line, demanding to know where she was and if she was safe. Taylor repeated the information she'd given to Jack but refused to give Dana any details about her whereabouts. She couldn't afford to assume that Jack's cell phone and hers were unmonitored. Right now, the fact that no one knew where she was or what her plans were was her only security. Jack and Dana needed to be kept in the loop, but only because they were, potentially, as vulnerable as she was.

Taylor didn't know at what point she had begun

thinking of Dana and Jack collectively as
"parents," but she had. They were not by any definition a *cozy* family, but they were *her* family.

She made another call, this one to Neil. It was a
risk, but there was no one else in Cold Peak she
could call whom she could guarantee *wasn't* under
surveillance. She needed someone to look out for
Buster if she didn't get back within the time frame
she had stated. She had paid for two weeks. In
theory it would be an easy enough matter to ring up
and pay for longer. The main hitch to that solution
was that if she couldn't get back in two weeks' time
that would probably be because she wouldn't get
back, ever. In the event that something did happen
to her, she needed to make sure Buster was cared for.

Neil sounded relieved when she identified herself. "I've been trying to call you about some information I found. I tracked down that server, and
you'll never guess who it was."

"The CIA."

"How did—"

"Don't worry about the server, and don't make
any more inquiries. Just drop it. There's something else I need you to do."

"Say the word."

"I've had to go away—a family emergency—
and I need you to look after my cat."

There was a moment of silence. *"Your cat?"*

"Buster. He's at the Cold Peak Cattery. I've paid

up until the end of the month, but if I don't get in touch with you before then, I'll need you to go and collect him. If that happens, you'll need to ring Pete Burdett. Just tell him Buster's my cat and he'll make arrangements from there. Get hold of a pen and I'll give you the number. And don't worry, this is just a precaution. I will be back."

He sounded a little shaken, but he got the pen.

When she'd double-checked that he'd written down the number correctly, she hung up.

Wearing the blond wig and using her fake identity, she caught a late flight out of Dulles. Using the alternate identity was a risk, but a calculated one. She was banking on the fact that even if the name she'd used had been flagged, Colenso would be slow to move so late at night.

The flight landed in Chicago just before midnight. An hour later she caught a connection to San Francisco.

Geographically, the West Coast was about as distant as she could get from Cold Peak and D.C. without leaving the country. From an investigative point of view it made sense, too. There were two angles she could research. The first and most important was the lead Jack had on the hit man who had shot her in D.C. The second was a wild card. Dennison, who had been listed on the file she'd gotten off Edward Tripp's computer as the South

American source who had informed on Lopez, had had a wife, a quadriplegic who had been a resident in a rest home in Eureka. Anne Dennison had died almost two years ago. Taylor didn't expect to discover anything new in Eureka, but the fact that she would be close to the town was enough to pique her interest.

As she waited for her suitcase to appear on the luggage carousel, she studied passengers and airport staff. Her spine tightened at the possibility that she had picked up a tail although, in all likelihood, if she was being scrutinized, it was by airport security.

Ever since she had left Cold Peak, she had been watchful. Fischer had tracked her as far as Cold Peak but, as deceptive as Fischer had been, he'd had no interest in terminating a federal witness who was important to his investigation. That meant that someone else had killed Letty and Hansen, then taken a shot at her.

In the drafty, open area, she felt naked and exposed. Her fingers itched to reach for the Glock, but she had left the handgun behind in a locker at Dulles. Without her badge, there was no way she could have gotten it through the security checks.

The only man who came close to Fischer's description was a tall European-looking guy, but he wasn't dark, he was blond. Frowning, she continued to study the passengers as she collected her case and loaded it onto her trolley.

She caught a glimpse of the blond man again as he talked into a phone. He was definitely European. At first she thought the accent was French, then he uttered a brief phrase and the harder consonants registered. The back of her neck crawled. He was talking English, but she was almost certain he was German.

The village of Marciano, Turin, Italy

Sixty-two-year-old Xavier le Clerc woke with a start, his father's name in his head. He stared through the murky darkness for long seconds, still caught in the grip of a dream where it was possible to reach out and touch a man who had been dead for more than fifty years.

Pushing the covers back, he rose to his feet and padded to the French doors that led to a small balcony. Opening them wide, he stared out at the mountain village that had become his refuge. The moon had risen. Its dim glow illuminated the narrow, cobbled street below and the simple villas and apartments crowded over tiny shops. He had lived in Marciano on and off for almost twenty years. He was far from being a local but, courtesy of generous annual donations to the tiny school and medical clinic, the locals had taken him in and had gradually come to view him as one of their own.

Closing the doors against the crisp night air, he

walked to the bathroom, filled a glass with water and drained it. This time the dream had been stark and clear. Sometimes the details differed, but certain elements were always the same: darkness, unbearable tension followed by a struggle, then the fire.

He doubted that the dream had any basis in reality. It was more likely a product of his imagination, but whether he dreamed or not, nothing could shift his certainty that Stefan le Clerc had died violently.

His father's body had never been found, but Xavier knew what he had been doing when he had disappeared, and why he had been murdered. Stefan had been hunting for justice, for his elderly parents, for his brothers and sisters and their families, and for countless others who had been swallowed by the death camps. The hunt had been intense and utterly personal.

He had had a name. It had taken years of searching and the last remnants of the le Clerc wealth to find even that, but his father had succeeded in picking up on the trail of an SS colonel tasked with removing wealth and assets from Jewish families in France. An ex-banker, Heinrich Reichmann had, ironically, been a former colleague of Stefan's.

According to the information he had obtained, Reichmann and his death squad had consigned countless families to the death camps—old people, women, children, babies. As part of the process, Reichmann had systematically confiscated all iden-

tification papers. Once the human factor was removed, he had harvested assets and bank accounts.

Stefan had obtained evidence that huge amounts
had been transferred, but the bank involved had
stonewalled him. Until he obtained documentation that proved the owners of the accounts were
no longer alive and that he had the authority to
access their accounts, legally they couldn't
disclose any information about those accounts.

Aware that Reichmann had cut a deal with the
bank, Stefan had been forced to drop that avenue
and had followed a trail that was more than seven
years old to Lubeck and an interview with the
daughter of the captain of the *Nordika*. The hunt
had eventually led him to America, where he had
disappeared.

Replacing the glass, Xavier padded back to bed.
Seconds later the phone rang. His mind suddenly
clear and sharp, Xavier answered the call. Only a
handful of his most trusted people knew the
number, which was unlisted.

"I picked up Taylor Jones flying out of Dulles."

The French was clipped, the intonation German, although Maximillian Schroeder was Swiss
by nationality. Before Schroeder had agreed to
work for him, he had been one of Mossad's top
agents, specializing in computer espionage. Give
Schroeder a computer hookup and he could access
almost any information network in the world. Ever

since Taylor had disappeared off WITSEC's scope three days ago, Schroeder had been coordinating surveillance on the East Coast with particular regard to monitoring flights. "Where are you? San Francisco?"

"Where else?"

Xavier's attention sharpened. Taylor had been one of Bayard's most competent agents. She'd had an eye for detail and a natural instinct that had broken cases open on more than one occasion. That instinct, combined with a bulldog tenacity, made her something more—a catalyst. "Any sign of Dennison?"

"Not yet."

Xavier terminated the call then made another, booking flights to the States. When the tickets were confirmed, he replaced the phone, dressed and began to pack.

He believed there was a certain order to life, that sooner or later, sometimes very much later, justice would be done. But not on his schedule. Always, it was in the time of *le bon dieu*. He had searched for Reichmann and the cabal for thirty-two years and poured millions into the effort. He had pushed to find and expose Alex Lopez. None of those things had happened on a scale that was acceptable to him.

Just months ago, Lopez had acquired a book from a safe-deposit box in Bogotá. Le Clerc had missed him by hours. Days later, he had almost had him in El Paso but, again, Lopez had been wily enough to elude not only him and his men, but a number of FBI and CIA personnel.

The instant Xavier had heard about the book, he had known what it was: Reichmann's ledger. The book had slipped through his grasp in Cancun. There had been a gap of years following Marco Chavez's death when he had assumed the book had been lost. Now Lopez had it and he was using it as a weapon against the cabal.

Over the past few months, Xavier hadn't detected any signs of Lopez inflicting damage either politically or internationally and the lack of news wasn't just puzzling, it was incomprehensible. Lopez was a master tactician and ruthless, and the book gave him an advantage he would never have been slow to utilize. It was possible he was negotiating terms with Helene Reichmann, despite the fact that the last attempt had ended in a bloodbath. It was equally possible that he was lying low, playing some kind of waiting game.

Either that, or he had lost the book.

The thought that the ledger, after all these years, was no longer in Lopez's hands sent tension humming through Xavier. It was the breakthrough he had been waiting for.

Zipping the suitcase closed, he carried it through to his study, removed a watercolor from the wall, tapped in the code that unlocked his safe and confirmed with a thumbprint scan.

He extracted the passport and identification papers he needed, relocked the safe and repositioned the painting. Opening his briefcase on his desk, he slipped the papers into a side pocket, along with a small, state-of-the-art satellite phone. The laptop itself was also wireless and fitted for satellite coms. Together the two pieces of equipment formed the basis of a traveling office that kept him informed and hotwired for communication, no matter where he happened to be.

As he picked up the briefcase, his gaze caught on a small grouping of photos on his desk. The most prominent was of his father just before he went into the French military. The second was a portrait of his family taken two years after the Second World War had ended, the third a black-and-white that he had taken years ago of Esther Morell in Bern.

Esther looked tanned and carefree, closer to twenty than the thirty-two she had been. The image was, he had always thought, deceptive, and revealed one of Esther's key strengths in the world of international banking. She had never looked like a player.

Esther had been in Bern at a point in his life when he had made the decision to go after Reichmann. He had never let himself dwell on what could have been. With the way he'd had to live, marriage had been out of the question, but Esther had tempted him.

Xavier had always been focused primarily on Reichmann and the cabal. Lopez had only ever been a side issue. But with Esther's murder, Lopez had elevated himself on Xavier's list.

Taylor Jones breaking cover was significant. For her to risk using an alternative identity that was traceable meant something was happening. She was a threat to both Lopez and the cabal. Where Taylor went, Lopez and Reichmann would follow. And Xavier intended to be there when they surfaced.

Collecting the suitcase, he switched off the lights, took the stairs to the ground floor and let himself out of the building. The walk through steep, cobbled streets to the shed on the outskirts of the village where his car was stored wasn't convenient, but it was a small price to pay for the safety of Marciano. The narrow roads in and out of the village could be construed as a trap, but he had weighed the risks and found them acceptable. Within minutes the powerful headlights of the Saab were slicing through the mist wreathing the winding mountain road.

Twenty-Five

At six that evening, Taylor drove north of Eureka and cruised past the address where she had been held hostage the previous year. The house had once been owned by Senator Radcliff, a former associate of Lopez's who had been shot during the operation to capture Lopez in El Paso. Radcliff hadn't just been a business associate of Lopez's—he had been Lopez's link to the cabal.

She cruised to the end of the cul-de-sac, made a turn and drove back toward Radcliff's house. Braking just outside the electronically controlled wrought-iron gates, she stared at the grounds, which were all that were visible from the road. A car appeared in her rear-vision mirror. Reluctantly, she took her foot off the brake and drove on.

A helicopter skimmed overhead, a tour operator

heading out to sea to catch the sunset. The chopping sound of the blades echoing off the hills triggered an unexpected fragment of memory—a balaclava pulled off an agent's head as he turned away, dark olive skin, a scar across his nose.

Pulling over to the side of the road, she reexamined what she remembered. Being jerked from the drug-induced stupor. Darkness, strobing lights and a helicopter, the sound deafening. She had been carried, handed into a chopper and strapped into a seat. Someone had spoken to her, although she had no idea what was said, but she did remember opening her eyes and seeing the balaclava removed. At the time she had thought it was J.T., Rina's partner and former agent, but J.T. didn't have a scar across his nose. Abruptly, she was certain it had been Steve Fischer.

She stared at the wild hills that tumbled to the Pacific Ocean below. She was certain Fischer was CIA, which would mean he would have working relationships with the FBI and other agencies. In light of the fact that a mole had already spoiled two major operations, he would have wanted to keep contact with FBI personnel to a minimum.

A car drove past, followed by a further two; commuters making their way home. Pulling off the verge, she headed back to Eureka. Instead of turning into a motel, she drove directly to a drive-through and paid for a burger and fries. Lately, she'd been surviving on takeout food, but she was too tired to shop and cook tonight.

As she nosed out of the drive-through exit, a man walking from the restaurant caught her eye. She braked and a car horn behind her blared. Releasing the brake, she checked traffic, turned out onto the highway, then glanced back at the restaurant parking lot. The man she had seen was medium height and stockily built. She hadn't seen his face, just a glimpse of a profile then the back of his head, but for a crazy moment she had been certain it was Edward Dennison.

Signaling, she changed lanes and pulled into a liquor store, taking a parking space near the exit so she could watch the vehicles turning out of the restaurant. A truck pulled out with two men in it, both wearing ball caps. The man she'd seen had been dressed in a suit, which had been the other thing that had reminded her of Dennison. In all his photos, she had seldom seen him in anything *but* a suit. Another vehicle pulled out, this one a sedan with tinted windows. Craning, she tried to see through the darkened glass. A window rolled down, revealing a woman behind the wheel and a car filled with kids.

Feeling rattled, she pushed the car door open and got out. Standing up, she would have a better view of the parking lot. The restaurant was busy, cars arriving and leaving in a steady stream. A flicker of movement to her right jerked her head around. Traffic was stopped at a set of lights. Two people were using the pedestrian crossing, and one of them was the man she'd seen leaving the restaurant. She studied him, still unsure. As he stepped onto the curb, he looked in her direction and she froze.

Pulse pounding, she lowered herself back into the driver's seat and closed the door. She didn't know if Dennison would recognize her, but if he was as thorough as his file had indicated, he probably would. She was still wearing the wig, so it was possible that if he had noticed her he would have simply registered her hair color.

Slipping on dark glasses, she watched as Dennison crossed the liquor store parking lot and walked into the store. When he came out he was carrying a bottle of Scotch. If there had been any doubt, it was gone. Twenty-two years had passed since his last Bureau photo had gone on record. He had gained a paunch and lost some hair, but it was Dennison.

The chances of her stumbling over Dennison were a million to one. Last she'd heard, courtesy of the FBI report, he was either dead or lying low. Dennison was obviously not dead and his *continued* survival was significant. If the FBI mole had at any point passed on to Lopez the fact that Dennison had informed on him, Dennison was a dead man. To her best knowledge that hadn't happened, which meant the FBI mole didn't work for Lopez. He or she worked for the cabal.

Dealing with Lopez was bad enough, but at least he was a known quantity. The cabal, quite frankly, sent a cold chill down her spine.

When it became obvious that Dennison was on foot, she grabbed her handbag, locked the car and followed him, keeping a discreet distance. It was a gamble. If he had a vehicle parked farther down the road, she would lose him, but she was betting that he was staying at a motel nearby since both the restaurant and the liquor store had had ample parking.

Two blocks down, Dennison turned into a motel. Keeping to a stroll, Taylor walked into the motel entrance just in time to see him disappear into a ground-floor unit. Keeping her pace leisurely, she checked out the room number and the model and plate of the car parked outside.

Keeping her sunglasses in place despite the fact that it was getting dark, she stepped into the motel office and requested a pamphlet. She didn't make any inquiries about Dennison; he wouldn't be using his own name and she didn't want to risk the receptionist tipping him off that someone was snooping around after him.

As she stepped out of the office, she glanced in the direction of Dennison's unit, then scanned the parking lot. In the few minutes she had been inside, the clear twilight had faded and the streetlights had turned on, throwing pooling yellow light over the clumps of shrubs and waving palms that decorated the entrance.

Walking quickly through the gloom, she turned out of the motel entrance and headed for her car. Unexpectedly, a lead had fallen into her lap. Just days ago, she would have handed the lead to Colenso, no questions asked. But that was before she found that she had been falsely tagged as the mole.

Colenso wasn't safe. She wasn't sure Bayard was, either.

Twenty-Six

Westport, California

Morning sunlight flooded the tiny laundry of the motel unit as Dana pulled items of clothing out of the dryer. Systematically, she folded and stacked pants, shirts and underwear in a neat pile on top of the washing machine. It had been years since she had done laundry for a man. Two days ago if anyone had told her she would be doing her dead husband's laundry while hiding out in a coastal beach resort, she would have said they were insane.

She pulled out the final item, a charcoal-gray cotton sweater, and folded it. The sweater had a designer label and a nautical theme, with a discreet anchor embroidered on one sleeve. The clothing indicated that, on the run or not, Jack was doing all right. It passed through her mind that either the fish-and-dive charter business was booming, or Jack was moonlighting. A small shudder went down her spine at the thought. She didn't go to church all that often, but she was a Christian. Everything in her utterly rejected the idea of taking someone's life. If she had known what Jack's real job had been, she would never have married him. But even though she still held the same view about the sanctity of life, after Lopez, Jack's past didn't pack the punch it should have.

A small sound in the sitting room made her stiffen. She frowned. Jack had walked down to the nearest mall to buy a newspaper. "Jack?"

She stepped out of the laundry, a pile of folded clothes in her arms. At first she thought it was Jack, because he was tall and lean, with dark hair, and her mind *wanted* it to be Jack, but the man standing just inside the sliding doors was a good twenty years younger. "If you want money, there's some in my handbag on the kitchen counter."

"I'm not here for money, Mrs. Jones, and I'm not working for Lopez." He produced his ID and set it down on the coffee table before stepping back so he wouldn't be visible to anyone approaching the unit. "My name's Steve Fischer. Check my credentials. I'm a CIA agent. Have a seat and I'll explain when your ex-husband gets here."

Her stomach tightened. Politely worded or not,

he wasn't asking, he was telling her. Setting the folded laundry in a neat pile on the coffee table, she complied.

"I'm going to unholster my handgun." His voice was low and flat. At a guess, the tone was supposed to be soothing, as he slid the gun out of his shoulder holster and chambered a round. "Don't worry about the gun, I don't intend on firing it. It's just a safety precaution because I know Jack's armed."

Dana's heart accelerated. Jack was armed? With exaggerated slowness she picked up the wallet he'd placed on the table. It looked real, but what did she know? Fischer had made a point of saying he didn't work for Lopez, but that could have been a lie. "What do you want?"

A flicker of movement distracted him. Seconds later the crunch of gravel preceded a shadow sliding across the small patio out in front. Then Jack stepped into the sitting room.

"Don't move," Fischer said quietly. "I've got a man coming in behind you, and one more in the next room. Place the newspaper on the floor and your hands on your head." A second man stepped inside, searched and disarmed Jack and took up a position on the patio, his weapon trained on Jack. Jack took a seat beside Dana.

Steve repeated the information he'd already given Dana and indicated that Jack should check the ID on the coffee table.

Dana stared at Fischer, while Jack studied the ID. "If you really are CIA, then you must know the agent I dealt with last year."

"J. T. Wyatt. We served in Afghanistan together. I hear he's becoming a family man in about six months' time."

Relief washed through Dana. Information about J.T. and Rina, especially on a personal level, was highly classified. Only agents who had worked closely with him and family members would know that J.T. and Rina were expecting a baby. "Do you still work together?"

"No, ma'am. J.T. resigned last year."

The correctness of the answer and the faint Southern drawl released a little more tension.

Jack looked confused. Dana briefly explained that J.T. had been the CIA agent who had rescued Rina, Taylor's best friend, from Lopez and Slater the previous year.

Jack fixed Fischer with a cold stare. "So that's how you found us. You had Dana watched."

"Not Dana. You."

"When I visited Taylor in the hospital. That's the only risk I've taken in more than twenty years."

Fischer didn't take his gaze off Jack, and the gun didn't waver. "If we hadn't gotten you then, we would have picked you up when she visited you down in the Keys."

Jack leaned forward, resting his elbows on his

knees, his hands hanging loosely, but Dana wasn't fooled. Jack hadn't liked being caught cold and he liked it even less that he had been under surveillance since his visit to D.C.

He gestured at the ID Dana still had in her hands. "You've been tailing me. You could have picked me up at any time. Why now?"

"I need information."

"If I knew where Taylor was, I wouldn't tell you."

Dana set the ID down on the coffee table. "I can help you find her."

Jack's hand clamped on her arm. "Damn it, Dana—"

Dana jerked free and pushed to her feet. She could be making a terrible mistake, but her gut reaction was to trust Fischer. "Taylor's got more chance of surviving with his help. *He* found us when no one else could, including Lopez."

She picked up her handbag, which she'd left sitting next to the couch. She handed her cell phone to Fischer. "The number's in the directory."

Jack's expression was cold as Fischer thumbed through the menu and checked the number. "You didn't need to do that. He's already got the number, just like he's got mine. He would have gotten it when he was down in the Keys."

Fischer handed the phone back. "I've had Taylor followed ever since she left Vermont. It's the whereabouts of Casale that I'm interested in today."

Dana frowned. "Who is Casale?"

Jack's hand gripped hers in warning. "I don't know where Casale is. Yet."

"But you've got a lead."

"That's right. And I'm not revealing my source."

Fischer dropped a blank card with a number scribbled on it on the coffee table, picked up his ID and backed away. "You have two choices. You can work with me, or I can continue to have you surveiled."

Either way, he would win.

Dana noted the flicker of movement off to the right as the man who had been positioned in the hallway moved into plain view. Like Fischer, he was dressed in low-key dark pants, a loose shirt and trainers, but there was nothing casual about the handgun.

Jack picked up the card. "If you listened in on all my conversations, you know as much as I do about Rico."

Fischer nodded his head at the man who had just walked out of the hallway. He slipped a portable radio from his pocket and began talking in a low monotone, repeating Casale's full name.

Jack's jaw tightened. "Knowing his full name won't do you much good. He's gone to ground."

The guy with the radio backed into the kitchen, keeping his gun trained on Jack. Fischer holstered his gun and followed him. "I'll be in touch."

Dana waited until the door closed behind them both. At some point, the man out on the patio had melted away. In the distance she heard a vehicle start up, then a second. She let out a breath. She was shaking. And those had been the good guys.

Jack's fingers squeezed hers and it registered that she was clutching on to him like a lifeline. Wrenching free, she pushed to her feet. "*Who is Rico Casale?* And just what have you been doing behind my back?"

Jack rose to his feet. "Whatever I can. But I don't have Fischer's resources." He slipped the card into his pocket. "Rico Casale is the hit man who shot Taylor in D.C. It's taken months of digging, but a couple of days ago I finally got the full name. It wasn't a phone conversation, which is why Fischer missed it."

Dana watched as Jack walked out onto the patio, bent down and picked up his handgun, checked the load and slipped it in the waistband at the small of his back as casually as if he were tucking a wallet into his back pocket. "Are you telling me that you've been making calls to criminals and *hit men*—"

His eyes flashed, the first real break in his control she'd seen. "I know you don't like this situation. I'm not happy about it, either. Being a hit man wasn't the best choice I ever made, but now it just might save Taylor."

He picked up the laundry and walked through to his room. Dana paused at his open door. Jack had his suitcase open on the bed.

She stared at the man she had once loved and married. Caught in the middle of another Lopez mess and on the run from both the good *and* the bad guys, all she could cling to was the fact that Jack Jones—hit man or not—had loved his daughter. "What now?"

"We pack. While I was out I checked with my source. Casale's gone to ground, my source thinks in Jersey. We're flying out of Oakland this evening."

Twenty-Seven

Eureka, California

At ten o'clock, Dennison checked out of his motel unit. Taylor, who had spent the night in the parking lot staking out his car, waited for a couple of cars to pass, then moved in smoothly behind him. Within a matter of seconds, he turned into a shopping mall complex. Minutes later, he exited with a bunch of yellow roses.

The next stop was a cemetery, and Taylor understood why Dennison had risked surfacing in a place where he could be, and had been, recognized. She had come back to Eureka looking for clues. Dennison was here for purely personal reasons.

His wife had passed away *exactly* two years ago.

Within days of Anne Dennison dying, Dennison had turned informant.

When Dennison drove out of the cemetery parking lot, he headed south. Later that afternoon, after two stops, one for gasoline and food, the second so he could use a restroom, Taylor followed Dennison as he turned off Interstate 880. She was both hungry and thirsty, and she needed to visit the restroom herself, but she couldn't risk leaving the vehicle. If Dennison slipped away from her now, the chance that she would ever find him again was remote.

Minutes later his destination became obvious. Oakland International Airport. After parking the rental, Taylor swapped the blond wig for the ball cap, unpacked her luggage and followed him into the airport. By now both Bayard and Burdett would know her general location and they would be monitoring flights. She could be detained if she tried to board a domestic flight, but it was a risk she had to take.

Dennison queued to check his luggage and her heart sped up when she realized he had bought a ticket to El Paso.

The excitement that had gripped her when she had first seen him and which had worn away over long hours of surveillance flooded back. She hadn't been a part of the operation in El Paso because she had been recovering from the hostage crisis, but she had read the reports a number of times. The operation had been critical but, like the two previous ones in Winton and Eureka, it had failed to net Lopez.

Her jaw clenched at the discomfort of having to lug bags with a full bladder, she stepped up to the counter, and asked if there were any seats left on the flight. Dennison had had his ticket with him, which meant he had prebooked. If the flight was full, she would lose him.

The woman checked her computer. There were two seats left, both in economy. Taylor paid for the ticket with cash and checked her luggage. Dennison had cut it close. The flight left in less than twenty minutes.

She followed him at a discreet distance to make sure he didn't buy a second ticket to an alternative destination. Dennison stopped to buy a newspaper and a candy bar, then perused the books. Despite the increasing pressure on her bladder, Taylor waited him out. No matter how badly she needed to make a trip to the bathroom, she couldn't risk leaving Dennison. It was possible that he had purchased the ticket as a ruse and would walk out at the last minute.

When the flight was called, he put the book he'd been studying back on the shelf, left the shop and ambled in the direction of the gate.

Sighing with relief, Taylor walked to the nearest restroom, chose the closest available stall and locked the door. Seconds later, she washed her hands and face, and took the time to check her appearance. With her hair pulled back into a ponytail, and the sunglasses and bill of the cap obscuring half of her face, she would be hard to identify. Add to that the generic, sexless look of the oversize shirt, denims and sneakers she was wearing, and she could have been any one of a hundred travelers she'd seen in the airport.

As she boarded the plane, she skimmed the rows of passengers. Dennison had a seat close to the front. She was near the rear. After stowing her hand luggage, she sidled into her seat, which was wedged between two harassed mothers with babies.

The sudden entry into a world of diapers and baby bottles was disorienting. For days she had been living on the edge. Two people had been murdered, and her life was threatened. She had found Dennison, an unlikely key to the puzzle of both Lopez and the cabal. Now, for the next two hours she was camped in a world she had briefly contemplated being a part of.

Taylor fastened her seat belt. As destinations went, for Dennison El Paso was a huge risk. After the unsuccessful operation and the manhunt that had followed, his face would be known. He risked being picked up by the local cops, and maybe even being detained at the airport. El Paso was the last place Dennison should go, which meant he had a strong reason for going there.

The first opportunity she got when she disembarked, she was going to have to buy a handgun.

The second the airplane taxied to a halt in El Paso and the seat belt lights went off, Taylor sidled out to the aisle and began working her way forward. A woman glared, and a man refused to move aside, forcing her to push past, but she didn't have time for politeness. Dennison was close to the exit, tucked in just behind business class. He would be one of the first passengers off. If she was slow disembarking she could lose him.

Minutes later, she joined the stream of passengers gathered around the luggage carousel. Luggage was already circling. She studied the milling crowd, boosted by people waiting for the arriving flight and tour operators picking up clients. She couldn't find Dennison.

He had been wearing a gray suit. He could have taken the jacket off, but she couldn't see anyone in either a gray suit jacket or the light-colored shirt he had been wearing.

A man bent to collect a case. He was wearing a blue ball cap, matching polo shirt, dark glasses, and he had a mustache. She registered the gray jacket draped over one arm.

It was Dennison.

Her pulse accelerated. There was no sign of the shirt, which meant he must have taken it off during the flight and dumped it on the plane. She hadn't seen him carry anything on the flight, which meant he must have been wearing the polo shirt beneath the light-colored shirt. He had probably had the ball cap folded up in his jacket pocket along with the fake mustache.

With his face on the El Paso PD's most-wanted list, she should have expected that he would change his appearance. Six months and a whole different life ago, she wouldn't have missed a detail like that. As a lesson in how dangerous Dennison was, it was salutary. She couldn't afford to forget that he was ex-Bureau turned criminal, and that he had been ruthless enough that Lopez had retained him to run the Colombian branch of the Chavez operation.

Dennison started toward the exit. Taylor checked the conveyor. Her case was filled with things that were important to her, but if she had to, she would leave it. She checked the entrance then glanced back at the conveyor. Her suitcase came into view. Threading her way through passengers, she intercepted the case, at the same time keeping an eye on Dennison, who had bypassed the exit and was walking toward one of the rental-car agencies.

She grabbed the handle of her case and started after him.

Twenty-Eight

Helene Reichmann waited for the maid to pour coffee. Afternoon sunlight glittered off the rings on her fingers as she added artificial sweetener to her cup. Her hands were well manicured, but despite all of her efforts they betrayed her age. She was seventy-one, although with cosmetic surgery and a rigorous exercise regime, most people thought she was in her midfifties.

After she had sipped her way through the first cup of coffee, she poured a second cup, picked up the television remote and selected a news channel.

A terrorist action in the Middle East led the news, followed by a breaking story about a local murder. Her interest sharpened as images flashed across the screen. Hot coffee scalded her fingers.

Normally it was the international news that most interested her, particularly the complicated weave of politics, greed and madness that drove various terrorist factions. Ever since she was very young she had been fascinated by the reasoning behind violence, the murky layers of anger and ideology. Invariably, there was one motivating factor: greed.

It was a motivation she understood very well. From the icy port of Lubeck and the ramshackle collection of tin huts Marco Chavez had called a refuge to the well-ordered opulence of her husband's mansion on Massachusetts Avenue, the lesson had been hammered home. Money was power. It changed lives, altered destinies and gave one the ability to create the future.

She set the cup down, barely registering the dark droplets that had spattered the expensive fabric of her cream suit.

Paul Seaton was dead.

The back of her neck crawled as the story segued into a brief biography of Seaton. Robert Onslow, another cabal member, had died several days ago of a heart attack. His death had been a surprise. He had been fit and healthy and hadn't had any previous record of heart problems, but he *had* been seventy-five. She hadn't gone to the funeral; nor, to her knowledge, had Paul or the other two surviving members of the upper echelon of the cabal, Stephen Ritter and Alex Parker. To do so would be to court media attention and discovery, and it went against the agreed code.

As always, she had made sure the code was adhered to by sending one of her people along to surveil the event and provide a list of the participants. Sometimes the finality of death stirred up old allegiances and loyalties and, with the increasing age of the ruling members of the cabal, she was ever vigilant.

There was no ambiguity attached to Seaton's death: it was murder. A .38 caliber bullet in the chest, another in the head. According to the report, the killing of the reclusive media magnate was brutal and senseless. No evidence of theft had been found, although Seaton's desk had been rifled through, so it was possible something of value had been stolen before the killer had exited the house.

With a jerky movement, she switched the television off and walked out into the hall. Mail and newspapers she hadn't yet had time to peruse were neatly stacked on a mahogany side table. She picked up the *Post*. Her gaze was caught by an advertisement on the front page, and any idea that two deaths within a week could be a coincidence dissolved.

She stared at the advertisement for a photographic service specializing in restoring old and damaged films—a cipher that belonged to another place and another time. Although the World War II cipher once used by German Intelligence had been used since. During a seven-year window when the cabal had first established itself in the States, before they had cut their umbilical cord to Chavez, they had used it to coordinate the trafficking of drugs and weapons with the cartel.

Discarding the *Post,* she picked up the *Times.* The advertisement was also featured on the front page. She studied the seemingly random arrangement of numbers and letters within the body of the advertisement. The first was different from the second. Lopez, in his arrogance, was communicating with her, but until she could find the key—

The sound of a voice jerked her head up.

She stared blankly at her personal assistant. Her driver was parked out front, waiting. She had appointments, meetings to attend, a four-o'clock briefing on the upcoming OPEC summit followed by a press conference. "Thank you."

Her voice sounded distant and hollow, but it was reassuringly precise. The facade she so effortlessly maintained was still in place.

She skimmed the advertisements again as she strode to her suite and changed. She hadn't made a mistake. Lopez had murdered Seaton and placed the ads on the front page of two major daily papers, where she couldn't miss them. The lead time for inserting advertisements was usually several days before publication, which meant the murder had been planned and precisely timed to coincide with the advertisements.

For the first time since the book had been stolen in Cancun, raw panic squeezed at her chest. The security leak that Taylor Jones had represented was irrelevant. Lopez *had* the book. He wanted her to know how much power he had over the cabal.

She had always suspected that Marco Chavez had set her up in Cancun. She had searched for years, and hidden the fact that the book had been stolen. Admitting the loss would have created an unprecedented situation, one that Ritter, her second in command, wouldn't have hesitated to exploit. He would have demanded her execution.

Over the years, when no blackmail attempt had been made, the fear that the book had been stolen by Chavez had subsided. Gradually, she had come to believe that the book had been discarded along with the rest of the contents of her bag and had probably ended up at the bottom of a landfill.

Now the murders and the coded advertisement confirmed that her first instincts had been correct. Marco *had* outmaneuvered her. He had had the book all along.

Now Lopez was exacting his revenge by killing the cabal members, one by one.

Two of the five upper echelon had died the past

week, both killed by Lopez, leaving herself, Ritter and Alex Parker. She could tell the remaining two cabal members, which would buy them time to get to safety, but if she did that she would have to admit that she had lost the book and hidden that fact from them. That she had thrown the entire upper echelon of the cabal to the wolves in order to preserve herself.

In a way, she decided, Lopez was solving her problems for her.

From the moment she had lost the book, the cabal, an organization that in recent times had become increasingly unstable, had become a threat to her. The threat could no longer be condoned.

The cabal was finished, but she would survive.

Lopez thought he held all the cards, but she held the most important one.

She knew who he was going to kill next.

She joined her assistant on the front steps. Outside, the day was sunny and warm, but the air had a crisp bite. In contrast to the lush, overblown display of spring, the roses, grouped in a formal arrangement around the front portico, were skeletal and barbed.

Her driver opened the rear door of the waiting limousine. "Where to this afternoon, Madame Ambassador?"

"The White House."

Twenty-Nine

El Paso, Texas

Taylor followed Dennison's rental at a discreet distance in the SUV she'd rented. Since driving out of the airport parking lot, he had been laid-back and methodical and completely absorbed with his own purpose.

He had made three stops in town. One at a mall to buy a bottle of water and a sandwich, another at a gun store, the third at a gardening supply store, where he had bought a spade.

Taylor watched as he loaded the spade into the trunk of the car. It crossed her mind that Dennison might be going to bury something—or somebody. Although the most likely alternative was that he was going to dig something up.

After ten minutes of cruising at a slow crawl through tree-lined suburban streets, he pulled over beside a small park. Driving past, her attention glued to the rearview mirror, Taylor took the first turn, parked the car, got out and walked, using the thick screen of trees and shrubs as cover.

She didn't have any qualms about leaving the vehicle, because she was certain that whatever Dennison was up to in El Paso, he had reached his final destination. When she had driven down the street, she had recognized the area from both the text and photographic images on Bureau files. They were very close to the address of the FBI bust the previous year.

Dennison was strolling through the park, the spade in one hand. He stared back at where he'd left his vehicle then began walking in a straight line away from it. Taylor shadowed him through the trees. When he reached the end of the grassed area, he turned around and retraced his steps, studying the ground and the trees. Eventually, he stopped beneath a large shade tree and began to dig.

Wishing she'd had the time and opportunity to buy a gun, Taylor worked her way closer. It was early evening. The air was growing perceptibly cooler as the sun set and the large trees shrouded the park in gloom. Dennison stopped driving the spade into the ground and began working to one side of the hole he'd dug.

He tossed the spade aside, bent down and pulled a wrapped object out of the ground. He glanced around, then opened what looked like a water-proof package and pulled out an envelope. Tearing the envelope open, he studied the contents.

Not documents, as she had first thought. A book. Dennison had a book.

His head jerked up. He stared almost directly at Taylor, although she was certain that, with the sun down and the light fading, there was no way he could see her through the thick screen of leaves.

She slipped through the trees, keeping pace with Dennison as he made his way back to his vehicle. She was certain Dennison had the book that Tito Mendoza once had in his possession. Lopez would have brought the book to El Paso to use as leverage, which meant it *was* important. Important enough to gamble with his own life, and to kill for. Important enough for Dennison to risk the trip to retrieve it.

According to Mendoza, the book contained the identities of German ex-nationals. If it did expose the cabal, it was possible it would also expose the identity of the mole who had set her up to take the fall.

She couldn't take the book off Dennison. She didn't have a weapon, and he was armed. She would have to follow him until she was in a position to either take his weapon from him, or obtain a gun.

As she neared the end of the belt of trees, a flickering movement ahead stopped her in her tracks. She recognized the blond man who had come off her flight in San Francisco.

Dennison had almost reached his car. She had to make a choice.

Stepping out of the cover of the trees, she walked directly toward Dennison. It was stupid, beyond dangerous. If she had been working as an agent, she would have been fired on the spot. The blond man was an unknown factor. And Dennison had no reason to spare an FBI agent, but she was banking on the softness Dennison had shown in taking flowers to his wife's grave. If she didn't try, she would lose everything.

A handgun appeared in Dennison's hand. It was nothing fancy, a common thirty-eight: inexpensive, reliable and deadly. It would kill her just as efficiently as a sniper's bullet.

She didn't make the mistake of moving. "If Lopez finds out you've got the book, he'll kill you."

As leverage, it was more conversation than threat. Dennison had cut his ties with Lopez. "I can help you. I have contacts—"

Dennison was moving steadily back toward his car. His focus shifted and his gun discharged. Simultaneously, she was knocked to the ground.

Her nostrils flared on the sharp scent of fresh sweat. She caught a glimpse of denim, dark hair, a muscular bicep. Digging the toes of her sneakers into the iron-hard ground, she lunged forward. An arm snaked around her throat, stopping her cold and his full weight came down on her, shoving all the breath from her lungs.

The blond guy was on the ground a few yards away, clutching his arm. Dennison was already in his vehicle. Sucking in air, she twisted, shoved at her assailant and froze.

For a full second her brain refused to work. Then the sound of Dennison's car engine screaming as he peeled away from the curb broke the stasis. She stared into Fischer's eyes, just inches from her own. *"He's getting away."*

"That's not your problem."

Dennison's taillights winked out as he swerved around a corner. For a split second what Fischer had said made no sense. Dennison and the book he'd dug up were very personally, very crucially, *her* problem. They were the keys to her staying alive—to getting her life, and Dana's, back—and after twenty-four hours of trailing Dennison she had lost them both.

She stared at the road. Dennison's concern now would be getting out of El Paso. There was a chance she could pick him up again at the airport. It was a long shot, but anything was better than nothing.

She attempted to twist and dislodge Fischer. The arm around her throat tightened, cutting off her oxygen supply. Long seconds passed and her head began to spin. A split second later he eased off on the pressure and air whooshed into her lungs. Dimly she registered that the hard shape pressing into her shoulder blade was a handgun. "You're saying Dennison's your problem?"

"That's right."

His voice was flat, his eyes cold, and any ambiguity about who and what Fischer was dissolved. A flicker of movement jerked her head around. It was almost full dark, but there was enough light to identify the dark-haired man who had stepped out of the trees and who had a handgun trained on the injured man on the ground. This time he hadn't bothered with the spectacles. If she'd looked past the glasses, which had probably been fake, she would have noticed he was fitter and more muscular than the average academic. *"Let me up."*

Fischer eased back on his hold, allowing her to breathe more freely, but didn't release her. "First I need your assurance that you're not going to run. It took me a while to track you out of Cold Peak."

"Just out of interest, how *did* you find me? This time I didn't have the computer."

"I put a tracking device on your SUV. When you changed to a rental in Springfield, that threw us. By the time we got the plate you were long gone.

We had to wait until you called your father to pick up on your location."

She went still inside. She had used a new phone, which meant they had tracked the call from her father's phone. "You know where Dana and Jack are."

"I paid them a visit in Westport right about the time Dennison left his motel in Eureka."

The matter-of-fact statement detailing the comprehensive manner in which Fischer had outmaneuvered not only her but Dana and Jack was chilling, and it achieved what it was designed to do—inform her that Fischer was in control. Now her only way forward was through him—*if* he would allow her in. She took a deep breath and let it out slowly. "I'm not planning on running. In case you hadn't noticed, we're going in the same direction." Toward Dennison and the book.

He eased off on his hold fractionally. Then, as if he'd made a decision, he released her and flowed to his feet. "Don't worry about Dennison. I've had a man following him for the past four days, ever since he flew out of Bogotá. Wells won't lose him."

She stared at Fischer as she pushed to her feet. He looked the same as when she'd last seen him standing outside the bank in Cold Peak and earlier on that same day, when she'd stepped out of his bed. But the shoulder rig, almost invisible against a black T-shirt, pulled him into perspective. "So, what do I call you? Steve, or Agent Fischer?"

His expression was unreadable. If she'd hit a nerve, she decided, she would never know it.

A third man had materialized from the cover of the trees and was methodically searching and disarming the injured man. Within seconds he had been moved back into the cover of the trees. It was fully dark, but with streetlights now lightening the gloom and the periodic sweep of headlights from cars, the danger that they were visible from the road was high.

Fischer produced an ID wallet and began to question the injured man, who identified himself as Maximillian Schroeder. His nationality was Swiss, not German as she'd thought.

Stepping back from Schroeder, Fischer shrugged out of his shoulder rig, placed the gun in the holster to one side and peeled out of his T-shirt. One of his men handed him a pair of latex gloves. Pulling them on, Fischer crouched down and cinched the T-shirt around Schroeder's arm, stanching the flow of blood. When he was finished, he rose to his feet, removed the gloves, then handed Schroeder his phone, which had been confiscated along with a handgun and an ankle knife. "I need to talk to your boss."

Schroeder's expression, though pale, was curiously devoid of emotion. He had answered some

of Fischer's questions, but he hadn't provided anything more than name, nationality and the details
of his travel plans. "I don't know what you mean."

"Xavier," Fischer said succinctly. "Xavier
le Clerc."

Wincing with pain, Schroeder agreed to make
the call. When he hung up his face was gray. "He's
not answering. I've left a message."

Fischer's regard was watchful. "What's your
schedule?"

"There isn't one. I wait. Le Clerc calls."

When Fischer took the phone and noted down the
number, Schroeder shook his head. "Don't try it. Le
Clerc doesn't answer calls unless he recognizes the
number. If you use my phone to leave a message,
he won't reply, he'll just change the number."

"How do you communicate if the number's
compromised?"

"I wait until he contacts me."

Fischer eyed Schroeder with a coldness that
sent a trickle of unease down Taylor's spine.
"That means you have a backup plan. Or a meeting place."

Schroeder's face was expressionless.

Fischer checked his watch. "We have Dennison,
and the book. If le Clerc wants in, he has until eight
tomorrow morning to contact me. After that, all
bets are off."

For a split second, emotion registered in Schroeder's eyes. "A meeting can be arranged."

"That's what I thought."

Fischer slipped a cell phone from his pocket and made a call, requesting a medical contact in the area. The two agents, Tate and Shaw, helped Schroeder into the back of a dark sedan parked directly behind Taylor's SUV.

Taylor dug out her keys from her jeans pocket, unlocked the car and climbed into the driver's seat. Fischer slid into the passenger seat. Without a shirt, and in the small confines of the car, he seemed to fill the space. As she fastened her seat belt, the back of her hand brushed against his bare arm, sending a small shock of awareness through her. She noticed Fischer had removed the gun from the shoulder rig and had placed both the webbing and the handgun at the floor by his feet. "How do you know le Clerc will contact Schroeder?"

"Because he's already in the country."

The slight Southern intonation didn't take away from the flat surety of Fischer's voice. Now she could see how Fischer had moved so seamlessly from the military into intelligence work—and into an assignment that, with his personal involvement, he should have been barred from. He had run rings around WITSEC and her because he was operat-

ing on another level entirely. Like le Clerc, he was
attuned to an international stage and a shadowy
underworld that most people doubted even existed.

"What happens if le Clerc doesn't show?"

"He will. He wants Reichmann's ledger."

A shiver went down her spine. *So the book
had a name.*

She merged into traffic, following Tate and
Shaw. Now that they were enclosed in the SUV, the
quiet was unnerving. "Reichmann being one of
the SS officers who hijacked the *Nordika.*"

He crossed his arms over his chest. "That's
right. Baron Heinrich von Reichmann, to be exact.
Head of one of the Third Reich's elitist breeding
programs, a colonel in the SS, and the architect of
the cabal."

The extent of Fischer's knowledge about the book
and the cabal reinforced what she now knew about
him. He was methodical, informed and focused. It
made sense that he would know a great deal about
the organization that had in all likelihood ordered his
father's execution. "Why did you break into my
apartment and install the spyware on my computer?
You're already working with Bayard—you must
have known I mailed copies to my work address."

She stopped for a set of lights. She could see
Tate's rental two cars ahead.

"If I'd gotten to your work computer in time,
you would never have been shot."

The back of her neck tingled. Of all the angles she had considered, protection hadn't been one of them. "How do you know that?"

The accepted story was that Lopez had put out a contract on her. Fischer was implying that he knew she was in danger at her workplace. She had only worked that out after she'd found the fake surveillance reports. She braked for a red light. "You're working with Bayard to isolate the mole."

"I'm sorry you got shot. I knew you weren't the mole, and I knew something was on. I should have realized the hit was in progress."

"How did you know I wasn't the mole?"

"I read your profile. It didn't make sense."

The light turned green. Frowning, Taylor accelerated, keeping the car ahead in sight. "You were searching for the mole, so you started surveiling me."

A cell phone buzzed. He took a call, his answers curt. When he was finished, he put the phone back into his jeans pocket, folded his arms across his chest and settled back in the seat. "I was searching for the mole *and* surveiling you."

The point was small, but it underlined the fact that he hadn't ever thought she was the mole. After everything that had happened it shouldn't matter that Fischer, at least, had believed in her. "Why did you sleep with me?"

Something flashed in his eyes and she had an answer she hadn't expected.

"If you don't want the answers, stop asking questions."

Taylor stared directly ahead, glued to Tate's tail-lights. She had been comfortable when she had viewed Fischer as emotionally locked down and ruthless. He had been a known quantity. Now the fact that he had slept with her because he wanted her had thrown her into a quandary. She didn't know if she could cope with the fact that he had been honestly turned-on.

He signaled that she should pull over into a parking space. A softly glowing sign indicated that the building was a medical center.

Taylor parked directly behind Tate and Shaw. Seconds later Tate popped the trunk and extracted a shirt from an overnight bag.

Pushing the passenger-side door open, Fischer stepped out onto the street. Tate, who was now wearing a jacket in deference to the evening chill, tossed him the clean shirt. Fischer shrugged into the shirt, buttoned it and slipped the handgun into the waistband at the rear of his jeans.

According to the sign on the door, the center had closed at five, but the foyer was lit. When Fischer rapped on the glass a tall, lean Hispanic man appeared and let them in.

Within twenty minutes Schroeder's wound was cleaned and bandaged and Dr. Mateo, an ex-naval doctor, had injected him with a painkiller and antibiotics. He handed Fischer packages from the dispensary: more antibiotics, painkillers and fresh dressings.

A cell phone rang as they were leaving the medical center.

Schroeder, a sheen of sweat covering his face, picked up the call. The conversation was brief. "That was le Clerc. He's agreed to a meeting tomorrow in D.C. Dupont Circle, Q Street and Nineteenth, twelve-thirty sharp. He'll find you."

Thirty

Dupont Circle, Washington, D.C.

In the milling, eclectic crowd of tourists and office workers, all enjoying the sunny fall day, le Clerc shouldn't have been noticeable. He wasn't tall, just over medium height, lean and tanned with dark hair graying at the temples. But to Taylor the qualities that had made him a legend for more than two decades marked him.

Fischer's hand landed on the small of her back, urging her forward. The touch was light, but warm enough to burn through the light cotton of her dress. Le Clerc wasn't alone. Two young, muscular men, dressed in suits, flanked him.

When le Clerc's eyes met hers, Taylor also recognized another fact: le Clerc knew what *she* looked like.

Instead of the handshake he gave Fischer, le Clerc held her hand in a brief clasp and executed a small, formal bow. "Ms. Jones. I'm glad to see you're recovered."

Le Clerc's voice was neutral, the accent generic European, which made sense. Since knocking over a Swiss bank in Bern back in the seventies, he had lived a wealthy but itinerant life. Rumor had it that he had resided in a number of locations, including a seagoing yacht, but his whereabouts had never been reliably confirmed.

"Please pass on my regards to Esther Morell's daughter."

"I no longer have contact with Rina."

Le Clerc lifted a brow as if he didn't quite believe her. The exchange was subtle and unexpected. Le Clerc was letting her know how informed he was, not only about her but about Rina, and suddenly Taylor knew that everything that had been surmised about le Clerc's relationship with Esther Morell was correct.

Back in 1972, directly before he had committed the series of crimes that had sent shock waves through the international banking community, he had been dating Esther. Given le Clerc's legendary talent for carrying out faultless operations, romancing the woman who had been auditing his affairs on the eve of the theft had been one of the riskier things he had done. Twelve years later, helping Esther steal billions of dollars from one of Lopez's offshore accounts had come a close second. The reason he had risked himself both times was simple: Xavier le Clerc had been in love with Esther.

Le Clerc shifted his attention to Schroeder, who was seated in the shade of an adjacent café, his arm in a sling. Tate sat a few tables away. Le Clerc's expression cooled perceptibly as his focus swung back to Fischer. Civility aside, he hadn't liked that his man had been hurt. "You have the book."

Fischer's expression behind dark glasses was remote as he scanned the lunchtime crowd. "We have Dennison and the book. Tell your man he can take Schroeder."

Le Clerc nodded his head at a muscular young man, dressed in a loose tank and baggy chinos, who hadn't made it past Shaw. As he walked slowly toward Schroeder, the tension escalated. Taylor had known that le Clerc would have more men stationed in the area. The question was, how many?

During the chartered flight out of El Paso last night she had learned enough about le Clerc to view him with more than a little respect. According to Fischer, he headed a tight, sophisticated network with established connections to MI6, the French Secret Service and Mossad. That was one of the key reasons he had survived. He acted outside of the law, but he got the job done without any of the international agencies having to get their hands dirty. Schroeder was an example of the quality and skill base of le Clerc's network. He was Swiss born, with a degree in political science from the Sorbonne. He was fluent in a number of languages, including Russian.

Le Clerc watched as Schroeder was helped into a nearby vehicle. "The book went on the market this morning. The bidding started at ten million." He smiled faintly. "U.S. dollars only. Europe hasn't yet woken up."

Fischer looked briefly at Tate. "We gave Dennison some rope, enough to get the bidding started and draw Lopez and the cabal in. So far we haven't had a hit."

Taylor watched as Tate drifted out onto the sidewalk. Dennison was holed up in a seedy motel in the Mexican town of Lucero, just south of El Paso. Since he'd checked in, according to Wells, he hadn't done anything except order in food, lay low and make phone calls. Lopez hadn't entered into the equation, closing out the slim possibility that Dennison had been running an errand.

Le Clerc's expression didn't alter. He produced a newspaper he had been carrying under his arm, unfolded it and handed it to Fischer. "Dennison may have the book, but the value is…compromised."

The front-page story was a speculative piece about two prominent but reclusive businessmen who had died within days of each other, one of a suspected poisoning, the second a straight-out shooting. It had been discovered that both homicide victims had had numbers tattooed on their backs, and the numbers ran *consecutively*. Even more bizarrely, the men looked alike, so much so that doctors speculated they could be twins, even though they came from two entirely different families. An investigation was in progress. DNA samples had been sent away for testing.

Taylor noted the date on the paper. It was this morning's edition, which meant le Clerc had probably bought it on his way to the meeting. At this point the dead men couldn't positively be identified as cabal members, but the chance that they weren't was ludicrously small.

Fischer handed the paper back to le Clerc. "There's a copy of the ledger."

Le Clerc folded the paper and slipped it neatly back under his arm. "And our friend has been putting it to good use."

It made sense. Lopez had taken the book to El Paso to put together a deal after the cabal had issued an execution order on him, but he hadn't wanted to risk losing his only chip in the big game. He had made a copy before he had left Bogotá, which meant Dennison's auction was a blind alley.

The reason behind Lopez's inactivity since El Paso was now also plain. He had been busy tracking down the members of the cabal. Now he had declared open season and was picking them off one by one, and with each death he was closing down avenues and destroying leads. The cabal were scrambling to protect the members that were left. In the space of a few days Lopez was invalidating years of surveillance and undercover work.

Fischer took his phone out of his pocket and made a call.

Le Clerc's gaze was sharp. "Keep your men in place. Lopez is taking out some key players, but he won't succeed in wiping out the entire cabal because of one simple fact. Reichmann and his daughter were never included in the book."

Fischer slipped his phone in his pocket. "She controls the accounts. That's how she's managed to retain her power."

"That's correct. In reality, Helene Reichmann *is* the cabal."

Taylor shook her head, trying to come to grips with the politics of a woman who sounded more monster than human. "What accounts?" To transcend the threat of the book, the money had to be huge, and the possible origins of that kind of wealth made her feel queasy.

Le Clerc looked faintly surprised. "The accounts into which Reichmann transferred the money he stole from the Jews. Estimates at the end of the war varied from one point five to three billion pounds sterling."

Taylor blinked. Pounds sterling was the English definition of a billion, which was another three zeroes on from the American. When le Clerc said a billion, he wasn't talking a thousand million, he was talking a *million* million. And those estimates were arrived at over sixty years ago, back in the nineteen forties. By now, even with minimal interest, the figure would be astronomical.

Suddenly the intense drive behind le Clerc's crusade came into sharp focus. He wasn't only hunting his father's killers. He was intent on achieving justice on a much wider scale by restoring the stolen wealth to the remnants of the families Reichmann had condemned to the death camps.

Le Clerc reached into his suit jacket and extracted a card. "You have Dennison. I want the book." He handed Fischer the card, which was blank except for a handwritten cell phone number.

With a brief inclination of his head, he turned on his heel and, flanked by his men, melted into the crowd.

Fischer nodded at two men sitting at a nearby table. Within seconds they'd merged into the lunchtime crowd, following le Clerc.

Fischer slipped the card into his shirt pocket. "It'll be interesting to see how long Sheldon and

Cole last. Le Clerc's security spotted them while we were talking."

Fischer's hand settled on the small of her back and they were moving again, this time in the direction of the car. The unsettling intimacy of the light touch started a tension of a different kind. In deference to the crisp, sunny day and the location, they were dressed as tourists, Fischer in a light shirt and pants, Taylor wearing a dress and low heels, but the charade that they were a couple was no longer required. Adjusting the strap of her bag from one shoulder to the other, she stepped slightly to one side, dislodging his hand. "I've just got one question. Why didn't either Chavez or Lopez use the book until now?"

"Marco didn't want a war, he preferred an insurance policy. Lopez didn't know about the book until Marco's accountant died and it surfaced in Bogotá."

Shaw, who had gone to get the car, pulled up at the curb. Fischer opened the rear passenger-side door. Taylor slid into the seat, then had to move over when Fischer moved in beside her, his thigh brushing hers.

When Fischer's gaze connected with hers, she was certain the contact had been deliberate. "We're picking up Tate."

Which meant Tate would take the front passenger seat. But that still didn't explain why Fischer had chosen to sit beside her.

Unless he had wanted to.

She stared at a passing cab as Shaw pulled smoothly into traffic. Maybe she was jumping to conclusions, but she couldn't deny certain facts. Fischer was in a position of command, running a team of seasoned professionals. He'd had no need to get personally close to her. Or sleep with her.

In sleeping with her he hadn't gained anything for his investigation. All he had done was complicate it. Added to that, having sex with a surveillance subject was not a career-enhancing move.

Her reasoning could be wrong. Fischer had fooled her in Cold Peak. Where he was concerned, none of her usual instincts functioned.

A small, rhythmic vibration registered above the noise of the vehicle.

Fischer picked up the call. "Damn. Tate's on Seventeenth and Corcoran. We've lost le Clerc."

"But not for long."

His gaze was remote. "That's right. We have the book."

Leverage.

In Fischer's world, she had to wonder if that was the only thing that counted.

Thirty-One

The following morning, Taylor studied the mottled leather binding of Reichmann's ledger, which Wells had delivered to Fischer less than an hour ago. The book was secured, and so was Dennison. In return for protection he had agreed to become a witness for the prosecution. Wells was transporting him to a safe house where, owing to the charges pending against him and the threat from both Lopez and the cabal, he would be held under armed guard for an indefinite period.

She had examined the book, reluctantly and with a sense of intrusion, because the content of the fragile faded pages was disturbing and highly personal. The reason le Clerc wanted it so badly was now evident. Reichmann's ledger wasn't just a careful accounting of theft, but of mass murder.

For le Clerc, and the remnants of those dispossessed families, its value—aside from exposing the members of the cabal—was incalculable. The book was hard evidence admissible in a court of law, and the beginning of the quest to gain closure, dignity and retrieve what was left of the money. Perhaps most importantly, it listed the specific camp each family had been sent to, providing physical locations for grieving relatives to visit.

To compound Reichmann's madness, after he had escaped Germany, he had continued on with the original purpose of the ledger, using it as his solution to control the members of the cabal by cataloging them in the same book that had been used to condemn thousands to death, a book that unalterably branded them all as criminals.

Fischer had looked at the ledger, as had Wells, Shaw and Tate. Their reactions had been uniform. Turning the pages had been like walking through a silent graveyard, and out of respect for the victims, they had each kept the journey short.

Placing the book back in its waterproof satchel, Taylor walked through to the bathroom and washed her hands. The impulse was knee-jerk. The book was an inanimate object, but both the Reichmanns and Lopez had handled it, and its purpose had been evil. Maybe soap and water didn't make much difference, but washing made her feel better.

When her hands were dry she walked back out into the sitting room. The motel unit was a near carbon copy of the one she'd stayed in just days ago—same name, almost the exact same decor. The only difference was the suburb they were located in and the fact that, this time, Steve Fischer was sharing the unit with her. She had the bedroom; he was on the couch. Shaw and Tate were sharing an adjacent unit.

She saw with relief that Fischer had packed the book into the armored briefcase it had been delivered in. Maybe she was being overly sensitive, but she couldn't wait until the book was removed. Every time she thought about it, the cold inhumanity of a man who had profited from mass murder sent cold shudders down her spine.

There was a brief tap on the door. Fischer got up from the couch where he had been making calls and working on a wireless laptop. After checking, he let Shaw and Tate in and holstered his gun. The fact that Fischer had remained armed underlined his tension.

Tate placed a grocery sack of delicatessen sandwiches and salads on the dining table. Taylor got out plates and poured glasses of water from the filter jug in the fridge. Fischer hung up on his latest call and took a place at the table.

The talk centered around le Clerc and his network, and the brushes they'd all had with the

Chavez cartel in South America when they'd been with the SEALs. Fischer had been Wells, Shaw and Tate's commanding officer. When Fischer had left, they had followed him.

Fischer's phone buzzed while they were eating. A third wealthy businessman with a lasered-off tattoo on his back, Alex Parker, had been shot to death in his car in the Appalachians. Evidently he had been driving to an isolated mountain cabin and had never made it. Apart from Helene Reichmann, there was only one upper-echelon member left. Fischer had been working to track his identity, which had been altered after the book had gone missing, but they were running out of time.

After the lunch dishes were done, Taylor tidied up the unit while Fischer showered. The enforced inactivity was grating. She had already read the newspaper that had been delivered that morning, and she could only watch so much TV.

On impulse, she picked up the shirt he'd left draped on the end of the bed and lifted it to her nose. The shirt smelled of Fischer, clean and male, and it sent unexpected emotion through her. Over the past two days, the enforced proximity had blunted the shock of what he'd done and she had gotten used to being with him. They weren't lovers and she didn't know if they would ever be again, but somehow that didn't affect the way she felt.

A card slipped out of the pocket and dropped to the floor. Bending, she picked it up.

Xavier's number.

She stared at the card then returned it to Fischer's shirt pocket. He didn't need the card. She had seen him enter the number into his phone.

When the sound of the shower running stopped, she left the bedroom and walked through to the sitting room. The bedroom was hers, but Fischer's bags were in there, and he used it to get changed. The cell phone, which he'd left on the dining table, buzzed. She carried the phone down the hall and handed it to him as he emerged from the bathroom, wearing dark pants but no shirt.

Seconds later, Fischer flipped the phone closed. "I have to go. Jack Jones and your mother are en route to Jersey."

Shock rolled through her. The one thing she had counted on was that Jack and Dana were safe.

She followed him into the bedroom. "Why Jersey?" The question was rhetorical: she already knew.

"Your father is after Rico Casale, the hit man who took the shot at you in D.C. Casale is based in L.A. but he disappeared a couple of weeks back. Jack found a guy who was willing to sell Casale out, a drug dealer working out of Jersey. Name of Aldo Fabroni."

He pulled on a dark T-shirt, placed a gear bag on the bed, unzipped it and stowed his gun and the shoulder holster.

"You're *using* them."

Fischer's expression was remote. "Jack had a choice. He could have handed the lead to me."

Her jaw clenched. Of course he wouldn't do that. He was used to working alone and the information was too important. He wouldn't trust anyone else to deal with the underworld in which he had once operated.

She reached for her suitcase, which was still mostly packed, dropped it on the part of the bed Fischer wasn't using and began shoving clothes and toiletries into it. "I'm going with you."

His hand clamped her wrist. "You're staying here. This has got as complicated as it's going to get."

She jerked free. "They're my *parents*."

"Shaw and Tate will look after you until I get back."

She sucked in a deep breath. Her chest felt tight and her eyes were burning. As much as she hated it, Fischer was right. He was doing his job. She had first-hand knowledge of just how effective he was, and she was hampering him. But that didn't make her feel any less panic or fear. She couldn't lose Dana, and she couldn't lose Jack, and she wasn't used to being powerless.

Fischer's hands closed on her upper arms.

"Don't worry about Jack and Dana. They won't get within a mile of Casale. They're safe, honey, believe it."

She stared into his dark eyes. *Honey*. Strange how it was the little things that undid her.

His fingers tightened. "I have to go."

Taylor spent the rest of the day watching television, rereading the newspaper and periodically running through sets of exercises. It began to rain, making the motel unit seem even more claustrophobic. By six that evening, despite the physical exertion, her nerves were shot.

She watched the news, checking for any hint that something had gone wrong. When it switched to sports, she turned the set off.

The phone buzzed, making her jump. When she picked up the receiver, it was Tate. He was ordering dinner. Did she want Italian or Chinese? She was no masochist; she chose Italian. With the wind howling, rain spattering the window and the possibility that the same guy who had shot her could put a bullet through someone she loved, it wasn't the best night to be reminded of her own shooting.

The fifteen minutes Tate had mentioned stretched out to thirty. When the knock on the door finally came, Taylor checked through the window before opening the door. In the murky light of the porch, for a moment she *saw* Tate wearing a ball cap and holding a sack of takeout.

When she opened the door, Colenso smiled and aimed a large handgun at her chest.

Thirty-Two

Ice formed in her stomach. In addition to the fact that Tate and Colenso were a similar coloring and build, Colenso was wearing his jacket. "So it was you."

He smiled. "Who did you think it was? Tripp?"

She didn't blink at the gibe. Colenso had always had an ego problem. His desire to score points off her wasn't surprising. However, the fact that he was the mole definitely was. In her wildest dreams, she wouldn't have imagined Colenso had either the intellect or the subtlety for the job.

Buying time in the hope that Shaw would magically appear, and feeling sick because she didn't think that Tate would, she looked past the black muzzle of the gun over his shoulder. He was alone, at least for now. That didn't give her much of an edge, but she would take any chance she could get. She stared into his eyes, which in the murky light were more gray than blue. "The bungled attempts *were* mounting."

He gestured with the gun. She moved back as he stepped into the room and kicked the door closed. The bland calmness of his expression registered. Colenso was a trained agent; he was competent and he had a gun. Without intervention by Shaw or Tate, it wasn't likely she was going to survive this. "You killed Letty."

"And called in the hit on you, milked your work computer and tapped your phone, although the calls were boring. You need to get yourself a social life. Although…" He stared over her shoulder at the bedroom where Fischer's shirt was still visible on the end of the bed. "Looks like you finally have."

"Did you send the calling card?"

"Nobody else, darlin'."

Rina had been right. Lopez wouldn't go near a piece of theater like that, but Colenso was all over it.

Motioning her back farther, he set the takeout down on the coffee table. The smell wafted through the room, turning her stomach. *"What did you do with Shaw and Tate?"*

She didn't know them that well, but their safety mattered. They were Fischer's men; they should have gone with him. Instead, they had stayed behind to look after her.

"Relax. I didn't shoot them. Too much noise, too much blood, and it would have wrecked the jacket." He produced a syringe and a vial, which contained a clear liquid. "It's an anesthetic. They're both taking naps."

Endless shadows, the sting of a needle. The smothering paralysis—

Stay calm. Stay focused.

This was what he wanted, to panic and demoralize her—to control her with fear.

Colenso went up another notch in her estimation. In his new position, he would have had access to her psych reports. He would know exactly how traumatized she had been.

"What do you want?"

He smiled. "You know where Dennison and the book are."

She wrenched her attention away from the syringe. Colenso didn't yet know that Dennison was in custody. It was information that Fischer had kept under wraps to buy time. Once the cabal members and Lopez knew the book was in the hands of the United States government, the situation would become even more volatile and they could lose the opportunity to capture Lopez and Reichmann. "I don't know where Dennison and the book are." That, at least, was the truth.

Colenso pocketed the vial and the syringe and lifted the gun. His index finger moved from the extended safety position to rest lightly on the trigger. "Try again."

Taylor's heart slammed in her chest. Colenso was experienced with weapons. Unless he intended to pull the trigger, his finger should remain in the safety position. "Fischer knows where Dennison is, but he didn't tell me. Why would he? He's CIA, I'm a civilian. But I do know how you can get the book."

"How?"

"I have Xavier le Clerc's number."

His brows jerked together. She had finally managed to shock him.

"Le Clerc's in the States?"

"I had a meeting with him yesterday. He's in contact with Dennison. By now he should have the book."

"Liar."

She shrugged. "Believe what you want, but if you shoot me, you won't ever get the book back."

Colenso's finger moved off the trigger. "Let me see the number."

"You'll have to let me go in the bedroom and get it. It's in the pocket of Fischer's shirt."

He followed her to the bedroom door, keeping his gun trained on her while she found the card. Keeping her movements slow and nonthreatening, she handed him the card and walked past him and back out into the lounge.

Colenso indicated that she sit on the couch. "Empty the contents of your bag on the floor."

Taylor picked up her handbag, which was beside the couch, and upended it. Her purse and the handgun Fischer gave her tumbled out along with a notepad, cell phone, pens, car keys, a comb and the miscellany of makeup that usually lived in a side pocket.

Colenso kicked her gun across the room and took out his cell phone. She kept note of exactly where the gun had ended up, and the fact that he hadn't noticed the absence of the magazine, which was concealed in another zipped side pocket. "You can't make the call. I need to do it. Otherwise le Clerc will ditch the number and your only link to Dennison and the book will be gone."

He placed the card on the coffee table. His finger was back on the trigger. "Phone le Clerc."

She picked up the motel phone, which was on a side table next to the couch.

"Use your cell phone."

She retained her grip on the receiver. Making the call via cell phone made sense. Colenso would retain his mobility, rather than being anchored to a motel room that could shortly become a war zone. "Le Clerc won't answer the call unless it comes from a number and a person he's expecting. The call itself will go to an answering service. He'll return it if he thinks it's safe. I'll give him my cell phone to call back on, but I need to call from this location. Then you're going to have to wait on le Clerc, and I don't know for how long."

Colenso was silent while he mulled over the logic of using the landline for the initial call. She needed to use the motel phone because it would leave a record of the call for Fischer to find. And, hopefully, once he realized it was le Clerc's number, a trail to follow.

Colenso checked his watch. Despite the chilly temperature, she could see beads of perspiration on his upper lip, signaling that he wasn't as calm as he appeared. He would be worried about Shaw and Tate waking up and raising the alarm, and that Fischer could walk in the door at any time.

She had also upped the stakes, which would have thrown off his carefully calculated plan. Colenso was a smart operator, but he didn't like surprises. Introducing the wild card of le Clerc, an old adversary who had been a thorn in the cabal's side for decades, had forced a more important objective on Colenso than simply killing her and taking out Fischer and his men.

Le Clerc wouldn't be happy at the breach of trust, but she had no alternative, and there was always the possibility that le Clerc could make productive use of Colenso's link to the cabal. The likelihood that Colenso would get close to a player like le Clerc was zero.

"Make the call."

She picked up the receiver and dialed. A split second later the call was picked up, not by a male voice as she had expected, but by a bland female voice that requested she leave a message.

Colenso frowned as she stated her name and cell phone number. He'd let her make the call, but he still didn't have any proof that she had reached le Clerc.

Letting out a breath, she hung up.

"Pick up your cell phone."

She found her cell phone in the muddle of items on the floor and placed it on the coffee table.

He put the phone in his pocket and pulled out the vial, which was partly filled with colorless fluid. "By the way, I think you know what this is."

Her stomach contracted.

The click of a briefcase. The cold sting of the needle—

"Ketamine."

"That's right. Technically it's an anesthetic. An interesting drug, but not really a killer." He produced a second vial. "After they drank the K in their coffee, they weren't really in a position to argue when I injected them with insulin."

Taylor's blood ran cold. The thought of being injected with ketamine filled her with horror, but insulin was worse. In the correct dosages it was a lifesaver for diabetics, but in large doses it dropped the blood sugar, causing diabetic coma, lack of oxygen, brain damage, organ failure and cardiac arrest. "You murdered them."

He checked his watch. "With the dose I administered, anytime soon."

A cold ripple of recognition went through her. Colenso was a killer. She couldn't afford the mistake of underestimating him again. With each kill he was growing in confidence. He had fooled her and everyone else in the Bureau, including Bayard.

Colenso produced a pair of handcuffs from his jacket pocket with all the flare of a magician producing a rabbit. "Hold your wrists out, and don't try anything."

His finger was back on the trigger. At this range he wouldn't miss.

He snapped the cuffs in place and stepped back. He checked his watch and jerked his head in the direction of the door. Pulling on a pair of latex gloves, he retrieved her gun, found the magazine in the side pocket of her bag and slipped both into his pocket. "Time to leave." He grinned. "Fischer should have found Casale by now."

Rico Casale had been dead for several hours.

Fischer studied the body sprawled on the floor of the second-story apartment in one of Jersey's more run-down areas. There were no signs of a beating or a trauma of any kind, but there was no mistaking the rigor, or the smell, of death.

He could hear Fabroni throwing up out on the sidewalk.

Fischer pulled on latex gloves and crouched down, careful not to touch the body while he systematically searched Casale. He was no forensics expert. At a guess Casale had been dead for several hours, long enough for rigor to set in, then relax slightly. And for the insects to find him.

A beetle scuttled away as he pulled aside Casale's shirt collar and studied a faint bluish mark on his skin. "There's a puncture wound on the right side of his neck."

It looked like Casale had been caught cold, probably from behind. Judging from the lack of any other marks or wounds, whatever poison had been injected had acted fast, immobilizing him. The way he had died didn't matter so much as *who* had killed him, but the fact that the killing had been achieved by a drug overdose, or poison, was interesting. In Casale's world, and this neighborhood, the gun ruled.

Straightening, Fischer took out his phone, turned it on and checked his calls. He frowned when he saw the number. Bridges, the agent who had come in to replace Wells, knew they were going after Casale. He wouldn't phone unless something had gone wrong.

Bridges picked up on the second ring. "Shaw and Tate are being taken by ambulance to Georgetown hospital. Looks like they've been injected with something."

"Prognosis?"

"Tate's not breathing—they're working on him. Shaw's in better shape, but not much."

His jaw clenched. "Taylor?"

"She's gone. I checked the motel phone. There was one call listed. She phoned le Clerc."

Fischer's phone rang as he boarded the chopper. It was le Clerc.

"I've just had an interesting call from Ms. Jones."

"Where is she?"

"The information carries a price."

Fischer's jaw tightened. "You want the ledger."

"I need the original. A copy won't carry any weight in an international court of law."

"It can be arranged. Where's Taylor?"

"At midnight she'll be in Portland, Maine." He supplied the address of a popular motel just off U.S. Highway One.

"Who has her?"

"He's American, male. The accent is West Coast. L.A., perhaps. He wants the ledger and he thinks I'm going to deliver it in exchange for Ms. Jones's life."

Not Tripp. *Colenso.*

The conditions were predictable, the timetable compressed. Xavier was to go alone and bring the original copy of the book. When he reached the motel he would receive instructions about the precise location of the handover. He would be watched. If anyone else was involved, the deal was off and Taylor was dead.

It was a given that the deal was a setup. The only certainty was that Taylor would be alive at the time of the handover, because Colenso couldn't risk losing his leverage before that point.

Fischer checked his watch. Four hours. "I'm going to need help." Colenso was smart—he would have backup—but Fischer was willing to bet that le Clerc and his team were smarter. The Frenchman's network was serpentine, elusive and motivated. They would blend in in a way the new agents replacing Shaw and Tate couldn't. If nothing else, le Clerc would guarantee the safety of the book.

"It can be arranged."

"Then we have a deal. Just one last thing. How good is your boy with explosives?"

Thirty-Three

Lubec, Maine

Helene Reichmann concealed her car on the deserted stretch of road overlooking the sea. A black van pulled in behind her. Several men dressed in black combat gear and equipped with night vision and automatic weapons flowed out. Within minutes they had dispersed, melting into the windswept trees that edged Ritter's driveway.

Moving slowly, she picked her way down the pitch-dark driveway, pausing frequently to allow her vision to adjust to the intense dark and to listen. Not that either senses would do her any good if Lopez had gotten here before them.

The lights of a lone two-storied beach cottage came into view and she quickened her pace.

Ritter's hideaway, built in a north-facing cove that not only carried a similar name but in its own small way mimicked the icy hell that the port of Lubeck in Germany had been, was tiny compared to the mansion he kept in Boston. Ritter liked his privacy, particularly when he came to the beach, and it was that hermit philosophy she was counting on. He employed a local woman to cook and clean, but he didn't have any staff living on the premises.

Security lights flooded the porch as she walked up the steps. Flexing her fingers against the cold, she pressed the buzzer.

Long minutes later, she wondered if she'd gotten it wrong and he wasn't here. Parker had been running for the mountains when Lopez had cut him down; it was possible Ritter was doing the same, although she would put money on the fact that Ritter wouldn't panic. She leaned on the buzzer again.

The door swung open a few inches.

Ritter's gaze was wary. "Helene?"

She flinched. "I told you never to call me that."

"What do you want?"

"In case you haven't noticed, we have an emergency on our hands."

He looked past her. "How did you get here? Where's your car?"

Helene took the impact of the solid cedar door as it slammed closed on her shoulder. Wedging one booted foot in the gap, she fumbled in her pocket, produced a gun and pointed it through the gap. She hadn't chambered a round, but the old fool wouldn't know that. "We need to talk."

The pressure on the door eased. Helene stepped inside and closed the door. "Into the library."

Ritter was an entrepreneur, a mathematical genius with an uncanny talent with stocks and shares. He had taken the small chunk of the cabal's money she had allotted him and built an empire.

He stared at Helene with his light gray eyes, and a shudder worked its way down her spine. He had always been odd, a little too brilliant and insightful, and with that uncanny instinct for the future. In her opinion, despite his prodigy status, at times he verged uncomfortably close to abnormal—and not in a good way. Sometimes she had been convinced he could read her mind. Years ago she had been almost certain he had guessed about the book.

His stare was fixed but slightly unfocused now, as if he was looking at something she couldn't see, a trait that had always infuriated her. When he spoke he used German, his voice halting and guttural, spinning her back to the months spent at the institute in Berlin, the long weeks cooped up on the *Nordika*. "You haven't come to talk. You've come to kill me."

She lifted the gun. The first bullet caught him

in the center of the chest, the second an inch off to the left. He died quickly, with surprisingly little fuss and hardly any mess.

Dispassionately, she stepped back from his crumpled form and the pungent smells that filled the room, and positioned the gun back in her pocket. One more loose end tied up.

Leaving the light on in the study, she systematically walked around the house and switched every other light off. When she was satisfied that the house was secure, she mounted the stairs and sat in the deep shadow of the first landing. The position gave her a clear view of the front door and the study.

Satisfied that the trap was set and that she had taken every precaution, she took out the gun and settled in to wait for Lopez.

Thirty-Four

Taylor came to lying on the chilly surface of a hardwood floor. She felt sick and sluggish and so cold convulsive shudders kept jerking through her. She also had a pounding headache. From the throbbing, localized on one side of her head, it was an easy bet that Colenso had dropped her on the floor.

"Take a seat."

Colenso came into focus, comfortably sprawled on a leather couch, a leather coat and a woolen scarf keeping the chill at bay. Memory flooded back.

When they had left the motel, Colenso had forced her to climb into his car at gunpoint. Le Clerc had rung back within minutes and she had picked up the call. He had asked to speak to Colenso. When

Colenso terminated the call, he had stabbed a hypodermic into her thigh.

He hadn't told her which drug he'd used. By the time he informed her that she was once more high on ketamine, she had been in no state to care.

He grinned, obviously having the time of his life, and waved his gun at an armchair situated off to one side. "I insist."

She pushed up into a sitting position. She was still cuffed, which made moving difficult. While she waited for her head to stop swimming, she took stock of her surroundings. The room was large, and strategically lit with lamps and wall lighting placed to highlight works of art and paintings. She didn't know a lot about antiques, but the few pieces she could see looked very old and expensive.

Outside she could hear the unmistakable sound of surf. A large bank of windows that presumably looked out over the sea but were presently blacked out by the night dominated the room. An empty fireplace occupied one wall, the pale, gray stone perfectly fitted and as cold in appearance as the temperature.

Using the arm of the chair to steady her, she hauled herself upright and sat down.

A gust of wind buffeted the house. The windows shuddered, shifting the garish reflection of Colenso and herself. "How long have I been out?"

Colenso checked his watch. "Approximately three hours."

She stared at a painting on the wall. Art was something she did know a bit about, courtesy of a narcotics bust where the currency had been stolen art. "The Degas looks authentic."

"It's real. So are the Picassos."

She examined the paintings positioned on the stark stretch of wall behind her. Not one Picasso; three.

"The smaller of the set was damaged in transit."

She stared at Colenso. "From Germany?"

He smiled. "Colombia. Although my father was on the *Nordika*."

Pushing to his feet, he walked across to an elegant side table and poured himself a drink from a crystal decanter. "Technically, my telling you that I'm a cabal member earns me the death penalty, but that was before Lopez started his little rampage. Now the rules have changed."

At a guess, Colenso was making them up as he went along. "He hasn't got all of the upper echelon yet."

His gaze sharpened. "How do you know that?"

"Le Clerc." She was bluffing, but anything that made Colenso feel less secure had to work in her favor.

He shrugged. "Lopez can't kill us all, only a

selected few, and most of them are past their used-by date."

The pronouncement was chilling, highlighting the real personality that Colenso had successfully masked for years.

Taylor worked her fingers, stimulating the blood flow as she skimmed the sitting room. Most of the surfaces were bare. She couldn't see Colenso's wallet or the keys he'd used to lock the cuffs, which meant he was either carrying them in his pocket or had them stashed in the briefcase she'd seen on the backseat of his car. "Lopez has finished the cabal. No criminal network can survive that kind of exposure. Reichmann will close you down."

He set his empty glass down. A muscle worked along his jaw. The silence drew out, punctuated by the increasing whine of the wind and the spatter of rain on the windows. "Who told you about Reichmann?"

Taylor spotted the briefcase, slotted beneath the elegant side table that held the decanter. Unless Colenso left the room, there was no way she could get to it to search for the keys. "That she really runs the show, and that she's not included in the book that she lost? Who do you think?"

His stare was intense. "What le Clerc knows about the cabal wouldn't cover the back of a postage stamp."

"But it's enough to take it down. Nazis operating on U.S. soil? The media will go crazy. The witch hunt will make McCarthyism look like an Easter egg trail."

"It won't happen."

"You can't stop it"

"Yes, I can." He picked up the briefcase, laid it on the table, flipped it open and pulled out a plastic Ziploc bag with a syringe in it. "And you're going to help me."

She stared at the syringe. "The damage control's a bit late. Lopez has already killed three cabal members."

He smiled. "Did you think we didn't know what Lopez was up to? As far as Reichmann's concerned, Lopez couldn't be doing a better job if he were on the payroll."

Her stomach sank. That answered one question. Colenso didn't work for the cabal as a whole; he worked directly for Reichmann. His interest was in protecting her. As long as she survived, Colenso was still in business. "Reichmann might be safe for now, but Lopez won't stop."

His stare was direct and cold. "He won't reach her. Reichmann is connected."

Radcliff had been a senator. If one member of the cabal had managed to step into the political process, it was a given that others had, too. Fischer was investigating on the basis that national security was threatened from within the country's security agencies. "What are you talking? Political? Or the Intelligence community?"

"Come on, Jones, you can do better than that."

Higher than the intelligence community itself meant he was talking the White House. "So, what now?"

He smiled. "We drive to the motel."

Colenso's cell phone buzzed. He answered, speaking in monosyllables, then hung up.

"Who was that?"

"Not lover boy."

Her stomach sank. He had seen through the ruse with le Clerc. He knew he was dealing with Fischer.

The phone rang twice more. Colenso's conversations were brief and concise; he was putting his men in position.

Colenso walked over to an occasional table, pulled on latex gloves and took her gun from his briefcase. He checked the clip, extracted his own gun from his shoulder holster and replaced it with hers, and suddenly the full scope of Colenso's plan was crystal clear. He wasn't happy just to reclaim the book. He was going to ambush Fischer, and anyone else who made the meeting at the motel. Using her gun, he would then stage the scene to make it look as if she was one of the killers. Once she was dead, he would plant the syringe on her, linking her to Shaw and Tate's deaths. His choice of ketamine—a drug that had sent her into months of therapy and had, arguably, lost her her job—made sudden sense.

The tabloids would love it. When interviewed, Colenso would make sure to emphasize her past association with Lopez, her problems with ketamine, and leak the false surveillance report that had "exposed" her as the FBI mole. In one stroke he would have cemented her role as Lopez's insider in the FBI and covered his own trail, and Reichmann's.

If the plan ran smoothly and Reichmann managed to influence her "connections," support for the investigation into the cabal could be scaled down or even withdrawn. Reichmann would remain anonymous and protected and Lopez and Taylor would go down in history as the villains.

The only hitch in Colenso's plan was the existence of the ledger, which was incendiary enough to guarantee a continued flow of support for the investigation. But if Colenso destroyed the original and Lopez's copy never came to light, that avenue to expose the cabal network would be gone. "What about Lopez? He's not going to stop."

Colenso shrugged. "Now that we know he's working to a list, every time he kills he presents us with an opportunity to take him down."

Us. The calmness of his statement reminded her that Colenso was working with a team. His men would already be in place at the motel he'd chosen.

She had never thought of Colenso as particularly clever, but he was. He was keeping her alive for now, but only because he couldn't afford to kill her until shortly before he did the other killings. If he shot her now, rigor would set in, negating the "evidence" of his staged murder scene. He needed all of the murders to happen within a window of an hour and, preferably, just a few minutes.

He picked up the briefcase and jerked his head toward the door. "Time to leave."

Minutes later, Colenso turned off the narrow country lane and onto a highway. Taylor stared at the landscape, now dotted with houses. A luminous sign indicated they were entering the city limits of Portland. Traffic thickened. They had to be close to the motel, so she didn't have much time. Colenso braked. Across the intersection a highway patrol car was stopped, waiting for the lights.

Suddenly, she knew what she had to do. Fischer would know it was a setup, but if he had to play by Colenso's rules he wouldn't stand a chance. If she could attract some attention, maybe even get them stopped by the highway patrol, she would have a chance at escaping. At the very least, she could delay Colenso's schedule and give Fischer the opening he needed.

The lights turned green.

"I feel sick." She leaned forward and used the

movement to fumble at the seat belt clasp. The belt went slack.

The patrol car flashed past. Sucking in a breath, she flung herself sideways, grasped the wheel and wrenched. The car spun sideways across the road. Horns blared, tires screamed. The gnarled branches of a tree appeared, suspended, in the headlights. A split second later the car hit the tree with a sickening jolt and she was flung sideways.

The engine screamed as Colenso put the car in Reverse. The tires spun, then finally gained traction, and the car shot back. Scrabbling for the door, she tried to get out. The door, which was locked, wouldn't open.

She heard the snick as Colenso unbuckled his seat belt. Instinctively, Taylor swung, using the cuffs. Blood arced from Colenso's mouth. She had a moment to register the recoil of his fist, then hot light exploded inside her skull and everything went black.

Thirty-Five

When she came to, the car was parked on a quiet side street, which meant Colenso had managed to get the car back on the road. Dimly, she could hear the sound of a siren in the distance.

Colenso climbed out, then reached in and pulled her across the driver's-side seat. "If you're awake, you can walk. If you don't walk, I'll shoot you now. We're close enough."

Apart from the glow of the motel light and the residential houses clustered around it, the street was pitch-black. Colenso—or Fischer—had taken out the street lighting. Hope surged. Her money was on Fischer.

His fingers bit into her upper arm as he pulled her out of the car. He kept a tight grip on her arm as they walked.

Taylor scanned the street. It appeared to be empty but, from the conversations she'd overheard, she knew Colenso had at least three men staking out the meeting, and probably more.

Keeping to the shadows, they turned into the parking lot.

Deliberately, Taylor dragged her feet. "How's your schedule?"

"We're on time. Hold out your hands." He jabbed the barrel of the gun in her throat, unlocked the cuffs and put them in his pocket. "Talk again and I'll shoot."

As they passed motel units with vehicles parked outside, her gaze was automatically drawn by a gray truck. There was no mud spattering the wheel rims or toolbox fitted to the rear of the cab. It wasn't Fischer's truck, but it was the same model and the same color. Her heart sped up as she skimmed the rest of the vehicles parked outside the units. They were mostly sedans, with the odd SUV just for variety. At a guess, the sedans belonged to the motel's business clients, the SUVs to tourists on holiday. The truck, a no-nonsense workhorse of a vehicle, stood out like a sore thumb.

As they got closer, she noticed the plate. It was a rental, and suddenly she was certain Fischer had placed it there. He had rented the same model truck that he owned and parked it outside the motel unit as a signal.

Movement flickered in the unit opposite where the truck was parked. Colenso's head whipped around. A series of detonations filled the air with thick, choking smoke. Time seemed to slow, freeze. A door was flung open and metal glinted. Simultaneously, a dark figure flowed up from one of the small gardens separating the units. *"Taylor, down."*

Fischer.

Colenso's hand came up. He was already firing, his grip viselike as he pulled her back toward him, using her as a shield.

Smoke swirled, stinging her eyes. The air stank of cordite. Fischer was down. Raw panic exploded, a fierce sense of disbelief. A dark shadow appeared next to Colenso, then a second. His men, she realized.

She heard the roar of a powerful engine and headlights cut through the smoke. A van braked to a halt; the passenger-side door slid open. A burst of gunfire split the air; one of Colenso's men went down. Colenso jerked her toward the van. The change in direction gave her the momentum she needed. Instead of pulling away, she surged toward the opening. As Colenso stumbled, off balance, she spun, grabbed the hand holding the gun and used her momentum to slam it against the side of the van.

Colenso grunted. The gun skittered across the asphalt. Tearing free of his grip, she flung herself clear.

"Bitch."

The door slammed as she pushed to her feet. The van accelerated out onto the road, fishtailed and shunted aside a vehicle blocking the exit. Gunfire erupted, the sharp thud of rounds hitting metal punctuating the roar of the engine as the van disappeared from sight.

She picked up the gun Colenso had used—*her* gun—and stumbled over to Fischer. He was sprawled on his back. For a heart-stopping moment she thought he was dead, even though she knew he had to be wearing body armor.

Relief poured through her as he wrenched at the Velcro fastenings of the Kevlar vest he was wearing and sucked in a breath. Colenso's sustained firing had knocked him over, but the ceramic plates in his vest had taken the brunt of the impact. He was winded and bruised, but otherwise unharmed.

Fischer spoke rapidly into a mike, bringing himself up to speed with the search for Colenso. When a dark shadow—one of his men—melted out of the trees, he pulled her to her feet, retrieved his automatic weapon, and urged her out onto the street and into the rear of a van similar to the one Colenso had used.

Fischer leaned in the door. "Bridges is staying with you."

Bridges, the dark shadow, stepped into the van

and closed the door. He pulled off his balaclava and held out his hand. "You can call me Matt."

She shook his hand. Young, fit, a Southern accent and very short hair. At a guess, ex-Navy.

She stared in the direction Fischer had gone. "What happened to Shaw and Tate?"

The warmth in Bridges's expression evaporated. "Shaw's in recovery, Tate's on life support. We'll know in a few hours."

Within twenty minutes, several of Portland's police cruisers had blocked off the street and a news crew had arrived. The last of Fischer's team, which for this operation had included a number of FBI agents, their faces blanked out by balaclavas, had piled into a second van and left. Fischer, a balaclava now in place courtesy of the camera crew, had wrapped up the formalities with the Portland PD. Colenso's men, the five that had been caught, had been charged with attempted murder, resisting arrest and a number of weapons offences, and had been taken to the Portland police station for processing. Since two had criminal records and one had a warrant out for his arrest, the likelihood that any of them would be released on bail was slim.

The operation had been high risk, and only partially successful. Taylor had survived, but Colenso had managed to slip the net.

Visibility deteriorated as a heavy, cold rain set

in. The news crew left, frustrated by the weather and the lack of action. The van door slid open, but this time it wasn't Fischer. Dana Jones, followed by Jack, climbed in out of the rain.

Taylor's throat closed up. Of all the things she hadn't expected to happen, this was at the top of the list. The meeting could only have been arranged by Fischer; no one else had the pull *and* the nerve.

Dana hugged Taylor, the pressure fierce. "Fischer's given us five minutes, then we have a rendezvous with a chopper at an airfield just outside of Portland."

That, at least, made sense. With Jack's past, Fischer would want to avoid the airport itself, because the press would be staking it out, expecting at least some of the personnel, maybe even the prisoners, to fly out from there. "Where to?"

Dana sat next to Taylor, keeping a firm grip on her hand.

Jack took an adjacent seat. "Florida."

Taylor glanced at Dana. "You're going with him?"

Her expression was wary. "For a couple of weeks. Maybe. I need some time out."

The van door slid open again. Fischer pulled off his balaclava. "Time to go."

Dana hugged her again. "Stay in touch. You've got my number."

A vehicle pulled up next to the van. Dana and Jack ducked into the rear passenger seats. Seconds later, Fischer motioned for Taylor to step out.

The rain had eased to a filmy mist that wreathed the sidewalk and trailed across the road. The crowd of onlookers that had gathered to watch the show had thinned, driven off by the rain and the fact that for the past hour, nothing of any note had happened.

Fischer dug in his pocket for a set of keys and depressed a locking mechanism. Ahead a vehicle beeped and lit up. Taylor recognized the gray truck that had been parked in at the motel. Fischer must have moved it out to the road, which made sense, because the motel was still choked with police cruisers and sealed off from traffic.

Climbing into the truck felt like going home, which didn't make any kind of sense, since it was a rental, and nothing about Fischer should represent "home."

Fischer pulled out from the curb. She studied the houses flashing by. A lone highway sign indicated they were heading west, not south—the direction she had expected him to take. "Where are we going?"

"Vermont. Cold Peak is about two hours away."

The sense that Fischer wasn't playing by the rules intensified. He had liaised with the Portland PD and the Bureau, but if he was following procedure he should have joined his men for the debriefing. "What's going on?" The question was rhetorical. She already knew they were out on a limb; she just had to understand why.

His gaze connected with hers, hot and edgy and undeniably male. *Question answered.*

"Burdett will have your head on a platter."

"It'll be worth it."

He handed her his cell phone. "If you want out, all you have to do is put a call through to Burdett."

Taylor set the phone back down.

Thirty-Six

At two in the morning, a creak on the stairs jerked Helene out of the dazed limbo she'd fallen into.

She stared at the deep well of darkness. There was nothing there.

She remained frozen, the gun locked into position, oblivious to the burning pain in her shoulders and arms. Lopez hadn't shown. If he had, her men would have opened fire and he would have died.

For long moments she sat, listening to the incessant sound of the wind and the sea. She checked her watch. It was time to leave.

Lopez had won this round. Somehow, with that uncanny instinct he had, he had known. Which meant she had to be extra careful leaving. He could be waiting for her outside. If he wasn't personally there, he would have someone waiting to tail her.

She'd made the mistake of underestimating him. He had known that she was aware of his killing agenda and that there was only one name left on the list. He had also known that she had chosen to protect herself at the expense of the others. Now—too late—it made a twisted kind of sense that he had stepped back on the last kill, leaving her to carry out the execution and saving him the trouble, but the irony didn't amuse Helene.

Using the banister to haul herself to her feet, she made her way down the stairs, wincing at the stiffness of muscles and joints that were no longer young. As she passed the pool of light in the study, she glimpsed Ritter's legs and remembered that he was dead. For a brief moment she regretted his loss. He had been dangerous but brilliant; she could have used his mind. For the first time in her life she felt truly alone.

Now, it was just her...and Lopez.

The glare of street lighting woke Taylor. She checked the clock on the dash. It was just after two in the morning and she'd been asleep almost the whole time they'd been driving.

Fischer stopped for an intersection and a familiar sign registered. They were in Cold Peak.

The light turned green. Fischer accelerated through the deserted intersection. "Tomorrow you can collect your cat and anything else you need from your place."

Smothering a yawn, she straightened. "And then what? Back on the Witness Security program?"

"Until we run Colenso to ground."

And then what? But she wasn't about to voice that question. Fischer was breaking the rules for one night. It wasn't good enough, but if it was all she was going to get, she was taking it.

Minutes later, Fischer pulled into his driveway.

Walking into the house was bittersweet. Fischer dropped his gear bag on the floor, kicked the door closed behind them and walked toward her. Taylor wound her arms around his neck. This time, for her at least, there was no ambiguity. What she wanted was clear.

His mouth came down on hers as he walked her backward in the direction of the bedroom. The first kiss was unexpectedly soft, the second even sweeter. Her palms slid upward, peeling off his T-shirt. Seconds later, her shirt dropped to the floor and the back of her knees hit the bed.

The bedroom was dark, the air faintly stuffy after days of the house being shut up. Light from the sitting room outlined Fischer's shoulders as he unhooked her bra and peeled off her jeans, glanced off the planes of his face as he pulled her toward him. Winding her arms around his neck, she arched into him and lifted her mouth for his kiss.

Reaching down, she unfastened his pants. He felt hot and sleek and smooth. He hadn't had time to put a condom on, and abruptly, she didn't want one. The decision was primitive and instinctual. She loved him; she had almost lost him. After tonight, she didn't know when she would see him again, if ever.

He cupped her face, his expression intense. A split second later they were on the bed and he was inside her. His mouth came down on hers and the night dissolved.

The sound of Fischer's phone woke Taylor. He was sitting on the side of the bed wearing pants but no shirt, his hair still damp from the shower.

He answered the call, then moments later flipped the phone closed. "Bridges has a reported sighting of Colenso."

She raised herself on one elbow. "Portland?"

"Just south. I have to go." He leaned over and kissed her, his mouth firm, the kiss brief.

Taylor watched as he pulled on a fresh shirt. "Is that a 'goodbye, honey, I'm off to work' kiss?"

He shrugged into his shoulder holster as he walked toward the bed. "That's an 'if I touch you again, I won't leave' kiss."

He leaned down. This time the kiss was longer.

"Don't leave the house unless you need to, and don't go into town. If you want to collect Buster, you

can use Tate's car, which is parked in the garage."
He extracted a set of car keys and some bills from
his wallet and left them on the bedside table. "If you
need food, order it in. I'll be back tonight."

"And Burdett?"

Unexpectedly, he grinned, teeth flashing white
against his tanned skin. "We'll talk about it when
I get home."

The front door closed behind him. Taylor listened for the sound of his truck as he backed out
onto the road and accelerated away, then pushed
back the covers and slid out of bed. According to
the alarm clock, it was just after nine.

She gathered up her clothing, took one of
Fischer's shirts from his drawer and walked
through to the bathroom. She needed fresh underwear, but that would have to wait until she picked
up Buster. On the way through town she could call
in at one of the malls and do a little shopping.

As she stepped under the warm spray of the
shower, she reviewed the pulse-pounding hours
she and Fischer had spent locked together. There
hadn't been a lot of time for conversation, but as
curt and unemotionally stated as it had been, the
phrase "when I get home" was unexpectedly sweet.

When she'd dressed and combed out her hair,
Taylor picked up the phone and rang the cattery.
Seconds later she set the receiver back down. Neil
had picked Buster up two days ago.

Perplexed that Neil had collected Buster early, when there was no way he could keep an eye on him when he was at work, she called the computer shop. An unfamiliar female voice answered. Neil had been sick for a couple of days and he wasn't due back in for the rest of the week.

Frowning, Taylor hung up and dialed Neil's home number.

When Neil picked up the phone, his voice was croaky but recognizable. He had collected Buster because when he had rung the cattery to check on him, the vet had said Buster had been sick and off his food. Since he was home with a virus, he had decided to collect Buster early.

Taylor got directions for his house and hung up.

The drive to the small cottage Neil rented took less than five minutes. Locking the car, she strolled to the front gate, automatically checking out the street, which was lined with an eclectic mix of modern bungalows sitting cheek by jowl with the old miners' cottages that had formed the original heart of Cold Peak. Stately oaks lined the street, softening the down-at-heel appearance of some of the houses.

She studied Neil's cottage, which was definitely on the down-at-heel side. Despite the sunny weather, the house was shut up and the curtains were drawn. Farther down the street she could hear the blare of a radio, and across the road a baby was crying. In contrast Neil's cottage was silent, although if he was as ill as he had sounded on the phone, that was no surprise. He was probably in bed and simply wanted to sleep.

She lifted the latch on the gate and stepped onto the mossy, overgrown path. Instead of walking directly to the house, she checked out the small adjacent garage. Neil's car, visible through a small window, was a sporty SUV painted metallic purple with ski racks and, from the look of the speakers at the rear of the vehicle, a state-of-the-art stereo system. The vehicle went with his character, slightly quirky and demonstrating his love of equipment.

She walked around the side of the garage and found a side door standing slightly ajar. When she stepped inside, she almost tripped over a cat cage.

Already on edge that the garage door had been left open, leaving Neil's car, which was in all likelihood the most expensive asset he owned, open to theft, she studied the cage.

She didn't own a cat cage, which meant either Neil had bought one, or the cattery had loaned him the cage when he had taken Buster. The fact that the cage was open made her frown, although it was possible Neil had carried the cage inside the house before opening it. Feeling even more unsettled, she did a circuit of the garage and checked underneath the SUV, just in case Buster had bolted and taken refuge in the garage. She was tempted to call his name, but an inbuilt caution kept her quiet. Neil's cottage was giving her a definite creepy feeling.

When she had exhausted all possibilities in the garage, she did a circuit of the house. As she studied the silent cottage, the breeze lifted and a tree branch scraped over the side of the house. For a disorienting moment she had a flashback to Letty's house and the moment she had stepped into the hall and seen the old lady's body. Tension tightened down her spine and a small, inane fact registered.

Neil was a computer buff. On the phone he had said he had a *virus,* not a cold or the flu.

Thirty-Seven

Fischer took a call as he drove. Tate was out of danger, although, like Shaw, he would be in recovery for days. The drug Colenso had used should have put them both into cardiac arrest. Their survival was owed to Bridges getting them almost immediate medical attention.

Relieved, he set the phone down and tried to concentrate on driving. After what had happened last night—and this morning—his normal level of concentration was shot. After months of meticulous planning, nothing about the investigation, or Taylor, was predictable.

The sun glanced off the windshield of a passing car, a spot of brightness in a dull day, and without warning, the road seemed to disappear. For an endless moment he was staring at a face, although this time it wasn't his father, it was Taylor.

The image dissolved, replaced by the windscreen of an oncoming car. He wrenched the wheel and the truck swung back onto the right side of the road. The car flashed past, fishtailing. His right front tire hit the verge and the truck slid sideways, plowing through a ditch before coming to a halt inches short of a fence.

Throwing the truck into Reverse, he depressed the accelerator. The tires spun and the rear wheels dug more deeply into the mud. Unbuckling his seat belt, Fischer shoved the door open, climbed out of the cab and adjusted the hubs. Seconds later, he put the truck in four-wheel drive and drove off the verge. As soon as he hit the hard surface of the highway, he adjusted the hubs for on-road use, did a U-turn and headed back toward Cold Peak.

He wasn't psychic. He had only had one other vision before, and that had happened when he had been eight years old and his father had died. Back then, the image of his father's face had been accompanied by a suffocating pressure in his chest. This time there had been no physical symptoms.

His phone vibrated. It was Bridges. Colenso's body had just turned up at the Portland morgue. He had been executed: a double tap to the back of the head.

Fischer's jaw tightened. "Call Bayard. Tell him his man is in Cold Peak. It's Martin Tripp."

* * *

Taylor stopped to listen. The wind rustled gently in the trees, emphasizing the damp chill of the day. Next door, she could hear the television playing out a morning soap. In the distance was the steady hum of traffic. The wind gusted, branches scraped against windows and dry leaves flipped along the ground.

She hadn't seen any sign of Buster outside, and she didn't have a cell phone, so she couldn't ring from the safety of Tate's car and ask Neil to step out of the house. The sensible thing to do would be to leave.

Moving slowly, she retraced her steps. She was beginning to feel faintly ridiculous. Neil was sick and obviously bedridden. Buster was probably sleeping on the end of his bed. Colenso had been sighted south of Portland that morning. It was unlikely he could have made it to Cold Peak by now.

On impulse, she stepped closer to the house and peered into a window. Through a gap in the curtains she could make out a pair of feet tied to the end of a bed. The metallic click of a round being chambered made her freeze. She let out a breath. "What are you going to do, Tripp? Shoot me in the back of the head?"

"I've thought about it."

"Shooting me in Cold Peak wouldn't be smart, and I think you're a lot smarter than you've ever made out."

"Put your hands on your head. Turn around and face me. That's better." He indicated with his gun that she move away from the side of the house. His gaze was cold and as steady as the hand that held the gun. "When I was twelve, tests showed I had an IQ of one hundred and seventy."

"And I bet your daddy's IQ was even higher."

"Both of my parents had genius IQ's."

She cocked her head on one side. "Helene Reichmann?"

Tripp's expression didn't change. "Don't try the psychological stuff. I'm better at it than you."

"If it wasn't Reichmann, who was it? I bet you lost someone near and dear. Three cabal members have been murdered—"

"Four. We killed the final mark."

A shadow flickered. Her gaze followed the movement. She caught a flash of white fur.

Tripp's mouth flattened. "Don't bother with the tricks—"

A sound halfway between a howl and a wail jerked Tripp's head around. Taylor took a gamble and launched at him, chopping at the gun. Tripp's fist caught her in the jaw, knocking her sideways. She hit the ground, twisting and rolling to lessen the impact. The gun detonated and dirt kicked up, showering her face.

She surged to her feet. Tripp leveled the gun for a second shot and seemed to slow, stop, as she looked directly down the barrel of the gun. A split second later the side of Tripp's head vaporized. Another round punched through his chest, but the insurance wasn't required: he was dead before he hit the ground.

Taylor stared at the lone figure stepping through the front gate, the Bernadelli still held in a two-handed grip and aimed at Tripp's prone body, and wondered why she was surprised to see Fischer.

With a shudder she wiped her palms, which were speckled with blood, on her jeans, and stepped around Tripp. When he had aimed at her the second time, her arms must have flung up to "stop" the bullet, although she had no memory of doing it.

Her legs were distinctly shaky as she walked toward Fischer

He had made the shot from the sidewalk with a handgun. That had to be more than seventy feet, yet he had been pinpoint accurate, aiming at Tripp's head.

Normally, in a high-risk situation, it was standard procedure to shoot for the chest area but a chest shot didn't ensure that the target was taken out, whereas the head shot did.

He surveyed the grounds and the house. "Is there anyone else?"

"I checked out the house before Tripp turned up. There doesn't appear to be anyone in there except Neil, and he's tied to the bed."

Still holding the gun on Tripp, he jerked her into his arms. "I thought I was going to be too late."

Taylor's heart squeezed tight at the rawness of Fischer's expression, at everything he hadn't said but which was plainly present in his eyes. And in that moment she decided the pros and cons of falling in love with him didn't matter; she loved him, period. She had obsessed about his motives for getting close to her, but the reality was he had been there for her in the exact moment she had needed him most. With Fischer's degree of accuracy with a handgun he could have chosen to wound Tripp and keep him alive, but he had made a choice; he had blown Tripp away, choosing *her* instead of preserving a major lead in his investigation.

Her arms clamped around his neck, the movement convulsive. She'd read that scent was the most powerful sense, and right then she could attest to that. Fischer smelled hot and edgy and wonderfully familiar.

Dipping his head, Fischer fastened his mouth on hers. Long seconds later he lifted his head and released her. "Time to go to work."

After Taylor and Fischer had conducted a comprehensive search of the property, Taylor located a kitchen knife and cut Neil's legs free. The cuffs Tripp had used to fasten his hands to the bed took a little longer, because she had to find the keys.

Luckily, she located them in Tripp's briefcase and didn't have to search the body.

Pushing to his feet, Neil stared out of the window at Tripp's body. "Is he dead?"

"Would you have a problem if he was?"

Neil turned away from the window, his expression stark. "No."

Fischer walked in the door, the gun still in his hand. "Muir's here."

Taylor recognized two of Cold Peak's finest with Muir—Driscoll and Hart—along with two other officers she hadn't met.

Within minutes the house was cordoned off, and Neil was taken to the Cold Peak medical center for a check over, although from an initial examination his only physical symptoms were chafing on his ankles and wrists and dehydration. Half an hour later, with the coroner's clearance, Tripp's body was bagged and removed, and the complications of jurisdiction had been smoothed out with a phone call from Fischer's boss, Rear Admiral Saunders. Muir wasn't happy. Cold Peak was front-page news, and the paperwork would keep him tied to his desk for weeks, but he couldn't argue with the fact that his double homicide had been solved.

With Tripp's body out of the way, Taylor and Fischer did a circuit of the house, searching for Buster. Taylor gave the flattened area of grass where Tripp had been lying a wide berth as she began calling. At the first call, Buster began to howl.

Crouching down, she parted the leaves of a dense rhododendron. It took long minutes, and Fischer retreating several yards, before Buster finally materialized from the shadows. Seconds later, she scooped him up. He was tense and on edge, his pupils dilated, but the reason he was so desperate was plain. He had lost weight, and if Tripp had picked him up two days ago, he probably hadn't been fed since.

Fischer opened the door of the cat cage. Taylor pushed Buster in, slammed the door and fastened it before he could double around and shoot back out. The moment was oddly warming. Not exactly your quintessential family snapshot, but close enough.

Thirty-Eight

The house in Portland, Maine, was relatively new, an expensive designer aerie set on a cliff overlooking a wild coastline. Xavier studied the waves surging in against dark rocks. Despite the extensive plantings there was clear evidence that there had been a large house here before. When he had rung the local council the previous day, his findings had been verified. This had originally been the site of the old Webster mansion, which had been built in the nineteen hundreds. It had burned to the ground in 1954, the same year his father had disappeared.

At the time the mansion had burned down the owner had been listed as Charles Everett Richmond. Richmond, a reclusive millionaire, had perished in the fire, and the house had passed to his daughter, Elizabeth, who had sold it soon after. The property had changed hands just once more, when Tripp had bought it.

Xavier's spine tingled as he studied the lay of the land, and his conviction that he had found the location of Reichmann's house—and the site of his father's murder—grew. According to the original plans of the Webster mansion, which he had viewed in the local historical society's archives earlier that afternoon, there had been a cellar beneath the house that had linked with a series of natural caves. He hadn't found anything resembling a cellar entrance in the house that presently occupied the site, which meant the entrance had to be somewhere in the gardens.

Fifteen minutes later, one of Xavier's agents, Tony, jimmied open the lock of a garden shed. Xavier stepped inside and immediately noted the unmistakable outline of a trapdoor.

Flicking on the flashlight he'd brought with him, he lifted the trapdoor, tested the first step of the ladder, then descended into the cavity and waited for Tony to join him.

The cellar was cavernous and empty. Breath pluming on the stale, cold air, Xavier conducted a circuit of the room, ducked beneath a beam and found a second door. Within minutes, Tony had broken the locks and Xavier stepped inside.

The beam of the flashlight caromed off thick

stone walls, and caught on the glint of a cap badge and the dull gleam of boots. For an electrifying moment, childhood fear and illusion fused, imbuing the sagging uniforms of Himmler's *Schutzstaffel* with horrifying life.

Emotion grabbed at Xavier, sharper and more intense than he'd expected as he trained the beam on the faded collection of uniforms and studied the evidence that his father had found. Evidence he had waited decades—and traveled thousands of miles—to find.

Within minutes the cellar and the connecting caves had been searched. Apart from the uniforms, a dusty table and a squat safe, circa 1920s, its door still hanging open, every room and cavity was empty.

There was evidence from the scrapes on the floor that heavy objects had been stored here. There was nothing to indicate that those objects had been the crates transported on the *Nordika*, although logic dictated that they must have been. It was inconceivable that Reichmann would have relinquished control of the wealth. After Reichmann's death, Helene would have had to secure the treasure and establish control of the cabal. The artifacts and gold bullion would have been transported to another location within days.

The safe was a different matter. It weighed a ton. Lifting it out would have required a great deal of effort for no discernible gain. Back in the fifties it was the kind of safe that had been routinely owned by thousands of businesses. The only aberration had been that Helene had left the uniforms behind.

The risk that the moldering clothing represented had been small. Colenso had owned the property and if anyone but Xavier had found the uniforms, they would have been no more than a curiosity. The mistake revealed arrogance and Helene's belief in her own invincibility, distinct flaws in an otherwise clinical approach. At a guess, she had enjoyed the knowledge that Reichmann and the officers under his command still lived on, if only in the hidden, tattered remnants of their uniforms.

Footsteps echoed. Light flickered as Tony ducked under the beam and paused in the doorway. "We've completed the search of the grounds. Sorry, no sign of a graveyard."

The faint hope that his father's body had been buried somewhere on the property was extinguished. "That's it, then." It was far more likely that Helene would have disposed of Stefan's body in a way that guaranteed he wouldn't be found. It was even possible she had dumped his body at sea, although that would have been difficult to organize without involving someone local in the process.

Tony trained his flashlight on the uniforms, his expression registering his distaste. "Why don't you check out the local cemeteries and parish registers. If Stefan died in the fire at the same time as Reichmann, it's possible his body was found before Helene could dispose of it. If that was the case, when the postmortem was finished she might have had the influence to destroy the paperwork, but she would have been forced to bury his body. Even if she managed to remove his papers and substitute a false name, the date of death would be the same as Reichmann's."

Xavier stared at the sagging uniforms and felt the first lightening of his mood since he had climbed down into this crypt. Sometimes his thinking was too serpentine. He looked for complications where there were none, which was why Tony was so valuable. He was blunt, efficient and, best of all, he had no time for European fatalism.

The grave, when Xavier found it five days later, was marked only by a bleached wooden cross on which the lettering had long since faded. Emotion swelled in his chest. More than eighteen cemeteries and sets of parish registers had been searched, but finally, twenty miles north of Portland in the village of Freeport, he had found Stefan le Clerc, and incontrovertible proof that his father hadn't died alone. He had taken Reichmann with him.

Fierce satisfaction filled him, not because Reichmann—or Richmond as the incised lettering on his headstone in Portland had proclaimed—

had been killed, but because his father had succeeded in his quest. He had found Reichmann, and he had stopped him.

For Stefan's name to be recorded by the parish meant that his identification had been recovered by the police before Helene could destroy it and, as Tony had surmised, she had been forced to bury him. Helene had subsequently destroyed the coroner's reports and police records, blocking any investigation into his disappearance through those channels. For the parish records to have survived meant she either hadn't been able to access them, or she had decided it was unlikely anyone would go to such extreme lengths to find his father.

Long minutes passed as he stared at the lichen-encrusted cross, at the grassy dip in the ground, and when the emptiness of loss couldn't be contained, he walked into the church. He paused in the dim coolness of the aisle, then took a pew and stared at the brilliant hues of a stained-glass window, at the gentle face and the iron resolve of a man who had given everything and finally found peace.

Thirty-Nine

Juan Chavez studied the apartment block from the concealment of his car. Two vehicles were parked outside apartment eight, which signaled that the two CIA agents who were minding Dennison were in residence.

He checked his watch. On cue, the van belonging to the take-out service that regularly delivered their food turned into the apartment complex to make the delivery. "Let's go."

His brother, Benito, climbed from the passenger seat, excitement and fear glittering in his eyes. In Juan's opinion the fear was good; the excitement was a liability.

Seconds later, they reached the side door that led

to the janitor's quarters. Motioning for Benito to stay outside, Juan tried the door. As expected, it was unlocked. Pushing it open, he glided into the room.

The janitor was eating his lunch, his back to the door. The sound of a radio cut out the small noise Juan had made opening and closing the door.

Extracting a cosh from his pocket, he walked up behind the old man and hit him with precision on the side of his head. Working quickly, he searched the unconscious man's pockets and took the keys he needed.

The front door of the apartment popped open. Dennison hit the remote, killing the television program he'd been watching, an exposé on drug cartels in Colombia. Not his favorite subject, even if it had been accurate, which it wasn't. For a start the contacts the interviewer had featured had looked more like gigolos than the sunburned plant bosses and enforcers that had made his life a living hell. Secondly, their teeth were in good shape, which meant they hadn't been chewing on coca leaves and lime. Thirdly, no one had mentioned the salted fish. At casa Lopez, and points south, they had been very big on salted fish.

Agent Grierson answered the door, paid the tab and set two paper sacks on the table. From the aroma, lunch was burgers and fries. No surprises there. For the past few days the schedule had been

the same, and so had the food. Grierson and
Mathews loved ketchup and fries.

Mathews walked into the kitchen, grabbed a
bottle of soda from the fridge, some glasses and a
bottle of ketchup from the pantry. He sat down,
pushed a burger toward Dennison and poured drinks.

Dennison opened his cardboard box and surveyed the burger. Grierson had gone out on a limb
and gotten chicken instead of beef. Moving awk-
wardly, because he had to eat cuffed, he extracted
the burger from the container and began to chew
his way through it. He didn't particularly like or
dislike burgers. To Dennison, apart from salted
fish, food was food, and with the constraint of the
cuffs, burgers worked.

Just as Grierson finished his burger the doorbell
rang. Wiping his hands with a paper napkin, he
answered the door. A third agent Grierson introduced as Pete Harris stepped into the room.

Grierson checked his watch and shrugged into
his sport coat. "Just to relieve the boredom, I'm
leaving. From now on, Harris is going to be taking
care of you."

The door closed behind Grierson. Dennison
stared at his new keeper. He didn't know if anyone
else had noticed—maybe not, because Harris had a
mustache, which distracted—but their facial features
were similar. Harris was younger and a little
leaner—okay, maybe fifteen or twenty pounds

leaner—but, apart from the mustache there was a definite similarity.

Possibilities swirled in his mind. As intriguing as the coincidence was, Dennison had no clear way to capitalize on Harris's appearance unless Mathews disappeared and Harris made him a gift of his gun and the cuff keys.

Mathews unlocked his briefcase, took out the cuff keys and tossed them to Harris, who put them in his pocket.

Dennison set his half-eaten burger down. *Strike two.* Mathews had always kept the keys in his briefcase, which had a combination lock, making the possibility that Dennison could get to the keys remote. Harris didn't have a briefcase.

Mathews's phone rang. It was his wife.

Dennison felt like he was standing at a black-jack table in Vegas, waiting for the next roll of the dice. He reached for a paper napkin and cleaned the grease off his fingers. Harris, who had poured himself a glass of soda, sat down at the table.

Mathews's conversation was disjointed, but Dennison could make out the gist of it. He and his wife were going on vacation and the car had just broken down. His wife was stranded at some garage. Mathews checked his watch. Dennison knew exactly what he was thinking. It was half an hour before Mathews's shift ended and the second new guy clocked in.

In the end, it was a no-brainer. Harris, more interested in finishing off Grierson's fries than Mathews's problems, or the fact that he would be breaking the rules by operating solo until Mathews's replacement checked in, told him to get his ass out of there before his wife divorced him.

Mathews looked uncomfortable. He was a stickler for the rules. The phone rang again. Thirty seconds later, he was gone.

Strike Three.

Ten seconds after the door closed behind Mathews, Harris reached for Mathews's fries. Dennison pushed to his feet, muttering that he needed to go to the john, grasped the neck of the ketchup bottle and brought it down hard on the side of Harris's head.

Harris slumped forward then toppled sideways, overturning his chair, his arm sweeping glasses of soda, take-out containers and French fries onto the floor. Cautiously, Dennison studied Harris where he lay, his feet tangled with the legs of the chair, a puddle of soda forming a stain in the carpet beside one outstretched arm. Blood glistened on the side of Harris's head, but he was still breathing, which was fine by Dennison. These days the only person he was interested in offing was Lopez, and he was no longer sure he wanted the opportunity: he just wanted out.

Working quickly, before Harris came to, he

slipped the agent's Walther out of his shoulder holster then checked for a backup gun. There wasn't one. Shaking his head at what he considered a sloppy practice, Dennison emptied Harris's pockets, found the cuff keys, a wallet, a set of car keys and a cell phone.

After unlocking his cuffs, he stripped off Harris's suit jacket, shirt and tie, and took the shoes. Dennison's loafers were tan, so he needed to change them. They didn't match Harris's pale gray jacket and blue tie. Maybe it was a small point, but in this business detail counted.

He cuffed Harris, gagged him with a towel from the kitchenette, then quickly changed into Harris's clothes.

Walking through to the bedroom, he checked his appearance in the long mirror set against one wall. The shirt was tight and the jacket strained across his shoulders. Harris was a lot leaner than he'd bargained on, but outwardly the fit looked okay. He fished in his trouser pocket and found the mustache he always carried, smoothed it on and stared at the effect in the mirror. It wasn't perfect, but close enough.

Within a matter of seconds he had shoved his clothes into his case and was out the door. He grinned when he saw Harris's car parked outside the unit. It was a Lexus. If he had time to do anything but save his skin, he would stop and buy a lottery ticket.

After almost twenty-five years of Lopez, finally Lady Luck had cut him a break.

Juan Chavez had counted: three agents had gone in, and three had left. Unless Lopez had made a mistake, Dennison had been left alone in the apartment. He drew his gun and, as a precautionary measure, got his fake CIA ID ready, then knocked on the door. Seconds later, when it was obvious no one was going to answer, he used the master key he'd taken from the janitor and let himself in. Benito crowded behind him. Juan stepped to one side, his gaze darting around the room, which at first glance appeared to be empty. For a split second, the fact that the agent who had just come and gone had looked a little like Dennison came back to haunt him. If that *had* been Dennison, they were both dead.

A muffled sound jerked his head around and down. Dennison was on the floor behind the dining table, cuffed and gagged. Juan's breath left his lungs on a rush. Lopez had told him that Dennison would probably have two men with him 24/7. That hadn't happened today. Something had gone wrong when they'd changed shift. Lopez had known about the changeover, which was why they had made their move. He had said the change in personnel would create the opportunity they needed, and it had, but not in the way Juan had expected.

Walking swiftly around the table, he jammed the barrel against Dennison's head, pulled the trigger twice and stepped back, grimacing at the mess.

Jerking his chin at Benito, he exited the apartment then barked a command when Benito neglected to close the door. The sound of a car turning into the courtyard made his heart pound. Ducking behind a screen of glossy shrubs, he indicated to Benito to stay still and quiet. The man who climbed out of the sedan was young, lean and wearing a sport coat: the fourth agent.

When they were clear of the building, he dialed the number he had been given and waited.

Lopez himself picked up.

"It's done," he said, automatically speaking in Spanish. He took another breath and this time worked to flatten out his voice, steady and smooth the way Lopez did. "Dennison's dead."

Forty

Costa Rica, two months later

Steve Fischer descended past fifty feet, keeping a check on his depth gauge. The water was murky, courtesy of a recent storm, the visibility no more than fifty percent. Below, in grim shades of gray and lavender, he could just make out the top of the reef. Beside him Taylor signaled to go left.

The stern of the *Nordika* reared out of the reef floor. The fisherman who had brought them out had been precise with his navigation. Jose regularly fished the reef. He knew where all the wrecks were, and still remembered the navy tragedy. Eight *Americano militar* dying in their waters wasn't an event that would easily be forgotten. Like everyone else along the coast, he had scanned the shores and checked his nets for bodies. The fact that none had ever been found had always been remarked upon, adding fuel to the mystery. According to Jose, with the Caribbean current sweeping in against the coastline, the bodies should have made landfall somewhere.

The *Nordika* still lay balanced on the edge of a ravine, its hull broken in two, its barnacle-encrusted rudder visible. Water welled coldly from the trench as Steve examined what was left of the deck area. The bridge was gone, and any sign of the onboard crane. The trench had already been searched by a specialist team and nothing further had been discovered, no bodies and no sign of the cargo the ship had carried. As a wreck, the *Nordika* remained as enigmatic as it had been almost twenty-five years before when his father had dived on it. At a guess, Reichmann and Chavez had offloaded the cargo and disposed of the crew at another location, then scuttled the ship over the trench.

Saunders had a lead on a small fishing settlement on the Colombian coast that had a deepwater anchorage, and the testimony of an elderly fisherman and his son who claimed they had seen the *Nordika*. The fact that Juarez was one of the few places a ship the size of the *Nordika could* anchor in close made it a strong candidate for the offloading of cargo and the execution of the ship's crew.

The discovery just days ago of a plank, which

had been used in the construction of a seaside shanty, and which had a partial swastika stenciled on one side, had finally provided Saunders with the leverage he'd needed. He had gone through diplomatic channels and pulled some heavy-duty strings. For the past two days the area had been sealed off while they had searched.

Juarez, Colombia
One week later

Steve watched as the team of forensic archaeologists painstakingly uncovered what had proved to be a mass grave, on not one level, but two.

The first level contained the remains of Todd Fischer, his SEAL team and the launch skipper. Identification of individual remains would take time, although the divers's neoprene dive suits had helped preserve the bodies. A further two bodies had also been found. At this point their identities remained a mystery, but it was conjectured that they could be local men who had been employed to dig the grave before being executed themselves.

The second level contained remains that were much older. From the scraps of clothing and the rotted documentation that had been found—the *Nordika*'s log and manifest—it had been ascertained that they were the original crew of the *Nordika*.

The discovery of the graves had sparked an international furor. People had started to arrive, filtering through Saunders's tight security. A Colombian woman who had been certain her son had died in the area, but had never been able to find him, came to the site. Representatives from the families of the naval dive team—Verney, Downey, Mathews, Hendrickson, Salter, McNeal and Brooks—were quietly waiting. An elderly woman from Germany, Bernadette Reinhardt, the granddaughter of the captain of the *Nordika,* Erich Reinhardt, had flown in that morning with her son.

Flowers had also started to arrive, piling up to one side of the open pit where they wouldn't interfere with the delicate work in progress.

Steve watched as the numbers around the grave slowly expanded, men in uniform, somber women in dark clothing. That morning he had positively identified his father's remains, courtesy of the tattoo on his Dad's right arm. The moment had hurt.

There would be a funeral service with full military honors back in Shreveport, a postmortem presentation of medals and an official apology. The record would finally be set straight, but as far as Steve was concerned it was over, here. Todd Fischer had already found his rest.

Chest tight, he crouched down and picked up a handful of the damp, crumbly soil. Rising to his feet, he let the soil slide between his fingers and remembered Todd Fischer as he had been, not as a soldier but as his father…and finally let go.

White rose petals and delicate sprays of jasmine blew across the muddy ground as Taylor slipped her fingers through Steve's. She was unwilling to intrude on his grief, but at the same time she was determined to pull him back from the solitary place he'd retreated to.

Steve had found his father and, against the odds, she had found hers. Her relationship with Jack wasn't perfect, but she no longer expected it to be. He was in the picture, despite his past, and was determined to stay for her sake and for Dana's. Dana hadn't said anything, but she didn't have to. The glow in her expression was all Taylor needed to see. Somehow, despite the passage of years and the twists and turns their lives had taken, she and Jack still fit together. More than that, they were *happy*.

Steve's fingers tightened on hers as he pulled her away from the lingering grief and sadness of the now-empty grave. His arm came around her waist as they picked their way through the expanding press of humanity that had sprung up around the site, his palm cupping her abdomen. Her stomach was still flat and there was no visible evidence of the small life growing inside her, but the baby was there, and already the center of the new life they were planning, courtesy of WITSEC.

They all had a chance at a new beginning, and they were taking it. Wedding arrangements were under way, although Taylor had stipulated that the ceremony had to take place *after* the memorial services. When Steve walked down the aisle, she wanted his focus firmly on the future, not the past.

His gaze met hers as they reached the mud-encrusted four-wheel-drive truck they had rented in Cartagena. He dug the keys out of his pocket and tossed them in one hand, and the grimness of the past few days dissolved, replaced by warmth and a piercing sweetness. "Time to go home."

And in that moment she knew he was finally free.

Wrapping her arms around his waist, she held him tight.

Freedom felt good.

Love felt even better.

* * * * *

*Turn the page to read an exciting excerpt
from the sequel to KILLER FOCUS
BLIND INSTINCT
Available February 2008*

One

The drone of a Liberator B-24 bomber broke the silence that hung over the forested hills and valleys that flowed like a dark blanket to the Langres Plateau. The plane dipped below ragged clouds that partially obscured the light of a full moon. Below, bonfires pinpointed the drop zone and a light flashed from the edge of the thick pine forest.

Morse code for "zero," the agreed signal.

The engine note deepened as the American aircraft banked and turned to make its drop. A pale shape bloomed against the night sky, growing larger as it floated to earth.

Icy air burned Marc Cavanaugh's lungs as he

stripped a leather glove from his right hand. Unfastening a flap pocket, he extracted a magazine for the Sten submachine gun that was slung across his chest and slotted it into place.

Fingers already numbed by the cold, he jerked on the parachute cords, steering himself toward the flashing pinpoint of light. He studied the thick swath of forest from which the signal had originated, the stretch of open country below—a ploughed field bare of crops. As he lost altitude, detail rushed at him: a tree, wind blasted and skeletal; a rock wall snaking across ground ploughed into neat furrows; the glitter of frost.

Shadows flowed across the field. Jacques de Vallois's men—he hoped.

Marc jerked on the cords, slowing and controlling his descent, then braced for landing. Seconds later he unlatched the harness and shrugged out of the straps. Stepping away from the distracting brightness of the chute, he dropped into a crouch, the Sten pointed in the direction of a flickering shadow to his right.

"Bénis soient les doux."

Blessed are the meek.

Cavanaugh let the muzzle of the gun drop, but only fractionally. *"Car ils hériteront de la terre."*

For they shall inherit the earth.

"De Vallois."

White teeth flashed, and metal gleamed as

de Vallois lowered a Schmeisser MP40. "At your service."

A brief handshake later and de Vallois barked orders at his men. A former attaché of de Gaulle, de Vallois was formidably skilled in clandestine operations. One of the architects of the French Resistance, he had worked tirelessly refining their systems and training recruits. He no longer wore a uniform, and it was unlikely that his efforts would ever be fully recognized, except posthumously, but de Vallois's determination was unshaken. He lived for *la France,* and he would die for her.

De Vallois said something in rapid French. With economical movements, two of his men gathered up the chute, which glowed with a ghostly incandescence. Within minutes the field was clear, the bonfires doused.

De Vallois jerked his head. *"Allons-y!"* Let's go.

Seconds later they were beneath the cover of the pines.

The parachute was buried in a hole that had been previously dug, the disturbed ground covered over with a thick scattering of pine needles. As high a price as the silk would command in Lyon or Dijon, the risk of being searched while transporting the parachute was too high, and de Vallois's men were too valuable. With the recent incarceration and execution of key Resistance figures, Himmler's SS and the Geheime Staats Polizei, the

Gestapo, were actively hunting insurgents and traitors against the Nazi regime. Over the past weeks, the activities of the SS and the Gestapo had escalated to a fever pitch.

Half an hour later they walked free of the trees and stepped onto a stony track. De Vallois checked his watch, then signaled them off the road.

Seconds later lights swept across the bare fields. An armored truck rumbled past.

Long minutes passed. De Vallois grunted. "Come. That is the last patrol of the night. Even the SS have to sleep."

Marc stepped up onto the road. The cloud cover had broken up, leaving the night even colder and very clear. Moonlight illuminated the barren fields and a stark avenue of pines.

Jacques grinned at the exposure. "Don't worry— my information is exact. My people understand that many lives are at stake."

A truck, its headlights doused, cruised out of a side road and halted beside them. Jacques opened the passenger door and gestured for Marc to climb in. "The only thing I can't guard against is a traitor."

REQUEST YOUR FREE BOOKS!

2 FREE NOVELS
FROM THE ROMANCE/SUSPENSE
COLLECTION PLUS 2 FREE GIFTS!

YES! Please send me 2 FREE novels from the Romance/Suspense Collection and my 2 FREE gifts. After receiving them, if I don't wish to receive any more books, I can return the shipping statement marked "cancel." If I don't cancel, I will receive 4 brand-new novels every month and be billed just $5.49 per book in the U.S., or $5.99 per book in Canada, plus 25¢ shipping and handling per book plus applicable taxes, if any*. That's a savings of at least 20% off the cover price! I understand that accepting the 2 free books and gifts places me under no obligation to buy anything. I can always return a shipment and cancel at any time. Even if I never buy another book from the Reader Service, the two free books and gifts are mine to keep forever.

185 MDN EF5Y   385 MDN EF6C

Name		(PLEASE PRINT)	
Address			Apt. #
City	State/Prov.		Zip/Postal Code

Signature (if under 18, a parent or guardian must sign)

Mail to **The Reader Service:**
IN U.S.A.: P.O. Box 1867, Buffalo, NY 14240-1867
IN CANADA: P.O. Box 609, Fort Erie, Ontario L2A 5X3

Not valid to current subscribers to the Romance Collection,
the Suspense Collection or the Romance/Suspense Collection.

Want to try two free books from another line?
Call 1-800-873-8635 or visit www.morefreebooks.com.

* Terms and prices subject to change without notice. NY residents add applicable sales tax. Canadian residents will be charged applicable provincial taxes and GST. This offer is limited to one order per household. All orders subject to approval. Credit or debit balances in a customer's account(s) may be offset by any other outstanding balance owed by or to the customer. Please allow 4 to 6 weeks for delivery.

Your Privacy: Harlequin is committed to protecting your privacy. Our Privacy Policy is available online at www.eHarlequin.com or upon request from the Reader Service. From time to time we make our lists of customers available to reputable firms who may have a product or service of interest to you. If you would prefer we not share your name and address, please check here. ☐

BOB07

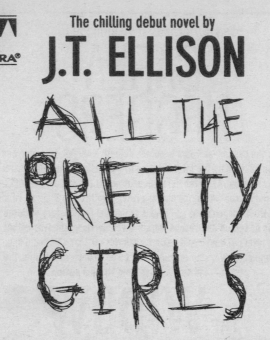

FIONA BRAND

32546 DOUBLE VISION	___ $6.99 U.S.	___ $8.50 CAN.
32289 BODY WORK	___ $6.99 U.S.	___ $8.50 CAN.

(limited quantities available)

TOTAL AMOUNT	$_____
POSTAGE & HANDLING	$_____
($1.00 FOR 1 BOOK, 50¢ for each additional)	
APPLICABLE TAXES*	$_____
TOTAL PAYABLE	$_____

(check or money order—please do not send cash)

To order, complete this form and send it, along with a check or money order for the total above, payable to MIRA Books, to: **In the U.S.:** 3010 Walden Avenue, P.O. Box 9077, Buffalo, NY 14269-9077; **In Canada:** P.O. Box 636, Fort Erie, Ontario, L2A 5X3.

Name: _____
Address: _____ City: _____
State/Prov.: _____ Zip/Postal Code: _____
Account Number (if applicable): _____
075 CSAS

*New York residents remit applicable sales taxes.
*Canadian residents remit applicable GST and provincial taxes.

MIRA®

www.MIRABooks.com

MFB1207BL